Arthur Sherburne Hardy

But Yet A Woman

A Novel

Arthur Sherburne Hardy

But Yet A Woman
A Novel

ISBN/EAN: 9783743303157

Manufactured in Europe, USA, Canada, Australia, Japa

Cover: Foto ©Andreas Hilbeck / pixelio.de

Manufactured and distributed by brebook publishing software
(www.brebook.com)

Arthur Sherburne Hardy

But Yet A Woman

BUT YET A WOMAN

A Novel

BY

ARTHUR SHERBURNE HARDY

Love is too young to know what conscience is;
Yet who knows not, conscience is born of love?
SHAKESPEARE, *Sonnet CLI.*

BOSTON AND NEW YORK
HOUGHTON, MIFFLIN AND COMPANY
The Riverside Press, Cambridge
1886

The Riverside Press, Cambridge:
Electrotyped and Printed by H. O. Houghton & Co.

The Dedication of this Book to

Mp Wife

is but the acknowledgment of the debt of

both it and its

AUTHOR.

BUT YET A WOMAN.

I.

THERE are some men who reach the downward slope of life without succumbing to Penelope, Phyllis, or Phryne. Such men are rare; nevertheless they exist, for M. Michel was one. Not that any strange play of chances had made his life exceptional; in its outward circumstances it had not differed from that of most men. It was M. Michel himself who was exceptional. During the forty years that had elapsed since he left the Lycée Louis-le-Grand many women had crossed his path, of whose charms he was not ignorant and to whose influence he was a debtor. More than once they had softened his convictions and purified his ideals, for he was neither a hermit nor a scoffer. Of that little circle of friends in which he moved, which the years had narrowed only to render it more essential, they formed an altogether necessary part, whose banishment would have dismayed him.

Still, for M. Michel, woman existed as it were *en masse*. As says the proverb, he admired the forest without seeing the trees. Indispensable to society as the flowers of the Luxembourg to the gardens in which he took his daily walk, it had never occurred to him to appropriate either the one or the other.

"Is not this delicious!" his niece said, one morning, showing him a rose wet with dew.

"Exquisite, but I prefer the violet."

"Ah, how provoking! Yesterday we had violets, and you preferred roses."

Yet M. Michel was far from being *difficile.* On the contrary, a certain large-heartedness dissipated his affections. He preferred neither roses nor violets, but loved only flowers. He admired neither one nor many women, but only woman. Indeed, some of M. Michel's friends had affirmed that it was precisely this eccentricity which rendered him so agreeable. In his society they escaped for a time that mania of appropriation which even a coquette tires, at times, of provoking; with him one could lower one's guard without danger, and indulge in a certain abandon with security.

If this man had ever inspired certain sentiments of another kind he had remained ignorant of them, if only because he did not reciprocate them. Doubtless, like others, he had had his opportunities without making them. With a good figure and manners, a loyal heart and gentle disposition, to say nothing of his *rentes,* it were strange had it been otherwise. But his sixtieth year found him still alone with his young orphan niece Rénée.

Without ever having thought of it, M. Michel's feelings of love and admiration for his niece, while genuine and sincere, were, apparently at least, of the same somewhat abstract character. His life, it is true, would have been desolate without her. She managed his household admirably; she presided at those little reunions of friends so dear to him at his age. In entering that large salon, whose tones were so subdued, everything indicated indefinably a reigning presence, and that, too, of a woman. A certain grace and refinement hovered, like the fragrance of a flower, over every trifle. He was far, too, from esteeming his niece only as an excellent housekeeper. Her wishes, her whims even, were law to him, and had need been he would have done a chivalrous deed as gallantly as any knight of the Round Table. For her he unlocked the doors of that library, that other world of unbroken silence, of which he once said, " It is a little space fenced off from illusions, maskings, and shadows ; here are no voices, only echoes, no action, only its photograph ; here no events transpire, but here is the record of all, and this alone is real and durable." Moreover, for her he stopped every Saturday night at the *Confiserie* of the Rue de l'École de Médecine, and brought away a white package tied with a blue ribbon.

Yet for all this, one night his niece said to him, " Be a little less good to me, and love me more, my uncle." Such a philosophy so puzzled the worthy man that he could only make a gesture of remonstrance.

But Mademoiselle Rénée was thoroughly in earnest, and had vaguely come to understand that life is not composed of generalities. So far from being content with the even affection and generosity of her uncle, she would have preferred him more exacting. In her quiet retirement with this old man her young heart rebelled against a peace for which it was not made ; unconsciously she had learned that happiness is only a relative. Looking one night from her window on the lights and glare of the great city, she exclaimed, " If he loved *me, Rénée,* I would make him cry with despair and happiness ! " So true is it that the human heart craves that tyrannous love which is selfish and imperious even, which in giving all takes everything, and is like an exarch's sword, with pain and pleasure for its two edges.

It had been raining all day, and a mist hung over the city. Wrapped in its folds, dome and spire assumed colossal proportions, and as the night advanced seemed to sway with their gigantic shadows. Water was dripping from every projection ; the doors of the cafés were closed, and their lights struggled feebly with the storm and darkness. This outside gloom made the salon of the

Rue du Bac even more attractive than usual. Dinner was over, the open fire was lighted, and Rénée was serving the coffee with her own hands.

Opposite her uncle, near the fire, sat M. Lande, an old friend and playmate of fifty years ago, now first violin at the Opera. The son of a farmer, Ernest Lande had never forgotten the kindness of his companion, the only son of the mayor at Brienne, — at that time a great dignitary in his eyes. Widely different as had been their paths in life, he had sought out this friend of his childhood after thirty years of buffeting, and found him unchanged. Thus it happened that for nearly twenty years he had enjoyed almost without interruption his regular evening before M. Michel's fire.

On accepting his coffee from the hand of Rénée, he always rose. He remembered well the little girl who had put out her cheek for a kiss at his coming, and lain asleep in his arms before that same fire. One day, when this little girl, instead of Baptiste, brought him his coffee, he was astonished to find her a little girl no longer. From that time he said " Mademoiselle," and a shade of constraint, mingled with deference, characterized his manner. This at first amused Rénée, and finally won her. It was a kind of homage, direct without ceasing to be dignified, to whose use her uncle was a stranger.

" Ah, mademoiselle," he said, taking his coffee, " how many more times will you do this for me ! "

"One would suppose you were going on a long journey, M. Lande."

"It is true, mademoiselle," he said half to himself; "some day I am going on a long journey."

"You, a journey!" exclaimed Rénée. "Are you to leave Paris?"

He looked up with a smile. "You forget how old I am growing."

Rénée was touched. M. Lande had not withstood well his years of buffeting. A tired heart is a poor ally, and his had been early tired. He had been well described by a critic as "one who would have achieved great things in Paradise."

"You are no older than my uncle," said Rénée, gently.

"And is your uncle then inviolable?" said M. Michel, coming to the rescue.

Rénée laughed as she went to the farther end of the room, where, in her favorite chair by the low lamp, she used to read while the friends conversed by the fire. This intimacy between her uncle and M. Lande she respected as if by instinct, and, once with her book, state secrets might have been discussed with impunity at the hearthstone.

The conversation to-night, if not upon state secrets, was somewhat confidential in its nature, and in these confidences between man and man there was something almost pathetic. Over matters on which women prattle innocently together like children, men philosophize in the third person. Open the inner doors of your heart and experience, and your friend grows silent; but sink your personality in abstractions, and he will discover your need, and cheer without wounding. In our strong need of each other we open the door wide to woman, unbandage our wounds, and cry " Give !" for we know her tenderest of nurses, if not wisest of physicians. But to our friend, with whom we sit before the fire over our pipes, we put on our best robes, though we be beggars, and ask alms for humanity. Playing this little farce together, which we both so well understand, how many hurts are soothed without once being named !

The room was yet unlighted, for the rays of Rénée's lamp in the corner hardly reached the fire. The flickering flames were going out; the fire itself was in its pensive stage, and threw a sunset glow upon the faces of its watchers. If it be true that the world we see reflects itself upon the face, it is also certain that there are some faces over which it seems to have little power. Furrow and sadden them as it will, a native light shines from the eye, which shadows and wrinkles serve only to intensify. Strangely, too, it is oftenest the simplest, one might almost say the softest, nature which refuses the world's seal, and wears its own to the end ; and Ernest Lande, gentle and timid as his eyes showed him to be, though

he had seen more of the world than falls to the
lot of many men, bore on his face fewer traces of
its influence than does many a stouter heart,
whose prided stoicism is often only a strait-jacket
which that very world it affects so lightly to despise has woven and hammered out for it as the
years went by. Practically his working days were
over; yet he was only the first violin at the Opera.
"If you had left your provincial heart at Brienne," a friend once said to him, "they would be
applauding you to-day at St. Petersburg." At
such a remark M. Lande would smile, and, like
certain monosyllables, his smile was a reproach, a
protest, an assent, or a denial, as occasion de-
manded.

From his earliest childhood he had given evidence of that passionate love of music which was
to dominate his whole life. He was the despair
of his father, who, loving him deeply, could never
seriously and determinedly thwart his natural pro-
clivity, yet never understood his nature, at once
timid and expansive, — a dreamer, who thought
more of the rustle of the corn than the fullness of
the harvest; so awkward in the duties to which
circumstances had assigned him; stealing away,
after the tasks of the day, in the shadows of the
hedges, to gain the town, where, perhaps, some
wandering musicians were singing the operas of
Scarlatti, or, silent and shy, with his beloved violin, to the secret places of nature, to listen to the

voices of the forest birds or the sounds of rushing waters.

But Père Lande was not severe. All this was a misfortune to be pitied, not a crime to be punished. Often, at vespers, something in Ernest's rapt face, as he sang in the collegiate choir, something in that clear and tremulous voice, spoke to him in a tongue he but dimly understood of a region other than that narrow one of raw products in which he lived, and made him silent and thoughtful as he walked home, with his son's hand in his broad palm. It was thus partly from a natural kindness of heart, partly also because he saw only too plainly that the hand which held the bow was not fashioned for the plow, that he yielded to Ernest's entreaties, joined with the influence of the curé, and consented to his departure for Italy. In this consent there was an undercurrent of silent protest, an almost mournful resignation prophetic of disaster, not wholly concealed that spring morning, when he waved his hand in adieu to the slender figure disappearing over the hillside with the light step of twenty years yet unsoiled and crowned with hope. And a year later it was with a certain irritable despair that he received tidings of Ernest's departure for Paris. "To seek his fortune!" he murmured bitterly. And who shall say that Père Lande's idea of fortune, broad, sunny lands, fields of yellow wheat sown with scarlet *coquelicots*, a snug roof covering vessels of golden cream and white cheeses, was an unworthy one?

Gérard might have taken him as a model for Youth in " Les Trois Ages " had he seen him, still light-hearted after his long foot-journey, with eyes fixed upon the thousand lights of the great city, which flashed and vanished as he followed the winding road, and whose distant hum seemed to call him also thitherward.

Thereafter matters went badly. With the unconcern of youth he married early a pretty face and a sour heart, and forthwith embarrassed genius with five children. Producing works destined some day to be discovered, he had none of those qualities which force the smiles of fortune or gain the ears of managers. Only after many years had an opera, begun in Rome and finished later in Paris, been produced through the exertions of friends, securing to him at the close of life a tardy fame and favor. But long before this the spirit had been broken, — broken by the prostitution of his talents to those ways and means of bare subsistence which his large family made necessary ; broken by the gradual flight — for it was not abandonment — of his hopes and ideals, and not least by the wife who early learned that art of subtle taunt which harasses a genius that cannot minister to coarse ambitions. Here was something more than what his friend called provincialism. For even a provincial knows how to steer,

and garners experience with his harvests. But M.
Lande could neither steer nor beat. The tricks
of success were beyond, nay, rather beneath, his
mastery. His friends rightly claimed for him
genius, but it was a genius that would have no
trade; and amid the rivalries, the deceits, the follies of this great capital, his life went in and out
like the streams among the hills on which he was
nurtured, — darkened by the shadows of the forest, but pure and untainted.

Upon his eldest son, Roger, this simple but
thwarted life had made a profound impression.
Accustomed from his earliest remembrance to the
querulous tones of his mother, the disorder and
often need which resulted from her improvidence;
drawn to his father by a love which had no other
outlet, and which in later years ripened into a
deep sympathy, he had read in his eyes a warning of which in truth his father was unconscious,
and which for this very reason was more impress-
ive. At once studious and ambitious, this life of
domestic unhappiness and struggle with poverty,
under which a weaker nature would have suc-
cumbed, or from which a more volatile one would
have turned in quest of diversion, slowly forced
him back upon himself. He wished to be independent of all this, to conquer success; and this
conquest seemed possible only by the suppression
of those instincts of the heart to which his father
ever yielded, innocently, but with the abandon of

a child. The influence of woman, the strain of the affections, the toil wasted in meeting wants incessantly renewed, all that in his own home he had seen frittering away the energies of talent and weighting the wings of genius, he wished to sacrifice, if sacrifice it was. He wished to live like Carlyle's Professor in his tower seat among the stars, above the city sweltering in passion and want below. It was this ambition which had driven him early from home into a bare attic in the Latin Quarter, which had kept closed for him the door of Bullier and the Valentino, and which gave him among his associates of the École de Médecine, who, in spite of their studies, were not insensible to the joys of the present, the sobriquet of "the man of the future."

This habit of thought developed with the intensity natural to his age into an intellectual cynicism, without bitterness because without real experience. His theory of life was an *a priori* one, but it worked well. He passed with credit, though without brilliancy, through his preparatory studies; and after his professional training in the hospital began to make himself felt as a man of resource and careful judgment, and subsequently, in his surgeon's practice, as the surest operator in Paris. Others were more famous, but in his reputation was that element of steady growth which already made him an oracle in the lecture room.

The glow of the fire had almost disappeared when the door opened, and Baptiste announced M. Roger Lande. Engrossed in his professional studies, he had resolutely avoided all society, even that of his father's friends. To his father's solicitations he said, "Of the world I see enough under the counterpanes," and to his friends he pleaded his duties. Summoned the month before to Beauvais to see an old nobleman stricken with the gout, he had met there M. Michel, who for twenty years had never missed passing August in Beauvais. While waiting the train for Paris, under the trees of the garden in front of the Casino, M. Michel had introduced himself as the old friend of his father, the surest passport to Roger's favor. Charmed, as was every one, with his manner and conversation, Roger had promised to renew at Paris their chance acquaintanceship, a promise which, perhaps, would not have been given had he known that it involved a presentation to Mademoiselle Rénée. On this his father's sixtieth birthday he made his second entrance into M. Michel's salon.

He was now a man of about twenty-five, his face pale but striking, though not handsome after the schools. His mouth was compressed and firm, his forehead narrow, his eye sad but resolute, brilliant but without vivacity. As he came into the light of the lamp and bowed to Rénée, one might have judged this man narrow in nature, even domineering, but daring, ambitious, and possessed of that rare power which to a certain extent controls events, but is not controlled.

He shook hands cordially with M. Michel, who said, " Monsieur, you see two old fogies talking treason. I was just saying that the price of success was happiness."

" Sometimes, also, it is that of knowledge," rejoined Roger.

Rénée's eyes were on her book, still she was not reading. Ordinarily the sententious wisdom of the old habitués of her uncle's salon troubled her but little. For her it had none of that meaning which experience alone imparts to it. Amid all those reflections which escaped so often from the lips of the old she moved serenely. But the advent of Roger Lande into the quiet and orderly routine of the Rue du Bac was the apparition of a new planet in the system. His voice forced her attention, and she found herself listening for his replies with expectancy. In the presence of this young stranger she felt a sympathy and an interest which his youth alone was sufficient to inspire by contrast with his surroundings.

Moreover, there comes a time when the spring buds are ready to open. It matters little whether it be the long summer sun, or but one of those hours of capricious warmth which are succeeded by frost and blight ; when their time is come they follow blindly the laws of their own growth. It is the moment for which they have lived, and under that warm breath they yield without reserve all those treasures so long prepared. It is so with the human heart. How many times an April sun violates its tender blossoms, which do not hesitate to obey the mysterious instincts of their nature! Counsels of experience, wise pleadings, stern commands, how powerless are they all to imprison this young heart, to combat that subtle force, at once so gentle and so persistent, under which resolutely and fearfully it unfolds and surrenders! Prudence, human conventions, reason itself, are all too fragile to contain this infinite need and desire, to restrain this hope, to tether and pinion this young life which must needs enter the struggle even with the certainty of being vanquished.

"Think of it! it is fifty years," said M. Michel, "since your father and myself played together in the fields about Brienne. Those were the days of illusions. We entered every door as if it were the gate of Paradise, for they were then all garlanded with roses."

"Some of which are not yet faded," said M. Lande.

"That is because we have put on the spectacles of philosophers."

"In which case the roses are in the spectacles," said Roger.

"You are wrong, my son," said M. Lande,

gently. "See here my best friend, this fire and this chair which I love, this hand which presses mine, — these are no illusions."

"I will not dispute with a man who has his proofs at hand," replied Roger, smiling. "Moreover, I am incompetent either as a witness or a judge. At my age we have companions; at yours, perhaps, they become friends."

"You think so because you will to think so," continued M. Lande gently. It was not his first argument with Roger on this subject. "But confess, now, it is not your desire. You have devoted yourself to your work, and you make light of sentiment, as if," he added, looking up into his son's face, "it were not the source of some good actions; but you will not confess that you have a heart without needs or without treasures. Last night was the close of the season, and the leader of the orchestra was sick. I took his place. Guess now what fancy entered the heads of these Parisians! You would never imagine it. At the end of the overture they rose on their feet and applauded the first violin, for a moment become leader. This gave me pleasure, after living so many years with these good people. But presently all this noise is over, the music is silent, the lights are extinguished, and this bit of favor thrown to an old man is forgotten. Not ten in the house will think of him again. And this is just; man grows old, but the world is ever young, full of new thoughts and plans, in which the old have no share. But should I not go out of that empty and darkened house to brood over these sad thoughts but for this fireside to which I come, — but for this friend who has the strange merit of being old also? For, believe me, in this world, which is ever slipping from under our feet, it is the prerogative of friendship to grow old with one's friend."

Touched by this simple eloquence, the two men remained silent.

"Nature provides well for us," pursued M. Lande. "Youth is the season of friendships, when we are prodigal with our affections, and thus it happens that of all those bonds so thoughtlessly formed some endure. It is an instinct of the heart which provides a store for the winter."

He spoke with an ease which was unusual, and, having finished, he rose, a little embarrassed at having said so much.

"You are going already!" exclaimed M. Michel. "But at least we will have our song. Come, Rénée, help us to convince this young heretic."

Rénée put down her book and went to the piano. Roger would have assisted her.

"There is no music, monsieur," she said. "I know it by heart."

And, without prelude, she began in a soft but clear voice to sing. Roger stood silently watching this peaceful scene. That voice penetrated the deep recesses of his heart, calling forth echoes which he did not seek to control. It was an old story of Switzerland, of the time of good Queen Bertha, a picture of childhood, home, and peace. To this man of the hospitals it opened horizons, which hung, like the mirage of the desert, over wastes of sand.

The song was over; he had bidden M. Michel good-night, who said, "You see, monsieur, we still live *dans le temps que la Reine Berthe filait;*" he was in the street again, buttoning up his coat against the mist and rain.

"*Bonsoir, M. le Docteur,*" said the concierge, as he turned into his own door. His reply opened her eyes with wonder: —

"Bah! it is all a dream."

II.

THE following week occurred one of M. Michel's reunions, and M. Lande was surprised to find, on his return from rehearsal, a note from Roger, begging he would accompany him. In fact, Roger himself was surprised to find he had written it. Accustomed to accumulate work, and to substitute a pressure of professional duty as a barrier between himself and society, his entrance into M. Michel's Saturday evening salon was an event for which certain malicious persons gave Mademoiselle Rénée the credit. And in this respect they were partly right, as he himself would have admitted. Quick to read character, none better than he could have dissected Roger Lande, — for it is not so difficult to know one's self as to confess to the knowledge, — and beneath his desire to lose himself in his profession, behind the armor which he wore, he knew the man, like other men, with nerves ready to tremble and pulses that obey smiles and frowns. Of the two classes who are cynics, one from observation, the other from experience, he belonged to the former. He was what he was because he wished to be, not because he could not help it. But, like many another, he

had not counted on the unexpected. It was the
old fable of the sun and the wind. In the struggle of life, amid the misery of the hospitals and
the secrets of his profession, he buckled up his
armor and lowered his visor; but the glimpse of
that sunny home and quiet fireside of the Rue du
Bac was a window opened out of heaven, and
through Rénée's eyes he beheld this other self,
which uprose, a sudden apparition, saying, " Thou
shalt not serve two masters!"

When they entered M. Michel's salon the guests
had already assembled. Most of its habitués were
of long standing. It had grown as a circle of intimate friends grows, slowly, and was emphatically
conservative. It possessed no representatives from
the gay society of the capital, for whom these
people would have been objects of curiosity preserved in alcohol. With the exception of M. de
Marzac, a well-known journalist, and Madame
Milevski, M. Michel's young half-sister, recently
returned from Russia, this little society repre-
sented the sediment of a life-time of social inter-
course. It was the residue of the evaporation of
forty years, and it had settled in M. Michel's salon
because in this quiet place there was no danger
that it would be disturbed.

To most of these people Roger was a stranger.
M. Michel, greeting him cordially, presented him
to two gentlemen with whom he was conversing,
M. de Marzac and the Baron Scherer, — the lat-

ter a cynic because he could not help it, a member of the Academy, and possessing the order of the Holy Ghost.

"M. Lande has but one fault," said M. Michel, — "that of being still young."

"It is one he will have the misfortune to overcome," said the baron with his smile; for notwithstanding his cynicism, the baron, who belonged to a past generation, possessed a smile which was part of a manner in which he wrapped himself, like a Spanish beggar in his cloak, and in which he secretly took more pride than in the cross of the Holy Ghost.

"Misfortune! On the contrary; and I have brought him to you that he may see in the man of sixty, two others whom I used to know and still recognize, the man of twenty and the man of forty."

"You give M. Lande a long time to wait for canonization," said a voice behind Roger.

He turned to recognize a woman whom he had not before noticed.

"Štéphanie Milevski!" he exclaimed, half aloud.

"Is this sanctity only reached at sixty?" and in her voice there was the sweetness and the mockery of a bird's.

"What we barely win at sixty, my sister, you surely will not dispute with us, since you may claim it already."

"Oh, with us sanctity is a birthright."

"And, being lightly acquired, is lightly held," said M. de Marzac.

It was a remark he would have recalled, but it was too late. Stéphanie turned quickly with the look and gesture of one who notices an adversary only to punish him.

"Interpret your riddle, M. de Marzac; we are dying to hear it. You protest? Well, I know its meaning, and you are right. It is a birthright which is often sold for a mess of pottage. You did not know, M. Lande," she continued, turning to Roger, "that M. de Marzac was a moralist. To tell the truth, neither did I. He is a continual surprise; he has always a leaf unturned. And that reminds me," she added to M. de Marzac, "have you seen Sartain's new book? No? It is very amusing. It is even said that you figure in it yourself."

"Ah! and in what guise?" he asked. He had begun in ill humor with some one, and had finished by becoming so with himself. Having lost his temper, he had lost also his guard.

"Well, if you are curious, of a lover with the motto, *J'en vis et je l'éteins,*" with which thrust she joined Rénée, who was talking with old M. Lande.

"In love as in war all is fair, is it not, M. de Marzac?" said the baron, compassionately.

"Certainly," he replied, coldly, "for love *is* war."

"You know Madame Milevski?" the baron asked Roger.

"I have met her professionally."

"A very safe way," said M. de Marzac, dryly.

"Is she so very dangerous?"

"Pardon me, here is the curé of St. Eustache; he will answer you. Shall I present you?"

"I have the honor to know him already," said Roger. "We also meet professionally, — too often, I fear, monsieur," he said to the priest.

"Not here, at all events," said Father Le Blanc; " and here we will teach you a secret not in your books, — that of perpetual youth. I tell you beforehand that you may follow the cue. You might misconduct yourself. Seriously, you have fallen into the pleasantest room in Paris."

"And its charm?"

"Faith, if you do not discover it, I cannot tell you. We are not paragons. Here, for example, is M. le Baron, an old courtier who somehow manages to believe in the present" —

"And Madame Stéphanie, who believes in the past," interposed the baron.

"Ah! Madame Milevski is here?" said the priest, putting on his glasses, and abandoning his classification of the guests which the baron's remark had interrupted.

She was standing in the centre of the room with Rénée. The most striking thing about her was a simplicity which had always been the despair of her imitators.   In a close-fitting dress of black, relieved by none of the accessories of a *robe à la mode*, there was an extraordinary freshness, almost girlishness, in her appearance, which did not suffer even from the close proximity of Rénée. She wore no jewelry except a dagger of brilliants fastening a lace scarf on her bosom.

When the curé had adjusted his glasses it was to receive one of those smiles which appear to the recipient as if vouchsafed to him only.

"Yes, it is she," he said.

"She tells me Sartain has a new book.   Have you read it?" asked the baron.

"Yes, it is very witty."

"Tell us about it," and the baron drew the two men to the sofa, where he sat down between them.

"It is a book destined to be popular," said the priest; "a book which, without breaking with morality, tolerates evil, makes conscience the child of custom, and prescribes to every one what he most likes.   It is called a Romance of the Century.   Well, it is also its philosophy."

"And that philosophy?"

"Is the study of self," said the curé; "a philosophy which M. Sartain seeks to make also a religion."

"I thought he was a good Catholic," said M. de Marzac.

"If so, he holds his faith in reserve, like yourself," the priest replied, laughing good-naturedly, "for a time of danger."

"Good-evening, father," said Stéphanie, approaching them, and holding out her white hand in her frank English fashion. "No," she added, as he rose; "to tell the truth, I am afraid of you. I know you have been reading a homily. M. de Marzac betrays you. Ah, for a diplomat, monsieur, what a tell-tale face you have!"

"I congratulate you on the skill with which you compliment your own divination," he replied, stiffly.

Roger, seeing Rénée left alone at this instant, crossed over to the table at which she sat. Baptiste was arranging some curious Sèvres cups destined for the coffee. "What a pretty picture!" he thought as he approached her.

"Will you allow me to sit down beside you, mademoiselle? I have been trying to reach you ever since I came."

"If you will be content with a divided attention, M. Lande. You see I must give to each one his proper allowance of sugar. I am obliged to think very carefully. Now this cup is for Father Le Blanc. You see I put three lumps into it. Think how sweet it must be, in such a tiny cup! There is scarcely room for the coffee. Baptiste," she said, leaning forward, "this is for M. Le Blanc, and this for M. Scherer. And ask my aunt if she will have coffee."

"Stéphanie Milevski! Is she your aunt?" asked Roger in surprise.

"Yes. Do you know her?"

"Oh, I meet a great many people whom I do not know," he replied, evasively.

"But you seemed so surprised," persisted Rénée.

"Did I? Well, she appears so young. No one would ever suppose her to be M. Michel's sister."

"She is young," said Rénée, looking over to where she stood. "Then, you know, she is only a half-sister. Where did you meet her, M. Lande? Here in Paris?"

"No, at Aix-les-Bains. Aix is one of my specifics. Have you ever been there?"

Rénée's manner had the ease and fearlessness of innocence. In this she differed from Stéphanie, whose self-possession was evidently also an accomplishment. She did not, therefore, notice Roger's evasion, which to the mere accomplishment would have been a note of alarm.

"No, never. Stéphanie has been almost a stranger to me. I have not seen her many times in my whole life. But M. Michel is very fond of her. Do you not think she is very charming? I feel already as if I had known her for years."

"That is probably one secret of her charm."

"Is it?" said Rénée, reflectively, and looking over at Stéphanie again. "That is M. de Marzac with whom she is talking."

"I have just been presented," said Roger, following Rénée's eyes. "They must be either the best or worst of friends, mademoiselle."

"And why, monsieur?"

"Because they seem to be continually at sword's points."

"Do they?" said Rénée, laughing. "If you had said M. Scherer, I should not have been surprised. They are political enemies. That is, M. Scherer has just given in his allegiance to the Orleans princes, and I think Stéphanie could more easily love the Bonapartists than forget treason to the king."

"You think it treason, then, to become an Orleanist?" Rénée's assurance amused him.

"M. Le Blanc says that change is always treason. But there! every one is served except M. Lande, and I must carry this myself," and she took up a little silver tray. "Pardon me; it is an old custom."

Roger watched her slender form as she went, and saw his father's face light up with pleasure. He had hoped she would return, but she lingered at the farther end of the room, and he saw Father Le Blanc approaching.

"I trust we shall see you here often, M. Lande," said the priest, seating himself beside Roger. "We old habitués have the right of invitation."

"It is a pleasure I fear I cannot often enjoy. My time is not my own, and, in fact, I have an appointment to-night which I must soon meet."

"Yes, yours is a busy profession and a hard one," the priest said, settling himself comfortably, and resting his fat hands on his knees.

"Yet I would not for that reason exchange with you, M. le Curé," said Roger, turning towards his companion, and looking into the black eyes which gave the lie a little to his thin white hair.

"And why not for that reason?"

"Because, while we are both at the call of men's needs, I go only to see those of the body, but you to know those of the soul."

"They are often the same, my son," the priest answered, sighing. "'The flesh lusteth against the spirit,' and," he added, as if perhaps he had made a dangerous admission, "the spirit lusteth against the flesh. We are too much discouraged because we are not able to do what we will to do; as if even in willing there were no spiritual victory."

"It is a victory which counts for little in this life."

"There is no life but the life to come," said the priest, solemnly. "You were speaking of an appointment," he resumed, after a moment's silence; "it is the excuse of the day. I will wager you are going to the conference of the Medical Society. Yes? See now, I thought so! In the next generation society will be given over to the fops; but in my day men of merit had also their appointments with leisure. Leisure, do I say? Such a salon as this was a school of instruction, where, without weariness, in an atmosphere of wit, learning, and beauty, men acquired wisdom as well as knowledge. The best of us, M. Lande, need another society than that of the faculties of science and philosophy, the society which polishes without disintegrating, which warms as well as enlightens. Do you remember the maxim of Vauvenargues? — 'One cannot be just if one is not human.' Well, the school of humanity is soeiety. It is dangerous to become a savant at the risk of ignoring the interests of the heart."

" One has not the time for everything."

" That is only saying one is not rich enough to buy everything. Time is a standard coin in every market, and that with which men make the worst of bargains ! "

" Evidently you think I am to make a bad investment to-night, since I am going to exchange two hours of it for the memoir of M. X——. But you are mistaken. It is precisely upon the affections of the heart."

"Oh ! " said Father Le Blanc, lifting his shoulders, " science has all the vocabulary of the passions ; but it produces only the moonlight of the theatre. You must go? " he said, as Roger rose. " I am sorry, but I count upon seeing you here again ; and this time," he added gracefully, " I ask you not on your account, but on my own."

Roger acknowledged the compliment with a bow, and went in search of M. Michel, to bid him good-night.

"I did not know you had met M. Lande before," Rénée was saying to Stéphanie. The latter stooped to arrange a bud that had become misplaced on Rénée's dress. "Oh, never mind that little flower," said Rénée; "it is always falling off. He told me that he met you at Aix-les-Bains."

A shade of anxiety passed over Stéphanie's face. "Yes, at Aix. There he comes now. I think he is going, and is looking for you;" and, crossing the room, she walked slowly towards the door.

After making his excuses to Rénée, Roger saw her standing at the coffee-table, which was near the vestibule.

She had taken one of the Sèvres cups from the tray, in an abstracted way, but a sudden, earnest thoughtfulness overspread her face, which that act alone certainly did not warrant. It was a not uncommon look, which sometimes transformed her; the soft eyes grew full of purpose; it was a transfiguration. "The reverie of a woman's eyes is always mistaken for thoughtfulness," M. de Marzac had said sneeringly; but in this case, at least, he was wrong. It was no woman in dreamland who stood playing with the china cup, in Roger's passage to the door; and even M. de Marzac himself had felt that subtle strength, a sort of reserve force, which, like the fragrance of a lace handkerchief, too delicate to be analyzed, yet too real not to be perceived, emanated from that lithe form.

As Roger passed her, her manner changed almost to indifferentism.

"Will you fill my cup, M. Lande?" she said, languidly.

Roger lifted the quaint silver urn from its stand over the flame, and slowly filled the cup which Stéphanie still held in her hand.

"So it seems we have met before," she continued in a low voice.

"Well, is it not true?" he asked, quietly.

There was a moment's silence, and as he replaced the urn he looked into her face.

"I have given you the word of a gentleman," he said, as if in answer to something he saw there. Their eyes met an instant.

"And I trust you with the faith of a woman," she replied, turning away.

On reaching the doorway at the foot of the stairs, Roger took his right to the quay, instead of turning up towards the École de Médecine.

"After all, I will not go," he said to himself.

On reaching the end of the Rue du Bac, he crossed the street to the sidewalk along the parapet overlooking the river. It was still early, and the streets were full of people. The lamps from the opposite bank threw their broad lines of light over the dark waters, and made a glare overhead, through which the stars shone as through a fine mist. He walked up the river, crossed the Pont de la Concorde, and entered under the trees of the Cours de la Reine. Here the lights and the loungers grew less frequent, and finding at last a bench in a secluded spot, he lighted a cigar and sat down.

A few weeks before, he was sitting in the garden of the Hôtel du Nord, at Aix-les-Bains. He had been summoned to attend a patient, whom he had sent to the baths, and, having returned from the consultation, was taking his coffee, after the *table d'hôte*, in the evening air. His table was in a distant corner, remote from the hotel entrance, through which the waiters were hurrying in and out, serving the many groups scattered in the less shaded portion of the garden, under the lanterns. The garden itself extended behind him still farther, but, at this time, was already deserted and lost in obscurity. Nevertheless, in the pauses of the conversation which floated out to him on the light wind, he thought at times he heard voices behind him. At last, in a lull of voices, when the rustle of the leaves ceased, he heard a woman's voice, asking, —

"But will the king consent?"

An unwilling listener, he took a match from

the table and lighted a cigar. Presently a woman emerged from the shadow. It was Stéphanie Milevski. Still concealed in the darkness in which he sat, he saw her distinctly as she followed the gravel path towards the hotel. At her side walked a priest, with a pale, intellectual face, who, on reaching the entrance, waited to permit her to enter first, bowed, and, passing through the hallway, disappeared into the street.

In all this there was an air of mystery which piqued his curiosity. What was the meaning of this strange interview, and who was this woman who talked with a priest of the consent of a king? Sooner than he anticipated, this riddle, which occupied him as he finished his cigar, had a partial answer.

As he followed the path along which Stéphanie had preceded him, his eye was caught by a white object, which proved to be a letter. The envelope was large, and carefully sealed. On entering the hotel he sought for some evidence of its owner. But there was no address; only, on the back, written across one end in pencil, " *To be forwarded to the king.*"

Who has not felt that resistless pressure which we call the force of events, which, without, often against, the voice of reason, impels us forward ?

He called a passing waiter, and asked who was the lady that had just entered.

" A young lady, with a priest ? "

"Yes."

"Madame Milevski, monsieur."

"Take her this card, and say that I am wait-ing."

During the delivery of the message he took his tablets from his pocket, and wrote a prescription. When he followed his guide to Madame Milevski's salon, he held it in his hand. The room was rather dimly lighted by a single lamp, instead of candles, and its soft light gave an appearance of luxury to the apartment. In the shadow, at the open window overlooking the garden in the rear, sat its only occupant. Through the thin lace curtain he could see the outline of her form against the black sky. As he entered she rose, and stood for a moment between the parted curtains, evidently expecting him to speak.

Sitting under the trees of the Cours de la Reine, recalling these circumstances of his first meeting with Stéphanie Milevski, he saw before him the same woman from whom he had just parted. As she stood silently holding in either hand the lace hangings, she made upon him then the same impression he had received a few moments before, as he filled her cup in M. Michel's salon. In her voice, in her manner, in her attitudes even, there was a strange confidence and naturalness, — which, except in children, is usually only the fruit of intimacy, — blended with a dignity which was almost imperious. But for the former, the latter might have been mistaken for the reserve of society; but for the last, the first might have been the innocence of girlhood. There was about her that fascination which invites yet restrains; under which men both dare and tremble.

"Madame," he said, glancing at his card, which she held in her hand, "I am a physician. Will you permit me to offer you the advice of one?"

She was looking at him curiously. Certainly he was not a fool, nor did he have the air of a madman.

"Taking my coffee to-night in the garden," he continued, looking steadily in her eyes, "I noticed that you were hoarse. A mere nothing, I admit," in answer to the interest he was awakening; "still, if you follow carefully the directions of this prescription, you will only have done a duty which you owe to yourself," and he laid the folded leaf on the table.

"Your interest, monsieur," she answered for the first time, coming nearer to him, "does me honor." There was a trace of irony in her voice.

"On the contrary, madame; and, by the way, this letter," taking it from his pocket and placing it in her hands, "does it perchance belong to you?"

A sudden pallor overspread her face, but she recovered herself instantly.

"Where did you possess yourself of this letter?" the irony deepening, though her voice trembled a little.

"It seems to me that is unimportant, since I have given it to you."

"Then I ought to thank you," she said, after a pause, in which she did not lower her eyes.

"I did not say so."

Despite her anxiety, an amused smile hovered about her mouth, as, taking the prescription from the table, she replied, —

"True, it is a professional secret."

He bowed, without answering, and took his hat from the table.

"Monsieur," she said, impulsively, "I have to thank you."

"No," he replied, as he stood at the door; "you have yourself said it is a professional secret."

"What you will not permit me to say, then, I shall feel," she said, softly. "One cannot be a friend, M. Lande, without having one."

III.

THE morning after Roger's visit to M. Michel's salon was that of the clinic at the Hôtel-Dieu St. Luc. It was that part of his practice which he most loved, for in it he was most master. There was none of the preliminary parleying, none of the diplomacy, indispensable to the private sick-room.

After the lecture was over and he had walked through the wards, he retired, as usual, into what had once been a consulting-room, but which he had transformed into a private office and library. Here the assistants made their reports and received his instructions, and here the Mother Superior sometimes conferred with him on the details of the hospital.

Sœur Ursule, three times chosen Superior, was what is ordinarily called a "remarkable" woman. All the mechanism of this vast establishment was under her eye. She overlooked everybody and everything, from the notary who managed the property owned by the Order in the city down to the smallest administrative details of the hospital proper.

"One would suppose," said Roger to a friend

who once made his morning round with him, "that this office of Superior would be much sought for. In the world this would naturally be the case. On the contrary, it is much feared. It is an honor, if you will; but also a respon sibility. Do you see this motto written over the door of every room through which we pass? GOD ONLY. It contains the secret of these sweet faces unmarked by worldly care or passion. You know well enough what disease and suffering will do for us; yet, for the five years in which I have daily passed in and out of these rooms, amid complaints and impatience, among the querulous and the bitter, I have not heard from these women a single reproach, or seen a glance of vexation. You do not live one such day in your own family. But what do they care for all these trifles which worry us! For them, they *are* trifles. This life is as nothing, and 'the pleasure of dying without pain is worth the pain of living without pleas- ure.' But to accomplish this miracle there is absolutely nothing adequate short of the faith which does not stop to reason."

On this morning Sœur Ursule followed him, after the clinic, into his private room.

She was nearly old enough to be his mother, yet in reality appeared as young as he. Her cheeks were like the south side of a peach, and if she had gray hairs they were hidden under her *bandeau.* She ordinarily said little, but her simplest utterances had force and beauty, for they were backed by her own personality. One always felt, when she spoke, as when one sees a shadow, that something more real lies behind it.

"Doctor," she said, entering quietly behind him, and closing the door, "you were very successful this morning."

Roger himself had been well satisfied. The two operations of the morning had passed off well, his thoughts had been clear, and his words at his command, as the applause of the students had testified.

"Yes, everything went off well," he said, sitting down at his table, and taking up the reports awaiting inspection.

"Moreover, you spoke well, doctor."

"Ah! you think so? I am glad of it;" and he began to open his papers.

"How much, in all this, did you think of the glory of God, doctor?" pursued Sœur Ursule, quietly.

"Pouf! so much only, I'm afraid, sister," he said, with a puff of imaginary smoke in the air.

"And that only will be left at the day of judgment," she replied, calmly.

Roger had learned not to argue with the Mother Superior. Having intuitions for premises, her logic was irresistible. "You are a bundle of foregone conclusions," he once said to her.

"I wish to see M. Laferme, if he is in," he said,

looking up from his papers. M. Laferme was the first assistant surgeon.

"I am going away for a week. Is there anything you wish to say to me?"

"No, monsieur, nothing, — except this bill. It is from Chatellier; the new instrument which you used this morning. It seemed to me that, as you said it was to be very rarely used, it did not properly belong to the hospital equipment."

It was not Roger's first experience with Sœur Ursule's prudent and economic management.

"True. I will attend to it."

"Is it a vacation you are taking?" she asked, her hand on the door.

"Yes, I suppose I may call it so."

"It is the first for a long time, and you need it. May it bring you happiness."

"Thanks, sister. And I know you mean it. If I had not a mother already " —

But Sœur Ursule had closed the door.

The explanation of Roger's sudden determination was a note from M. Michel.

"After you had left us, last night," it ran, "we formed an altogether unexpected project. M. Le Blanc and your father remained with us after all the others had gone, for to-morrow we go to Beauvais for a month or more, as usual; and this year Madame Milevski will be with us. Rénée begged M. Lande to accompany us, and he consented, provided M. Le Blanc would go also. To our surprise and delight, he too consented — for a week. It was now my turn to propose something; that you should join us. Your father shook his head dubiously; still, I do not despair. Furthermore, let me add, you owe a duty to the ladies, who will otherwise be in the hands of three antediluvians."

Baptiste handed him the note at the door of the hospital. A vacation was something which had never occurred to him. "After all, why not?" he said to himself. "It will make me glad to get back;" and, tearing a leaf from his tablets, he wrote, —

"I accept with pleasure. But I must make some arrangements, and will come down to-morrow."

The following day he was walking down the platform of the station, in search of an empty compartment. As he passed the long line of coaches, he perceived in one of them the red face and white hair of Father Le Blanc.

"Ah, what good fortune!" the latter exclaimed, making room for him.

Roger was equally pleased at the prospect of companionship. He had made a favorable impression upon the old priest, and those whom we please are apt to please us.

"I thought you had gone already, monsieur."

"Well, well, well! How pleasant this is!" the priest said, folding his glasses and laying them in the book he was reading. "You understand, I was to go yesterday. Beauvais,—I thought it was in the west, and went to the St. Lazare station. So I missed our friends altogether."

"Then you have never been to Beauvais." "

"Never, never!" said the priest, energetically. "And you?"

"Yes, I have been there, but not for pleasure. M. Michel, I understand, has a beautiful house on the lake."

"Ah! there is a lake? Yes, we shall enjoy ourselves," said Father Le Blanc, with evident satisfaction. "We have a charming party."

".You are an old friend of M. Michel's."

"Yes, since he first came to Paris. That is saying much and little: much, because he is the most agreeable of friends; little, because he makes friends of every one."

"That is an art few possess."

"True. Only with M. Michel it is not an art at all. That art by which one never disputes the qualities which those about us pretend to possess, and, on the other hand, never asserts any for one's self, like other arts, requires calculation; and M. Michel has none. He fulfills its conditions without suspecting it."

"Perhaps it is a family trait. I should think M. Michel's sister possessed the art also."

"Madame Stéphanie? Oh, she is quite another person."

"Yet she appears to make friends easily."

"Yes, but in a different way. And against what odds!" said Father Le Blanc, lifting up his eyes with an expressive gesture of his hands. "For woman the art of pleasing is a kingdom for which all her sex are pretenders; and as for ours, with such a woman as Stéphanie Milevski, one is not content with friendship."

"You have arraigned the whole world against her," said Roger, laughing.

"Yet I take the world only as I find it. Women make friends like princes, by gaining thrones and dispensing favors. Only, more generous than princes, finally they surrender their thrones also."

"And M. Milevski? I do not hear of him."

"M. Milevski is dead. M. Michel's father married, late in life, a second time, in Russia. Of this marriage Stéphanie was the only child, and to M. Michel she has been much like a daughter. She was educated here in Paris under his supervision, after which she returned to Russia, to live with her mother on her estates near Kief."

"And her mother is dead?"

"Also. But, before dying, she married Stéphanie to a Russian nobleman of the new school, who, shortly after, became compromised with the emperor, and was exiled to Siberia."

"Then madame has a title?"

"She had one, but it was forfeited on her husband's exile. It is said that the estates were also confiscated, and that madame was forbidden to reside in Russia. On receiving the Czar's order, she drove alone, in the dead of winter, from Kief to St. Petersburg, with a single servant. Notwithstanding this defiance, she obtained an audience, and kept her estates. There is a story that the Czar gave her a cross set with diamonds, as a token of his good-will, and that she asked permission to have the cross changed to a dagger, ' lest your majesty's clemency make me forget my husband,' she said. The Count Milevski was already dead; he died on the journey to Siberia. But then, we cannot believe all that is said. Still," added M. Le Blanc, reflectively, " I would believe many things of her. She puzzles me; and, for an old man, that is saying a good deal. The young look into women's eyes to see their own reflections; the old, to see the woman."

" You make a very agreeable definition of age," said Roger. " Most men, in that classification, die young."

Father Le Blanc laughed, which he did with his shoulders and trunk. As a laugh it was not infectious, but conveyed a sense of satisfaction. As Rénée said, " When Father Le Blanc laughs, I feel happy myself."

" Yes, she puzzles me," he resumed. " Now, with Mademoiselle Rénée it is different. She is like the brook at its source; one sees the bottom. But Stéphanie!" and he shook his head, — " it is the river; one sees the reflection of everything. but of what is beneath the surface, nothing — except that there is something."

Roger was not averse to giving M. Le Blanc the reins of the conversation; partly because he was interested, and partly because he was curious.

"She is certainly very beautiful."

"Ah!" said the priest, holding up his hands, "and what beauty! I am a bit of an artist, M. Lande; indeed, I was an artist before I was a priest. I will tell you why she is beautiful. Do you know?"

"I have not studied her," said Roger.

"Well, do so. It will repay you. Her beauty is not faultless; that is, it is not absolutely regular, — not the *style magnifique*, as the Greeks have it. They knew what they were about, those Greeks, and gave such to the gods alone, and to certain of them only. Such beauty pleases the judgment; it is too correct for the heart. But of Madame Milevski, my friend, the judgment must beware. She does not please it; she destroys it," he said, with a little shrug: "for in her beauty is that factor of weakness and incompleteness which touches the heart."

"She does not appear to know all this. At least, no one would suspect her of it."

"Nonsense!" exclaimed Father Le Blanc. "There is a spirit which whispers in the ear of every beautiful woman as she leaves Paradise.

But, as you say, she does not appear to. Now, I will prove the contrary. Have you noticed her dress?"

"Hardly; except, possibly, that it was simple."

"Exactly, but designedly so. It fulfills the condition of a perfect dress, which is only an accessory, having little value in itself, covering what it does not conceal, and calling attention to that which it embellishes. But, without beauty, such a style would be frightful! What are all the eccentricities of fashion but the devices to conceal and supplement nature? Madame Stéphanie flies in the face of all these follies: first, because she knows she can dare to; and second, because, like a king who has the air of one, she has the good taste to dispense with her decorations."

At this instant the train emerged from the forest, disclosing the valley of the Seine.

"*Ah! la belle France!*" cried Father Le Blanc.

Half-way up the slope of the hills, the view of the valley below, bathed in the warm sunshine, with the broad river, like a ribbon of gold on its green bosom, was indeed beautiful. The priest leaned his head back upon the cushion, lost in contemplation, and neither spoke. Presently the little worn volume on his knee dropped to the floor. Father Le Blanc had fallen asleep.

Roger took up the book, and, as he laid it on

the seat, glanced at its title. It was the "Phædo" of Plato. For a long time he watched the placid breathing of his reverend companion. "After learning to live, we have no longer the time," he thought. "After all, in learning to live, we learn also how to die."

Then there was a scream from the engine, a rush of steam, a babel of echoes from the station buildings, and the guard, opening the door, shouted, "Beauvais! messieurs; Beauvais!"

"Bless me!" exclaimed Father Le Blanc, "we have arrived already? I owe you a thousand apologies. The sun being full in my face, I closed my eyes, and must have slept a little."

At the station they found a phaeton and Rénée's two Breton ponies.

"How far is it?" the priest asked the driver.

"A short half hour, monsieur," said the latter, touching his cap.

"Ah, that will be delightful. We shall see the sunset."

Beauvais was one of those places of which the traveler sees nothing. The railway, after threading its way among the houses of the lower town, between high walls of stone and across narrow streets, ill-paved and unattractive, plunges at once into a tunnel through the promontory which juts out into the lake, as if in contempt of the beauties of nature. Rénée's ponies dashed down one of these steep, narrow lanes at a pace which caused Father Le Blanc's hand to tighten on his "Phædo," and took the wide street along the lake, called the Avenue du Quai. There was no ripple on the blue waters. A few pleasure-boats floated at their buoys, their silken flags hanging idly, and the columns of thin white smoke from the barges moored at the quay rose undisturbed by any breath of air. Beyond, the spur of Mont St. Jean, from whose wooded sides appeared here and there the red roofs and awnings of half-hidden villas, stood out like a challenge into the lake, making a little bay for the boats of Beauvais. Imagine an arm, bent; the closed hand is the promontory of St. Jean, which slopes backward gently, and nestling in the curve of the elbow is Beauvais.

At the end of the quay the ponies turned under the trees into a broad avenue leading up the hill, which they took gallantly. On one side was a soft earthen road for cavaliers ; on the other they passed, now and then, the high iron gates of a villa. A sharp turn to the left led them into a wood almost black, so dense were the trees, and so thick the foliage overhead.

"A little slower, my friend," said Father Le Blanc ; "we wish to enjoy the scenery."

"Oh, there is no danger," responded the driver ; "we are there."

A gleam of light ahead broadened, the trees became more open, and suddenly, almost without warning, the ponies passed through a gate into the glow of sunset, circled a level stretch of lawn dotted with trees, and stopped, pawing and shaking their shaggy manes, at M. Michel's door.

"Doubtless it is safe," said the priest, alighting, "nevertheless, they have wicked eyes, those ponies."

M. Michel was on the steps, and hastened down to greet them.

"Why, my good friend, it is you, after all," he exclaimed, taking Father Le Blanc's satchel; "we thought you had abandoned us. And you have brought M. Lande with you."

"Faith, it was not I who brought him," laughed the priest; "quite the reverse. At all events, we are here," and he led the way up the steps with the air of a man who is at home everywhere. Rénée met him at the door.

"We had given you up," she said, with surprise and pleasure on her face. "I have been scolding you terribly. How did it happen? Where were you yesterday?" Then she caught sight of Roger. "We are very glad you have come," she said, naively; "we had begun to have doubts of you both."

"Come, now," interposed M. Michel, "let these travelers rest; they must be tired, and will have barely time before dinner. Baptiste! take these bags, and show the gentlemen their rooms."

Going up the stairs together, following Baptiste, Father Le Blanc made a little explanation. "She obeys her impulses, — like a child, — then, you see, with M. Michel, who knows so much and sees so little, what can you expect! She has no mother."

"One is tempted to say, so much the better!" Roger answered.

While dressing for dinner he had an opportunity for reflection. Except for the fops, as M. Le Blanc would say, who give all their mind to it, dressing soon becomes purely mechanical, — an automatic process which leaves the mind a rover. Like those of most workers, his reflections took the form of plans: in thinking, he matured something. But here, in Beauvais, sleeping quietly on the lake, with all his professional cares forty miles away, he could think only of M. Michel, in whose house he was; of Father Le Blanc, who carried "Phædo" for a breviary; and of Rénée and Stéphanie, with whom he was to dine. Still, he formed plans. To talk much with Father Le Blanc, whom he liked; and as to that brook and that river of which the priest had spoken, not to listen too long to the music of the one or search too curiously into the depths of the other; thus making plans like the rest of the world, ignoring that potent factor, self, whose value remains still unknown, even when, after three-score years and ten of vain endeavor, it reënters the impenetrable darkness whence it came.

IV.

PERCHED on the crest of Mont St. Jean, M. Michel's villa overlooked the lake on three sides. From its wide veranda one might almost throw a stone into the waters at the base of the cliff, where a narrow beach received the miniature surf which the southeast wind dashed upon its slope of pebbles. Wreathed in vines, the posts and arches of this veranda formed so many frames for the landscape.

"This is my picture gallery," said M. Michel to his guests, who had adjourned, after dinner, to the piazza. "Why should I pay twenty thousand francs for a Corot or a Bouguereau, when I have here these pictures which never need retouching, and which change with every passing cloud;" and while he was speaking, the shadow of a great cloud, like some monster of the lake, moved in the glitter of the moonlit waves over its surface.

Leaning on the railing, Rénée stood under one of the arches, the shadows of the vines over her.

"You have no softer web of lace, mademoiselle, than the moonlight makes for you," Roger said, joining her.

"Yes, how pretty it is," answered Rénée, looking down on the tracery it had woven over her dress. " Do you see that black tuft of trees, M. Lande, just beyond that point of land where the boat is ? "

" It looks to me like a ruin."

" Yes, it is a ruin.   You can see the gray tower very plainly in the sunlight; but it is so buried in the foliage, I did not think you could distinguish it now.   We often go and take dinner there."

"Ah !   Then it is inhabited."

" No, we take our dinner with us.   It is a real ruin, and it has a real story, which makes it more interesting."

"Is it too long a story to ask you to repeat, mademoiselle ? "

" It is not so very long, but it is very romantic."

" Then I am the more interested to hear it."

" You are ? " she said, giving him a look of grave surprise, " I did not think so."

" You did not think so ?   Why ? "

" I hardly know why," Rénée said, a little shyly. " I suppose I did not think you were a very romantic person," she added, laughing. " I read the story in an old book I found in my uncle's library. It was such a surprise to me to think that it had all happened here, so near to us. Our own lives seem very commonplace beside those of such a story."

" Except as such lives, when brought so close to ours, remind us of what is possible for us all."

"I carried the book to my uncle, and read the story aloud to him. He was as still as a mouse," said Rénée, smiling. "But what do you think he said after I had finished? 'Thank you, my child, it is very amusing.'"

"Then you think it would only amuse me? Your conclusion rests on a premise which I should dispute."

"What premise?"

"That you know me better than you do."

"We often know people very well, whom, in the ordinary sense, we do not know at all," Rénée answered, straightforwardly. "You make a certain impression on me, as every one else does, without any will of my own, — that is all."

"Then it is my misfortune to have made a wrong one," said Roger; "but I can readily disabuse you."

"Readily? How?"

"By telling you, though you have not told me this story, why I should be interested in it, and —and why you are."

"You think it is some romantic folly," said Rénée, resentfully.

"I do not know what it is; but certainly I think better things of you than you do of me."

"Well, then, disabuse me. I am waiting."

"Now you are disposed to laugh at me, while I, on the contrary, am very serious," said Roger. "Every day, almost, in my profession, I read such stories as you find in the old book.   The characters do not live in castles, and the heroes are not knights, but the drama is the same; the accessories only differ.   And these accessories, of time, and place, and manners, they are only the frame of the picture; it is the vulgar eye that is attracted by them solely.   How many times, as I have set out on my morning visits or entered the door of the Hôtel-Dieu St. Luc, I have wished that I had some poet with me, who should strip all that I was about to see of what was local and accidental, and write anew the story of human suffering and endurance.   Besides the inheritance of suffering, transmitted from age to age, there is another, — the *capacity* to suffer.   Is not the consciousness of this capacity the secret of your interest in the story of the ruin?"

"I do not wish to suffer."

"No, not for the sake of suffering; but, as Lamennais says, 'there is something wanting to the perfect life, which does not finish on the field of battle, the scaffold, or in prison.'   And when we read of such lives, we feel we are in the line of succession; the consciousness of our own powers fills us with a nameless longing; we rebel against a life which offers us no opportunities to die, to suffer, to be silent, for that love of kindred, country, or God, which redeems us.   I know this enthusiasm has a morbid side; but it commands sympathy, for its source is in the recognition of our own nobility, and the sublime consciousness that we are all eldest sons in the heritage of humanity, in its virtues as well as its follies."

"How strange you are," said Rénée, looking at him.

"Why? Is not what I have said true?"

"That makes it all the stranger."

"I do not understand you."

"I mean, as I said before, that you make a certain impression upon me. It is not necessary for one to speak to make a declaration of faith; there is the manner, the tone, the not speaking, which are more eloquent still. You surprise me, because you contradict that general impression. I don't know how to explain myself better; and I cannot, without telling tales, — that is, without gossiping."

"Well, then, let us gossip a little."

"You contradict yourself," Rénée said, after a pause. "M. Lande says that you are altogether absorbed in your profession. Yet you leave it suddenly, for no reason whatever."

"For no reason, mademoiselle?"

"For a reason you have never tolerated before as sufficient. You astonished M. Lande by accepting our invitation. Then, at Paris, at my uncle's, you say sharp things, like M. de Marzac, which do not at all agree with what you have been telling me. I had begun to think you were very cynical."

"It is possible to have very little respect for individuals, and at the same time to build a creed on faith in humanity," said Roger. "Men are like the planets; as parts of a system they behave themselves well enough, but any one of them, freed from the restraints of all the others, would rush to destruction. But I interrupt you."

"M. Lande says that you hate society, and Father Le Blanc that you were made for it."

"I might admit them both right without contradiction; but what do *you* say, mademoiselle?"

"How should I know?"

"Well, is there anything more?"

"Oh, a great deal," said Rénée, laughing. "I heard some one say that you were cold"—

"Yes, I know her."

"And another, that you had no religion"—

"Him, also," said Roger.

"But Sœur Ursule says quite contrary things of you."

"Then you know Sœur Ursule."

"Yes, indeed, very well, M. Lande. You know when I go back to Paris, in the autumn, I am going to enter the Congregation of St. Luc."

"*You*, mademoiselle!" Roger cried, with a sudden movement towards her, as if he were about to seize her by both wrists, "what is M. Michel thinking of?"

"Of my wishes and my happiness," she answered, quietly.

"But I cannot believe it," he said, impatiently. "Have you reflected? Have you thought " —

" What questions you are asking, M. Lande."

"True! I acknowledge it. But you do not understand, you do not know what I do."

" Your father once told us you had the greatest reverence for the Sisters of St. Luc. Then I have five years of novitiate in which to learn all those things which you know and of which I am ignorant, and — and to know myself better."

Standing opposite her, Roger was looking straight into her face. It was a searching look, and for the first time Rénée's eyes avoided his, and fell.

"It is a sublime folly!" he said, in a tone of mingled weariness and protest.

"Did I not say rightly you were inconsistent?" said Rénée, looking up again. "You bring us back to what we were speaking of. I see lives of sacrifice and devotion, which I wish to emulate. I feel that very capacity to endure of which you spoke, and which you just called sublime, without adding that it was folly; and I wish to consecrate that endurance to the highest service."

" Mademoiselle, you have the right to silence me, for I have none to criticise or to deter you. Nevertheless, understand me, for I am not inconsistent. If, like the Sisters of St. Luc, you believe this life was given us to abjure, you are right. Forget it, abjure it, shut your eyes to all it holds,

and fix them only upon the world to come. But
if, on the other hand, it be given us, not to renounce, but to conquer " —

" But, M. Lande," interrupted Rénée, " have
you ever seen those who have better conquered
self and the world than the Sisters of St. Luc? "

" It is not conquest; it is crucifixion. Strong
character, like a strong muscle, comes from activity, from warfare, not from retreat."

" You live in a world wider than mine; I do not
pretend to know it. But mine, if narrower, is the
same. I think it would be the same in the cloisters of St. Luc, and that there, also, would be opportunity for conquest. Do you think that, in the
world you know, one can better prepare for the
world to come than in those cloisters ? "

" Mademoiselle," said Roger, " we use the same
words and phrases, but with different meanings;
so different that it seems hopeless for me to attempt the reconciliation which I believe is possible. For your future world, I answer, no — for
mine, yes. You remind me of Sœur Ursule.
She talks of renouncing this life, of the life to
come, of absorption in God; and I, too, use the
same phrases, while our thoughts are far different.
Of that life to come, of which she speaks, I, perhaps, know less than she; but, whatever it may
be, I shall enter it myself, and not another, else
for me it has no personal interest. I do not
understand Sœur Ursule's transformation. The

worm, in becoming the butterfly, loses its identity. The moment after, as the moment before, my death, I shall be I, with such strength after as before, and with such weakness, — courageous then, as now, by subduing fear; knowing then the pleasures of duty, as here, by sacrifice; generous then only as now, by conquering selfishness, and winning victories only by fighting battles. Goodness and virtue! I cannot value nor comprehend them, if they cost nothing. Costing nothing, they disappear altogether. Without the struggle and temptation of Gethsemane, Calvary itself would have no meaning. Give me some other view of this life to come, mademoiselle. I will not ask to understand it, but only to conceive of it. But as it is, I wish to enter it a man, not an anchorite; and in it I expect to be strong only as I conquer weakness, and able to grow only as there is weakness to conquer."

"And heaven?" said Rénée.

"When you say heaven, it is as if you said eternity. I admit it, but I do not comprehend it. It is the goal; but, when reached, it is the end of everything."

"And I wish it to be the beginning," said Rénée, looking over the lake, as if she would discover the everlasting hills on its farther shore. Her voice had a troubled tone in it. Was it moonlight or tears which Roger saw in her eyes?

"Rénée!" said M. Michel, "we are going in.

There is a dew to-night, and we wish you to make
a game of cards with us."

"Not to-night, uncle.   I am tired."

"Ah, true!" said this worthy man, "you are
tired.   Well, rest yourself, and sleep well, for to-
morrow we shall be busy."

But Rénée lay awake a long time that night,
thinking, within the white folds of her bed-cur-
tains, which, in a serious pleasantry, she used to
call her cell.   And this novice-to-be fell asleep,
saying, "I know him better than they all."

When Roger approached Rénée on the piazza,
for what proved to be the longest talk they had
ever had together, it was with that feeling, "here
is some one whom I shall like, and who is worth
knowing."   Yet he had not expected to enter at
once upon a subject so personal, or, at least, so
serious.   There is usually an ascent, more or less
difficult, more or less obstructed with *banalités*,
which must be climbed before one reaches the
upper levels of conversation upon which Rénée
had entered so naively.   She had no fund of
empty phrases, none of the current coin of society; and, if she was not easily embarrassed, it
was because one had intuitively the good sense
not to compliment her.   When she spoke, her
words were the exact reflection of herself; there
was no doubt of their sincerity.

From the very first, this young face in the corner of M. Michel's salon had interested him.   As

he talked with her uncle before the fire, he looked over at times to find those gray eyes, at once so grave and so sweet, and to see that smile which came and went as a ripple passes over still water, while she turned the leaves of her book. But if he was interested in Rénée, he had not then begun to wonder what she thought of him. Not until she told him so quietly of her approaching novitiate, did he say to himself, with that secret annoyance which betrayed him, "she tells me as if it would give me pleasure." When he found himself alone in his room, that evening, demonstrating to an imaginary M. Michel the unwisdom of yielding to her wishes, and finding fault with the world in general for its topsy-turvy condition, Rénée's face, in the black veil and white bandeau of the Sisters of St. Luc, came so often before his eyes, that it was not easy to believe his argument altogether abstract and impersonal. And when he woke the next morning, it was with the consciousness of something on his mind which would not keep the truce of silence and forgetfulness he had resolved upon.

The dew was still on the leaves, when, after finding the salon empty, he stepped out upon the piazza. It was not Rénée, but Father Le Blanc, who stood under the arches.

"Bonjour, M. Lande," he said. "It seems we two are the early risers."

"Are we the first?" asked Roger.

"Yes, it seems so.   Habit is incorrigible.   But what a reward we have!" said Father Le Blanc, with a gesture which took in the whole scene. "Nature is like a woman.   In the morning she is fresh from her bath, at noon she is in her working dress, and at night she wears her jewels.   As for me, I like them both best in the morning."

As he spoke, Baptiste appeared at the door.

" Will you have breakfast here, messieurs?"

" Nothing could be better.   That is " — turning to Roger.

" Oh, by all means," he said; and on a light wicker table was soon laid a white cloth, fresh strawberries with crème St. Gervais, rolls from the morning's baking, and two fragrant cups of coffee.

" We are altogether too early, I fear," said the priest to Baptiste.   " At what time does M. Michel breakfast in the country?"

" He has his coffee at six, monsieur."

" Diantre! at six!"

" And breakfast at ten.   He keeps exactly the same hours as at Paris."

" The same as at Paris!   Then he is now writing?"

" Yes, monsieur."

" M. Michel is writing a book, is he not?" asked Roger.

" Yes, he is writing a book."

Roger had asked the question with the thought that Father Le Blanc would give him some information about M. Michel's labors, of which he was ashamed to be ignorant; but the priest's answer seemed to imply a profound secret. Looking up inquiringly, Roger caught his eye, which twinkled with amusement.

"Ma foi!" he laughed, "I know no more than you. It is about Egypt. They say, when he took the first volume to the Librarie Baillière, the publisher said to him, 'M. Michel, I have an idea. Take your MSS. to M. X——; he is the only man who can read your book, and you will thus save yourself the trouble of having to publish it.'"

Roger laughed. There was a vein of kindly humor in the priest's composition which endeared him to every one: and, as he knew him better, the courtesy which distinguished him mellowed into a sort of comradeship.

"I believe I could sit on this piazza all my life," said the priest, helping himself to the strawberries.

"You would soon begin to miss your daily work."

"True enough; I shall miss that long after I can no longer do it. Work is a great blessing," — passing the cream to Roger, — "after evil came into the world, work was given as an antidote, not a punishment. The punishment is pain, a rascal whom I feel even now in the joints of my limbs," said Father Le Blanc, drawing his soutane close over his knees, and finishing his sentence with a shake of the head. "Better there than in the heart," he added. His heart evidently troubled him little then, as he finished his coffee with a smack of satisfaction.

After breakfast he proposed a walk down the path to the lake. Winding among the trees, broken now and then by irregular flights of stone steps, this path was a succession of sudden views at different heights, till, turning at last the steep base of the cliff by a long détour, it opened from under a thicket of acacias, upon the beach. The sun, now far above the horizon, had dissipated the morning mist, of which stray thin remnants only hovered here and there in the curves of the shore. Father Le Blanc sat down on a wooden bench under the projecting rock, overhung with mosses and glistening myrtles.

The sudden view was so beautiful that neither felt the necessity of speaking. To break the peace of that summer morning required an effort, as if one feared the ripple of the beach, the songs of the birds, and the dripping of the dew from the leaves, would all cease at the sound of one's voice. On the farther shore Roger saw the broken masses of the ruin just above the rounded outlines of the forest. Gray and sombre amid the green foliage, under the blue sky, it seemed to him almost a prison into which Rénée was about to enter.

"I see only the back of your head, still I fancy there is speculation in your eyes, M. Lande," said his companion, at last.

"I was thinking, M. Le Blanc," replied Roger, turning around, "of what Mademoiselle Rénée said to me last night."

"Ah!" said the priest, with a quick look, "and what did she tell you?"

"That she was about to enter the Congregation of St. Luc," answered Roger, looking intently at his companion.

"Yes, it is an old project."

"And you approve of it?"

"My approval has not been asked, — that is, formally."

"Yet you are an old family friend."

"True," said Father Le Blanc; and he might have added, "older than you," thought Roger to himself. Still he persisted.

"She is very young to take such a step; very young, and very ignorant."

"She has a long time; there is a long novitiate."

"But that novitiate is passed altogether under such influences as to leave no real choice. It would have only one result."

Father Le Blanc shrugged his shoulders.

"Then, as to ignorance," he continued, without noticing the interruption, "Mademoiselle Rénée is innocent, but innocence is not ignorance. Ignorance, if you will, of the lesser and worser things of life ; but such ignorance is often only one side of a profound knowledge."

" When I said ignorant, I meant ignorant of herself, of her own nature, capacities, and heart."

" Oh ! if one were to wait for that reason, there would be no Sisters — and no doctors. In all choice of this kind there is an element of uncertainty."

" Which, if action is not forced upon us, and events give us time, is a reason for prudence and deliberation."

" Exactly so. I admit it. But here is a case, a special one, — we are not talking generalities. You counsel reflection and prudence. Good ! But this has a limit. Mademoiselle has this plan for years, though she has but recently announced it ; and she is twenty. How much more time do you counsel for her ? "

" Knowledge comes from experience, not time alone," replied Roger. " Twenty years with M. Michel, of this strange, quiet life, will not disclose to the heart of a young girl what the woman will be. She is a young plant, growing alone in a secluded garden. Such a life tells her, perhaps, that she has needs, but is not able to name them. It is precisely this ignorance which is dangerous, when, conscious only that something is lacking, she listens to the first voice that breaks the silence, or follows the delusions of her own imagination."

The priest made no answer, though he did not have the appearance of one who was convinced.

"Shall we go in?" he said, presently.

Half-way up the path he stopped, and, turning, laid his hand on Roger's shoulder.

"My son, this first voice that speaks to mademoiselle seems to her a voice from heaven. Let us wait a while patiently, lest, perchance, we strive against God."

Long afterwards Roger remembered these words, and thought of Father Le Blanc's delicate use of the plural.

Had he been accused of loving Mademoiselle Rénée already, he would probably have resented the charge energetically, and, in so doing, would have made a confession. At the mere thought of her, as she stood a picture in one of M. Michel's frames, the world seemed larger to him. Her face was not more fair, her eyes no clearer, than many another's; and certainly it would not have been to this little girl, who said, "how pretty it is!" so simply, that Roger Lande would have gone for the secrets of life. Yet she held in her hand the key to that world which he thought to ignore, — the world of a woman's love and dreams. What a mission has this woman who meets us unforeseen, and who, standing in our narrow pathway, silent, with her finger on her lips, yet says, "Lo! all things are made new."

Nature suffers no infringement of her laws with

impunity.   Resolute and ambitious, this man will
check the outward flow of his feelings, and isolate
himself from human sympathy.   Straightway she
curses him with vanity, and in his prudence even
he becomes a slave to his own illusions!   Contact
with his fellows is the source of his life, and without it self-dependence becomes self-consumption.
This contact is the moment of generation, when
the circuit closes and the sparks appear.

Old M. Lande, at the fireside of the Rue du
Bac, was a beggar for this food of life.   Once he
said to Roger, —

"You are going to make your profession, and
what is incident to it, everything" —

"Yes."

"You will make a mistake, — I have tried it.
There is no mistress who will compensate for solitude.   I say I have tried it.   Music! the divine
priestess whose lyre echoes the harmonies of
heaven, is sufficient!   But, no!   The revelation is
fragmentary, and, in satisfying, it also saddens.
She brings melody into life, but cannot make life
melodious.   What, then, will you expect, if I
have found her wanting?"

Poor M. Lande!   Nothing daunted by experience, for he knew all the while that somewhere in
the wide world was one who, God willing, might
have made out of the broken sounds of life a
song, and of life itself a melody.

V.

WHEN M. Michel was selected as the guardian of his young step-sister, and given to Rénée as a substitute for her natural parents, Providence moved in one of those mysterious ways which no one understands, and which, in this case, some people even openly called in question.

Yet M. Michel least of all was impressed by his new responsibilities. In the case of Stéphanie this responsibility was somewhat less direct, and was mainly limited to the selection of a school at which she was to receive her French education. When, every month, he had visited his young sister at the Convent of Notre Dame, and had received the report of the Superior, he wrote to madame at Kief that " her daughter was all that could be desired," as if this was a matter of course, and there was nothing to be thankful for.

As for Rénée, when his brother besought his protection for his only child, he simply went to Lyons to bring her to Paris, and requested Baptiste to find a maid for mademoiselle.

" If he had charge of the MSS. in the National Library," said Madame Valfort, one of his friends,

"he would not close his eyes out of the room."
For she did not share M. Michel's optimism.

Fortunately Rénée did not belie the wisdom
of Providence. There was more truth than M
Michel suspected in his oft-repeated remark, " You
are a good girl, my child."   And, for a good girl,
Rénée's life had its advantages. She had the best
masters, and, at twenty, was far better educated
than others of her age. If she lacked the companionship of her sex and years, with its inevitable mixture of good and bad, serious and silly,
on the other hand she had passed, in the freedom
of her uncle's salon, the narrow confines of the
conventional system of education. From childhood to the verge of womanhood she had grown
up among these friends of her uncle without ever
making a formal entrée into society. To the question of a new-comer, there was always some one
to answer, " That young girl? Oh, that is the
niece of M. Michel."   And this society had been
a second education, which kept pace, year by year,
with her books, and was not the least of her teach-
ers. If it wanted some elements of childish pleasure, still, among these older companions, it afforded
her glimpses of a broader and larger life than is
to be seen in the school-room, for all its descrip-
tions of China and definitions of the soul. So that
while still inexperienced she could, in some respects, have entered that hot-bed called society
with a sturdier constitution and with less danger

than usual. Among these older people, in this somewhat stately circle, she had not been exposed to those sudden intimacies which ripen the fruit too fast, and exhaust the heart by foolish and false emotions.

M. Michel's friend, Madame Valfort, long ago had been a great beauty. But her intelligence and good sense was beyond the reach of years, and saved her from living only on a remembrance. Equally with M. Lande, but in a different way, she demonstrated the fact that age does not depend upon years, but upon temperament.

Rénée had been for her a source of perplexity, not to say anxiety; and many a kind word and motherly hint had she given to M. Michel's niece, for which the latter had been grateful. If, thanks to Rénée, her uncle had discharged his trust in a manner that gave Madame Valfort an agreeable surprise, the time had at last come when her perplexity was redoubled. She had seen the lorgnettes directed to M. Michel's box, when Rénée, ignorant of all that passed around her, had ears only for the song of Romeo, or eyes only for the dagger of Phædra. More than once she had been importuned for an introduction, though far too loyal to so presume upon her privileges as to introduce a lover into her friend's salon.

" Really," she said to him, one spring day, " all this must have an end. You cannot go on so forever." And after some conversation designed to assist M. Michel's mental vision, it was arranged that in the following winter Rénée should make her social début under her auspices.

When she made her announcement, Rénée seemed less pleased than she anticipated. Still, she gave Madame Valfort a kiss, which reassured her.

"I have told Rénée of our plans," she said to M. Michel, shortly afterwards.

"Oh, by the way!" he said, lifting his spectacles over his eyes, "since I saw you she tells me that she has a plan — a serious one."

"A plan! What do you mean?"

"She wishes to enter a convent."

"A convent!" said Madame Valfort, smiling faintly. "What an idea!"

"The dear child is very determined. It seems she has thought of it for a long time."

"Who can have put such a thought into her head? It is preposterous."

"It may be so," replied M. Michel, who in an emergency always seemed unexpectedly to know what he was about; "but she has settled it."

"Settled it! Why, what can you mean, my friend?" hardly knowing whether to be most astonished at Rénée's audacity or at M. Michel's complacency.

"She has talked with Sœur Ursule of St. Luc, where she goes sometimes with clothing and food for the sick, and she wishes to begin her novitiate

soon — this winter even. It would be a great
sacrifice for me, my dear friend " —

" And a greater one for herself ! "

" That is what I do not know. You think
so ? "

" Decidedly," said Madame Valfort, with em-
phasis, having regained her composure. " But
leave her to me. We have at least six months,
and in that time she will change her mind."

" It is quite possible, I admit," M. Michel answered, letting his spectacles fall again.

In the mean time Roger entered on the scene.
When he first came into the salon of the Rue du
Bac, he was not altogether a stranger to Rénée.
His name certainly was a familiar one. Often had
she heard M. Lande speak of him to her uncle as
they conversed before the fire, and this introduction of the son by the father was sure to have
been a flattering one. All that his own life had
failed to realize, M. Lande saw in Roger. He
never tired of rehearsing those qualities which he
himself lacked, but which Roger possessed ; and
the success and reputation which had been denied
him were even dearer in his eyes as achieved by
his son. When he thought of him it was always
with this halo of honor about his head, as he
would think of one of the apostles. Not that he
was wholly blind to his defects, but he spoke of
them tenderly, as the shadows necessary to the
relief of a strong character, and as something

which time would soften or transform. When, then, Roger himself appeared, Rénée knew him already.

In nothing did Rénée so thoroughly reveal herself as in this desire to enter the cloister. She had been nurtured in solitude, and in solitude the soul declares its true faith, — it is a candidate for nothing. If Roger was right in calling her desire a folly, he was also right in calling it sublime. This offer of her life was, indeed, neither a renunciation nor a flight. She knew too little of life's pleasures for true sacrifice, too little of its sorrows to wish to avoid them. The act she contemplated was simply an aspiration, but this aspiration was the index of her soul. The vows of chastity, humility, or poverty would have been for her only a declaration of faith. To many a tear-stained sufferer this convent door is the Jordan, over which it passes into the Land of Promise and of Peace; and to many a sin-stained penitent it is, like the Rubicon, the symbol of a new and great resolve. But for Rénée it was only the door, nothing else, — leading into a new room surely, but as easily as when from ten years old she became eleven. It was simply a matter of a new dress and a birthday cake.

In the way of this aspiration suddenly appeared two obstacles — Madame Valfort and Roger Lande. The former troubled her but little. As an obstacle her opposition was like a hill over which our road winds, but to which we scarcely give a thought. As to the latter she felt a vague uncertainty and anxiety, as when launching upon an unknown sea we perceive its horizon veiled in mystery, and feel the strength of those great currents which hurry us resistlessly we know not where.

While Roger was breakfasting with M. Le Blanc on the piazza the morning after his arrival in Beauvais, and M. Michel was writing his second volume on Egypt, Rénée, in her white morning dress and slippers, stole quietly down from her chamber to Stéphanie's door.

Evening thoughts grow cold in the night. That which then troubles us, when the imagination is most active, increases the pulse and produces fever; in the morning the fever abates, the mind is more clear, reflection more dispassionate, — but this reaction produces despondency. Rénée had been troubled by her conversation with Roger. Maturing quietly in her own mind, her plan had appeared to her in that conversation in a new light. She had seen it from a different standpoint, and, while she had not been convinced, she was perplexed, — like all who, having settled a question satisfactorily, are disturbed at the appearance of unlooked-for factors, and are thus obliged to doubt a decision which before seemed natural and simple.

For the first time in her life she felt keenly the need of some one besides M. Michel, some one to whom a long explanation, a statement prepared as for a referee, would not be necessary, some one who would divine her trouble without making her confess it. It is a long time before we outgrow that childish indecision which renders choice so difficult; and in this first great responsibility she turned instinctively to one who should, in deciding with her, help her to share it.

But M. Michel, when he kissed her cheek at breakfast, never knew whether it was hot or cold. Even had she been in Paris it is doubtful if she would have consulted Sœur Ursule. Partly for the reason that she felt that Sœur Ursule's decision would necessarily be incomplete, and, being very honest, this would not satisfy her; partly, it must be confessed, because when she thought of Sœur Ursule the color in her cheeks deepened, and she felt a little frightened. Living so long without thoughts which frightened her, this first secret one, which she hardly knew how to name, almost made her ashamed.

When she knocked at the door she had not really thought of speaking with Stéphanie of this, though she would have feared less to talk with her than with any one else whom she knew. Yet in this morning visit she was making one of those shy advances which a friend would so quickly perceive.

"Where are we going to-day, Rénée?" asked Stéphanie.

"My uncle wished to go to the château," said Rénée, looking about the room. Two days before it had been like her own, very pretty, but very simple, with its fresh white bed and curtains that gave it a modest and maidenly air. What had Stéphanie done to it? It seemed more cosy, even luxurious. Perhaps it was only the effect of Stéphanie herself in her pale blue surah *robe de chambre*, trimmed with white lace, as she sat before the dressing glass while Lizette combed her hair.

"How do you go? By carriage?" she asked.

"That is the best way," said Rénée, "because at night the wind often dies out, and we should be obliged to row back. We will send to the town for our carriage, and I will drive over the ponies with M. Lande."

"What a manager you are."

"There must be some management. You know my uncle would not think of such things, and, when the carriages came, no one would know his place."

"True enough," said Stéphanie, smiling. "And coming back, have you arranged that?"

"Would you like to drive my ponies?"

Stéphanie was watching Lizette's fingers as they gave the last touches to that simple coiffure which men pronounced classic, and certain women, after having endeavored in vain to imitate it, pronounced childish, even ugly. For not all faces

lend themselves to that rare agreement between
the subject and the style, which gave to Stéphanie's toilette that natural accent which, more than
anything else, was the secret of its success.

"Very much. I have not driven since I left
Russia. And I will take M. Roger back with
me, and surrender M. Lande to the others. I want
to talk with him."

Following Lizette's fingers, she caught Rénée's
eyes in the glass, and there was that in them
which caused her to say, "That will do. You
may go down for my chocolate."

When Lizette had closed the door, she went
over to Rénée.

"What is the matter, my child?" she said, kissing her cheek and sitting down beside her in the
large easy chair.

Rénée looked at her silently, as if to say, "Why
do you ask me?"

Stéphanie's manner was winning, not because it
was tender, like a mother's, but because it inspired confidence. She knew Rénée well enough
to feel that the shortest way was the best, and
that circumlocutions were needless.

"Something troubles you," she continued, taking her hands. "Do I add to it in speaking to
you?"

"Not yet," said Rénée, courageously.

"I do not wish to do so at all, my dear," said
Stéphanie, drawing Rénée towards her to hide a

smile; "but I think I know what troubles you.
Is it not Roger Lande?"

"Partly."

"And what else? Tell me, dear."

"Sœur Ursule."

"Rénée, do you love him?"

"No!" she said, releasing herself suddenly.

"When one thinks as you are thinking, one
is beginning to love."

"I was afraid so," Rénée said, looking up.

"Afraid? Why should you be afraid? Are
you afraid of loving?"

"I had not thought of it. Moreover, I have
my doubts whether you are right."

"Ah, Rénée, you make me only the more sure.
I do not think you are a thoughtless child to be
deceived by a passing emotion, and something else
which I have in mind I know you are not. One
does not question one's heart seriously, except it
is already lost."

"How can you say so," said Rénée, half rebellious, half ashamed. "You talk to me as if you
wished to persuade me to believe it."

There was certainly more than curiosity in the
question.

"No," said Stéphanie, quietly. "I wish you
to know yourself."

"I should not know myself, if you were right."

"Tell me truly, Rénée, have you begun to question your plan to enter the convent?"

"Not really.   I was thinking of it."

"But what leads you to think of it again?   Is it not he?"

"No," said Rénée, quickly, "it is what he said."

"And if I said it, would it have the same weight with you?"

"I do not know," Rénée answered, after a pause.

"What did he say?"

"Perhaps I do not say it rightly, but it seemed to me as if he said that besides devoting one's self to God, there was something better.   Only I know he meant there was a better way than mine."

"Well, is that impossible?"

"I do not know.   I know one can live a good life in the world, but I thought of a better one."

"But why should we not all choose this better one?   Do you think God has made a world which can be maintained only on the condition that nine-ty-nine live a lower life, while but one lives the higher?"

"I did not say that because the world would stop we cannot all enter a convent, but because not all are able to live this better life."

"It is the same thing," said Stéphanie.   "God made the world."

"Aunt Stéphanie," said Rénée, very earnestly, after a pause.

" What did I ask you, Rénée ? "

" Do you really believe, Stéphanie, that I can live a better life in the world than in the convent ? "

" I believe that better lives are so lived, and that God has given us love to make it possible. Now will you answer me a question as frankly ? "

" What is it ? "

" Would it make you glad if you believed my answer true ? "

" I cannot believe it yet, — I do not know, — whether it is true or not."

" No, but if it were."

Had Lizette been there she would have noticed this strange pertinacity, and would have looked in the glass to see her mistress' face.

" I am not good enough to become a Sister," said Rénée, impulsively. " I believe I should be glad."

" Have I troubled you, Rénée ? "

" If you have, it is my fault," she said. " I have no right to ask you to agree with me. I wanted you to help me."

" Well, now I am going to. I see farther than you do. In some respects, at least, I know better, and I am going to advise you. The convent is a long way off ; you have really six months to decide in, — more if you wish. But Roger Lande is close at hand. What if he should begin to love you ? "

"But he has no right "—

"It is not a question of right, but of fact. Could you prevent it if you wished to? I do not mean that you are at the mercy of every man who should say he adored you. Fortunately most men are so constituted," she said, with a trace of bitterness, "that we can dispose of ourselves without incurring much risk of destroying them. But Roger Lande is not a common man, Rénée. If once he had begun to love you, it would be too late. He could not say then, as you do now, ' No, I am going to retire from life.' "

"But what can I do, Stéphanie? I cannot fly."

"No, you cannot fly. That would be absurd."

"It seems to me that, instead of helping me out of trouble, you wished to convince me that I was surrounded by it," said Rénée.

"Rénée," said Stéphanie, taking her hand in both her own, and looking into her eyes, " I have been in trouble myself, and I have found that the way out is to recognize first that one is in."

"You make me laugh in spite of myself," said Rénée, almost in tears.

"Then we are quits, dear; only you are more honest than I, for just now, when you amused me, I did not dare to. I mean this," she resumed, " I do not say to you, ' Wait! Time will decide for you; it is nothing.' Just fears cannot be reasoned away, or kissed away, and time never decides anything. On the contrary, look into your own heart; listen to what it tells you. It will advise you in this better than Sœur Ursule — or than I. Yours, and his, they are both alike. Hide from them, and they will find you; thwart them, and you will break them. You would know then what you now call trouble; and between this and that there is the difference between the mist that the morning sun drinks up and the clouds that hide his face at night."

"Stéphanie," said Rénée, after a little, "had you been thinking of me, or of — of M. Lande, I mean before this morning?"

" A little," she said, smiling.

" Was it because of anything — anything that I " —

" My dear child, no! Never! Here is Lizette coming."

Rénée threw both arms round her neck.

" Promise me not to speak of it again. I must think it out for myself. Will you come down with me and prepare the lunch we are going to take?" she said, as Lizette opened the door.

" Love, love, love!" said Stéphanie, sitting down, when she had gone, in the chair before her dressing-table, and looking at the face reflected in the glass. " It will drag him out of his seclusion, and prevent her from entering hers." But if this was all she said, she was evidently thinking of more than this.

" Is not madame satisfied ? " asked Lizette, after standing with her tray what seemed a long time.

" Yes," said Stéphanie, letting drop the silk screen over the glass, like a curtain that falls upon a play that is finished.   " Put it here beside me. I am very hungry."

VI.

THE day of the excursion to the Château of
Beauvais was all that its morning promised. Nature was in her generous mood, and filled it with
happy surprises. She sent cool breezes from the
lake to temper the midday air, and while, seated
around the wooden table in the smoke-browned
room of the farmer's house attached to the château,
Rénée's guests were doing justice to her luncheon,
one of those brief showers, which fill the air with
perfumes, and from which the landscape emerges
with fresh coloring and sharpened outlines; and
when the evening sun, streaming through the
trees on the crest of Mont St. Jean, furrowed the
water with crimson lines, she had stilled the breeze
and scattered the clouds, and had made ready one
of those summer nights in which the silent proc-
esses of growth make the very air warm with a
luxurious life, and our own pulses throb with hers
to a nameless sense of desire and peace.

"I am going to drive Rénée's ponies home,"
said Stéphanie, as the carriages drove up to the
door. "Will you trust yourself with me, M.
Lande?" she asked, turning to Roger, as she
stepped into the phaeton and took the reins.

She had scarcely spoken with him all the day long, and her invitation surprised him; but he accepted it with pleasure. In spite of his resolve, Stéphanie excited his curiosity, and, while he had exchanged so few words with her since their first meeting at Aix, her very reserve was a fascination.

As Rénée had said, there was an ease in her manner which made one feel as though one had known her a long time; still, he agreed more and more with Father Le Blanc, that this knowledge, like the reflection in the river, apparently so real in its perspective, was only a surface illusion. Perhaps, too, in fortifying himself against curiosity, he had anticipated the manner in which it would be aroused, and, coming from an unexpected quarter, the enemy's force is not always recognized.

The process of becoming acquainted with some people is a restful one: every day brings its own disclosure, which completes the intimacy and fills out the character; one by one appear those tender tones and melting shades which soften and fuse its contrasts. And there are others, like a picture whose foreground we feel to be unimportant, whose horizon alone fascinates and entices us. What is near and apparent but renders us the more eager to penetrate this encircling mystery. M. Michel certainly seemed insensible to any such peculiarity in his sister. He treated her, as he did every one, with that charming courtesy, almost gallantry, belonging to certain of his race, — that race of literary men who, absorbed in their ideal world, slip out into life occasionally only, as one would make a visit, to say, " Madame, I trust you are well," or, " Accept my congratulations."

Roger was not guilty of a vulgar curiosity to know her life, or her past. But the woman, — what was she? What he had heard from Father Le Blanc, what he had seen at Aix, — these things he thought of, not for themselves, but only as they contrasted with her quiet dignity and reserve, and increased the desire to understand the woman. The question he asked himself, as he thought of her, was less what she had done or been, and rather what she might do and be. Indeed, those very occasions on which he had observed her, so different were they; her moods, too, so variable were they, that one might well ask for the single answer to all the forms of this enigma. In the garden of the Hôtel du Nord he might have seen a woman meeting her lover; delivering the letter to Stéphanie Milevski, the actor in some court intrigue; trifling with M. de Marzac, she was only a woman, beautiful and brilliant, a little venomous, even, but ever mysterious; later, as he poured her coffee, imperious, distrustful, even dangerous; and then, suddenly, as once before, at Aix, trustful, frank, with a trace of tenderness. Doubtless,

to this nature, as to all, there was the one skeleton key which unlocks all its wards, the one word
which explains all its contradictions. What was
it? For natures, like melodies, have their key-
note, and through one's moods, however varied,
runs a central fibre of character, like the string in
a necklace of many-colored beads.

After the ponies had started she gave him the
reins, and leaned back against the cushions.

"What a night!" she said.

The stars were beginning to come out; not
clear and cold, as in winter, but veiled in an air
heavy with warmth and odors, and filled with
murmuring sounds. The silence of a winter's
night suggests the temporary death that reigns
over nature; the mother's bosom is still because
it is cold. But in this summer silence her warm
breath is on our cheeks, and we hear the very
buds swell.

"I supposed you wished to drive," he said, taking the reins.

"No, I wish to talk with you."

"I thought so," replied Roger, to whom this invitation began to have a significance.

"Why? Is your conscience so sensitive?"

"It is about myself, then, that you wish to
talk."

"Yes, and no. I am going to commence with
an allegory. You remember you once did me a
favor."

"For which you thanked me."

"Are you so afraid of having me as your debtor? If you insist upon reversing the rôles, I warn you I might prove an exacting creditor."

"I think the account is closed."

"You amuse me," she said, laughing. "Do you intend to go through life with your accounts always balanced? But seriously, M. Lande," she said, sitting up, "I have something to say to you, and I wish you to listen to me patiently. I return to Paris to-morrow. Letters which I received this morning call me back unexpectedly, and it may be I shall travel. At all events, it is uncertain when I shall see you again, and I cannot make up my mind to be silent, even if my concern should prove groundless, or if, in discharging this duty, I am less delicate than you were. I have a friend — a young girl. She has a strong character, and is capable of strong feeling; but she has lived apart from the world, almost in solitude. The very angels would smile to hear her confession. Left to herself, she will continue her life as it begins."

"You mean that she will enter the cloister."

"Precisely; and on that question I do not wish to exert any influence. I might regret to see her take the veil; for though her character, developing thus in all its purity, should so remain unscarred, I should miss something in it. I admire moral beauty most when it is also moral heroism.

That is, I prefer character beautiful because strong, and strong because capable of resistance, not because superior to temptation. Be that as it may, the latter is more difficult. Should she enter her convent, however much I might regret it, concern for her would cease. And if she did not " —

" Well? " said Roger.

Stéphanie paused a moment. She was approaching the more difficult part of her undertaking.

" A friend of yours, M. Lande," she continued presently, " meets this friend of mine. Carry him this message. Do not ask for an explanation, for he might refuse your right to it, and you would thus offend him ; but ask him to reflect upon what he may do, even unconsciously, — on the responsibility he may assume. Tell him to remember how, from morning to night, we are ever scattering the seeds whose harvest we cannot foretell, and oftenest never know. Tell him to remember that soil in which they fall, the human heart, — that soil so rich that of all these seeds none utterly perish. Will you tell him this ? " she said, earnestly.

" Yes, I will tell him."

" And if," she said more gayly, looking into Roger's grave face, " he should even then be offended, tell him he is wrong to be so, since, instead of preaching a sermon, you were content with simply repeating the text."

" I will answer for him," said Roger.

"I am glad to hear you say so. You increase my confidence. You must use the whip, M. Lande; our friends are overtaking us."

"They will be sorry to lose you so soon."

"And I shall be sorry to go, for some reasons. But in one respect I have an unfortunate temperament. I exhaust things too quickly. Now that I have been in Beauvais a day, I am not sorry to go; in a week it would almost be necessary."

"That is not temperament, but only a habit."

"Perhaps so," she replied. "But temperament lies back of habit, and determines it. One is the mould of the other. I thought of it this afternoon as I was looking with M. Le Blanc at the view from the château tower. I saw it all in a glance, while he discovered its beauties gradually, one by one. I was ready to go when he was in the midst of his enjoyment. When one takes in everything so rapidly, there is no time for real pleasure, — everything becomes a matter of course."

"That is weariness; every temperament can be harnessed," said Roger, for the sake of the argument. "The power to take in rapidly ought no' to prevent us from enjoying."

"Well, it does; if only because possession always diminishes enjoyment. Besides, it makes very little difference, in such a case, what ought to be. You cannot prescribe an enjoyment to a patient who has no capacity for it. It would be a great advance in your art if you could ; inasmuch as we live in its midst, and are obliged to see it constantly, even when we cannot feel it.   But our conversation is very doleful ; let us change it."

A long pause followed, which would have been embarassing, only there was no self-consciousness in it.

" How strange we are ! " said Stéphanie, breaking the silence.   " We sometimes tell strangers more than we do our best friends."

" That is only natural," he replied.   " To our friends we are either known so well that we have no need to speak, or so little that we fear to."

Then followed another silence, an important part of some conversations, and one in which the argument makes the most progress.

" We talk a great deal about friends and friendships," Stéphanie said, thoughtfully, " and after all we have none.   It is easy to describe the ideal friendship, and it is because we are not ready for our part of the compact that it is not realized. But we are prone to lay the blame on others, if blame there is.   Ideal friendships are for ideal people.   As we are, pride and self-respect forbid our tearing away all the veils of the soul that friends, such as they are, may know us completely : and when we complain that there are none, we are lamenting our own unfitness, and in recognizing that clearly, we ought to find reserve a virtue. Too much friendship is dangerous, even fatal."

"'Be at peace with many, nevertheless have but one counselor of a thousand.'"

"Are you quoting? You are so often epigrammatic that I am doubtful."

"Your compliment is a dubious one. Epigrams are brilliants usually bought at the expense of truth."

"But you do not answer me."

"Was I quoting? Yes."

"Who?" asked Stéphanie.

"Jesus, the son of Sirach."

"That is really curious. That book is one of my brother's favorites. He says it is a complete code of morality. And he sometimes quotes from it very appositely. Do you know Madame Brèda? No? Well, she is very bright and, in a superficial way, well-read and agreeable. When M. Michel published his first volume on Egypt, she took an immense interest in it, and the amount of torture she inflicted upon him must have been incalculable, since it resulted in what, for him, was so keen a thrust. She is a tireless talker. She bought the volume, and insisted on conversing with him about Egypt on every occasion, and, finally, even on his writing something on the fly-leaf. I happened in his study one day, and, seeing the book on the table, was curious to know how he had gratified her. Opening the cover, I found this : —

"'As the climbing up a sandy way is to the

feet of the aged, so is a wife full of words to a quiet man.' "

" Did he send it? " asked Roger, laughing.

" No.　I remonstrated, and he yielded.　He had written it in a moment of exasperation, and had then forgotten all about it.　But, to go back, your proverb is a wise one, and I would add to it, — a thousand times listen to his counsel, but seek it once only.　Friendship, here, is a staff, and when it breaks it is under the load of our own infirmities."

" It seems to me you are returning to a doleful subject."

" Yes," she said, impetuously; " I cannot help it."　Then, leaning back in her corner, and looking up to the stars, " It is the night, — it is stronger than I."

" When my mother was dying, M. Lande," she continued after a moment, in a voice so quiet it seemed that of another person, " a street singer, under the window, sang the prison song from ' Il Trovatore.'　I did not notice it especially at the time, though I was conscious of it.　From that day I cannot hear that song without feeling again as I did at that moment.　It has the power to reproduce, against my will even, the conditions of that mental state, and when it reaches my ear, no matter where, no matter how suddenly, I have the very sense of suffocation in the throat, and that strange swelling at the heart which oppressed me then. I can think of that scene, even dwell upon it, without experiencing these sensations; but this song seems to have become wrought into my very body and to control it, so that now, when the first cause of these sensations no longer exists, when even the remembrance of it cannot renew them, at its first note I feel as I then felt, and as I should feel if suddenly brought face to face with a mortal peril. This is what I mean when I say this summer night is stronger than I. Like that song, it has the power to remind me of another night, — no! not to remind me of it, to reproduce it!"

"Life would be hard for you in any event," exclaimed Roger, involuntarily; "it makes upon you such deep impressions."

She laughed with one of those swift changes of voice and manner which characterized her, and, as the ponies turned under the trees of Mont St. Jean, turned the conversation to lesser things.

At the steps he gave her his hand to alight.

"Good-night and good-by," she said. "I shall take the early train. Of our ride remember only this, that you gave me a promise and are an ambassador."

"But I shall see you this evening."

"Oh, certainly," she said, as he opened the door.

When Lizette that evening went, as was her wont, to undo her morning's work, she found her mistress leaning upon the window which overlooked the sleeping lake, with her head bowed down in her hands, and her face bathed in tears. If she was surprised she did not show it, and to the order to pack the trunks and to be ready for an early start, she answered as usual, " Yes, madame."

The next morning at breakfast Stéphanie was absent.

Several times during the week telegrams from desperate or impatient patients arrived for Roger; but he remained faithful to his plan, and resisted all appeal. This brief rest was grateful to him, and he missed less than he had anticipated the pressure of his daily routine.

Having discovered each other's habits of early rising, the little party of five gathered every morning about the table on the piazza, and, alike to the younger and the older, the long day without duties or engagements was a pleasant vista.

" *Nec cupias, nec metuas,*" said Father Le Blanc, one morning.

The second volume on Egypt progressed, it is to be presumed, satisfactorily, for M. Michel appeared every morning at the door of his library with a genial smile, and spent the remainder of his day in France with his guests. A boat ride on the lake ; a drive through the environs ; a visit with Rénée to her sick poor ; — " I am doubly armed against misfortune," she said ; " I have my priest and my physician ; " — a hard-fought strug gle at piquet after dark ; long talks about nothing and short ones on the state of politics or the drift of religious and scientific thought ; a duet in the evening, when M. Lande opened the dingy box which contained his treasure and Rénée uncovered the piano ; these were the simple pleasures which, for such different reasons, made the days happy ones for each. *Hæc olim meminisse juvabit*, was Father Le Blanc's constant refrain.

With that fine perception which is not acquired if it is not native, both Rénée and Roger had avoided all reference to the subject of their first conversation. It was a question for events, not for arguments, to decide. Either would have felt a moral jar had the other reopened it so soon, while each knew the other had not forgotten it.

In this quiet life, regulated so simply by the natural tastes of these five people, some of what Madame Valfort would have called the proprieties of society were lost out of sight. On the part of M. Michel, because, if left to himself, he naturally dispensed with them ; on the part of Rénée, because untrained to their slavery ; and as to Father Le Blanc, this society was ideal enough to ignore conventionalities, and he would have apologized for their absence only to a stranger. Thus it happened that Roger often found an hour alone with Rénée on the piazza, acted as assistant gardener, and filled with her the morning vases, or strolled with her to the wood-cutter's cottage to

visit the paralytic boy to whom Rénée was a guardian angel, — happy hours ! which Madame Valfort, with all her tact and good nature, would
have marred, even had she herself assumed the
rôle of dragoness.

But all things come to an end; only, when the
end comes, things are no longer the same. Father
Le Blanc and M. Lande, two old men who knew
how to appreciate true happiness, had laid in a
store of sweet recollections ; in this sunny atmosphere the armor which Roger had worn as the ambitious, even selfish, physician, proved cumber-
some, and some of its pieces were laid aside ; in
the spring-time of life, he, with some deliberation,
Rénée, with some dream-like consciousness, had
sown hopes; and M. Michel had added two important chapters to his second volume.

VII.

AFTER the departure of her guests, Beauvais did not seem to Rénée quite the same place. Nor would it ever again be what it had been.

Since first, as a little girl, she had passed the summer months among its cool forests and beside its placid lake, it had been a sort of Paradise for which she yearned all through the winter, and of which an excursion now and then into the environs of Paris reminded her tantalizingly. There she came closer to the great heart of Nature, to which as children we are so near, — whose constant beat of sympathy the noise of the world may indeed drown for a time, but which in later years we hear again gladly, falling asleep at last to its loving murmur.

All kinds of bonds and fetters tied her literally hand and foot in Paris; pavements and sidewalks, asphalt and Macadam, all kept her feet from the warm, moist earth which they loved; roar of wheels and clatter of hoofs drowned all the inarticulate speech of wood and stream which address the heart in their own alphabet; and through the blaze of the gaslit night, or the smoke and dust of the day, scarce a moonbeam or a sun ray could filter pure and uncontaminated.

And there were fetters of another kind, conven
tionalities and proprieties, which put the very residue of nature, left in that hive of artificial life, beyond her reach. No wonder that we laugh at the
rustic, and no wonder that he laughs at us. Our
education has made us aliens to the brotherhood
of Nature, and only Nature's touch makes us kin.

But at Beauvais, if the lake invited her, she
could go out to it ; not in a carriage, to stare at it,
as in the Bois de Boulogne, but to dip her hands
in its cool waters, and let its waves rise and fall
about her ankles ; if the woods called her, she had
only to open her window and listen, or go out
under their shadows and dream. Here she was
free. There were no eyes, prying or cold, to cen-
sure her or to laugh at her. For Nature is like a
mistress, — we love to be alone with her; even as
our mother, there is between us and her the sanctity of close relationship and communion. Before
the world of houses and carpets with which our
factitious wants have surrounded us ; before the
world of towers and spires which our heavenly aspirations have builded us, we are ashamed to
stretch ourselves out at full length upon the soft
damp mosses, lest we hear the sneer of the dilet-
tante or the reproach of the pietist.

Rénée did not philosophize over her pleasures.
She was not yet beginning to lose them or the love
of them. And, deprived as she had been of those
ties which sweeten girlhood, perhaps the overflow

of her soul was more than usually directed into this channel. Certainly there was one injunction of Sœur Ursule's which she did not fully understand, and against which she found it hard not to rebel.

" It will be all the easier for you," said this holy teacher, " who have not felt in all their intensity the power of earthly ties, to develop and purify the influences which unite us to Heaven. Do some appear to abjure these ties readily? This power is bought at a great price. For they had first placed in them all their reliance, to find them in the end stained with sin and dimmed with tears. You, my child, are spared this ordeal, and Nature will be easily conquered; not because you have found her a broken reed, but because you have not learned to lean upon her."

Conquer Nature! Yes, it was well enough to say so in Paris, among the sick and suffering of the Hôtel-Dieu St. Luc, — but in Beauvais! under the branches of those great trees, it was as if one should say to the bud swelling in spring-time, " Conquer this force which expands your petals and works in your thousand cells, for it is the principle of disease and decay, and only when you have subdued it shall the true flower blossom in an immortal life and bear fruit in eternity. '

This was a mystery which Rénée solved by not thinking of it.

And yet Beauvais was no longer the same. Not

a ripple had deserted the lake; every star was faithful, and appeared at night in its surface as before; the waters on the shore, the wind among the leaves talked still with one another, and Father Le Blanc had not carried away in his cassock a star, a leaf, or a pebble. Yet all was changed. After all, the wealth of Nature is not hers, and her face is but the mirror in which we see our own. Love has but to shoot a single arrow, and straightway we charge the universe with hope, and dewdrops become opals.

M. Michel remarked that when the migration season arrived Rénée made none of the usual objections. He had delayed his return later than customary, for he had become very much absorbed in the land of the Pharaohs; and this delay was due to the absolute quiet of Beauvais, — for social requirements were few, — a quiet which left him undisturbed on the Upper Nile. There was also another circumstance which prolonged his stay. He was growing old, and yet had got no further than Neferkara of the VIth dynasty. He felt that time was pressing, and that he must hasten. Certain admonitions were not wanting. They were, it is true, gentle ones; a little unsteadiness of vision, a little dullness of touch; but they foretold the time when judgment too would waver, and imagination and memory grow dull. But M. Michel kept all this to himself. It was one of the aggravations of his character that he did not seek sympathy. All relationships become closer and dearer through our poverty as well as our wealth. A friend must need sympathy as well as be capable of giving it, else we never have the pleasure of giving, which is the golden side of the shield of gifts.

But if M. Michel was ever ill, he turned his face to the wall. Unlike most of those who live in health on independent resources, but who in sickness are either fretful and exacting or gentle and craving, he enjoyed neither fretting nor worrying, and craved only to be let alone. On doctors, as a species, he placed no reliance. "A wise physician," he used to say, "is a John the Baptist, who recognizes that his only mission is to prepare the way for a greater than he, — Nature." This, however, would not have prevented him from summoning all the doctors in France for Rénée, if she were ill; and he would have explained this inconsistency by saying that Rénée, more fortunate than he, could respond to that most potent medicine of the materia medica, faith in the physician, — a remedy which a wise physician, however conscious of his impotence, carefully husbands to the last.

But the leaves were beginning to fall; the winds were growing colder; certain sessions of other spectacled worthies were about to take place in Paris, and the return could no longer be delayed.

"I wonder whether Stéphanie has returned,"

said Rénée to her uncle, as they rode up together in the train.

"Returned? Where has she been?" asked M. Michel.

" Why, don't you remember? I read you her letter only the other day. She did not say where she was going."

" To Kief, perhaps."

" I wish we might see more of her, uncle."

" Probably we shall, my child. There have been reasons for the contrary in the past. After the count's death she remained at Kief, secluded. Moreover the health of her mother gave way suddenly, and she devoted herself to her care. When she died," and M. Michel laid down his paper and looked out of the window, as if he could see the event of which he was speaking, " there was another reason for retirement. You know it is not long since she came out from this seclusion, and in that time, quite naturally, she has traveled a good deal. Probably, as I said, this winter we shall see her more frequently."

" Did you know the Count Milevski, uncle?"

" I went to Kief to the wedding. Do you remember? It was not long ago."

" I remember you went away. Tell me something about it, uncle; I am interested."

" There is nothing to tell, especially," said M. Michel. " They were married, and the wedding was as usual."

Rénée, who was a little tired, in one of those moods of tenderness which sometimes came to her when with M. Michel, and which embarrassed him not a little, had nestled close to his side and laid her head upon his shoulder. These appeals to him in his capacity as father really touched him, and he usually responded by a more than ordinarily tender kiss on her forehead, after which he relapsed into constraint, and, putting his arm around her awkwardly, sat very still without moving a muscle.

"And then?" said Rénée.

"The count took his wife to St. Petersburg to present her at court. It was shortly after their return that he was arrested."

"You know I never asked you about these things. I never should dare to speak of them with Stéphanie. Why was the count arrested?"

"No one knows fully why it was. He had been in high favor with the emperor, and it was said that Stéphanie was warmly received at court. Her mother wrote me of her reception, and of how the emperor gave her some token of his goodwill. Then, suddenly, her husband was denounced, — by whom, no one knows. Such things are done very quickly in Russia. He was summoned to St. Petersburg, and in less than a week was on his way to Siberia. All this broke the good mother's heart. Stéphanie was the child of her old age, and she had planned for her a great future. Then, on the journey, the count died."

"I should think it would have broken Stéphanie's," said Rénée.

"It was a terrible shock; but hers was younger. At her mother's age it is more sad to have our plans fail, for we have no longer the time, then, to repair them, or to form new ones."

"But what had M. Milevski done?"

"No one knows exactly; except that he was associated with the Socialists. The trial was a secret one."

"But could not Stéphanie do something? Had the count no friends!"

"Ah! Russia is not France, my child. Moreover, it appears that she did everything. She appealed herself to the emperor. The count had hardly left St. Petersburg before she arrived there to plead for him. But it was useless. Then he died, suddenly. After that, what remedy was there, even if the emperor had been willing to apply it?"

"One can have justice," said Rénée, indignantly.

"After all the worst is done? Justice cannot restore life. In such a case reparation is beyond the power of man, and is in the hands of God." And then, after a pause, "The count's estates were also forfeited, but they were afterwards restored."

"I would not have accepted them!" said Rénée.

"Well, no; neither did Stéphanie. But her

mother arranged that. She did not wish to see her daughter left a beggar. She was prudent, and looked into the future, and the proposal which Stéphanie would have rejected, unbeknown to her, she accepted. In lieu of the estates, she received a sum of money; not an equivalent, still a large sum; and, at her death, this came to Stéphanie as a part of her inheritance."

"She must have loved her husband very much," said Rénée, after a long interval of silence.

"Oh, undoubtedly," replied M. Michel.

Evidently this last step in the conversation had carried him beyond his depth. Even Rénée laughed to herself over the calm assumption of his answer. She remained so long thinking over what she had heard, that M. Michel supposed her asleep, and being unable to open his paper without disturbing the head on his shoulder, resigned himself to his own thoughts, and was soon in the land of the Pharaohs.

Thus it happened that two people, while making the journey from Beauvais to Paris, passed the time, one in Russia, the other in Egypt.

Baptiste, who had preceded them by a train, met them at the station on their arrival at Paris.

"Madame Milevski called this morning to inquire when you were to return, mademoiselle," said the old servant, "and learning that it was to-day, she wrote this note."

"Ah, I am so glad!" exclaimed Rénée, tearing it open eagerly. It was very short.

I am delighted that I am to see you so soon.   I shall come to-night to kiss you, and to propose a plan to you.   STÉPHANIE.

"What can it be?" thought Rénée.

In the evening, after dinner, she listened at every roll of wheels in the Rue du Bac, till at last a carriage stopped in the street, and a moment later Stéphanie herself appeared at the door.   Rénée threw her arms around her neck.

"I am so glad to see you again!"

Stéphanie kissed both her cheeks, and they sat down together before the fire.   For very different reasons, these two women were beginning to lean upon each other.

"And Beauvais; is it charming as ever?" asked Stéphanie.

"Yes, but I missed you very much."

"What! with your ponies, your boat, and your château?"

"When I think that perhaps I have seen them for the last time!"   Stéphanie noted the "perhaps."   "I really love my ponies; this morning I laid my cheeks on their warm noses and thought of Sancho."

"How would you like to play Sancho in reality?"

"What do you mean, Stéphanie?"

"I mean that I should be the Knight of the Woful Countenance," not in search of adventures, but to forget them, she thought, "and that you should be my squire, and that we should take a little journey together into Spain, under the cork-trees."

"Really?"

"Why, yes, really," said Stéphanie, smiling at Rénée's enthusiasm.

"What do you think M. Michel would say?"

"What I do; that it would be delightful."

"Is this the plan you spoke of in your note?"

"Yes. But I shall not go without you; it rests with you."

"Oh, if it only depended on me!"

"Well, does it not?"

"Madame Valfort" —

"Leave that to me," interrupted Stéphanie.

"I would rather arrange it myself," Rénée said, after thinking a moment. "You know she wished me to be presented this winter. Of course, I am under no obligation, except as she meant it kindly; but, under the circumstances, if I should decide to go with you, it would be better for me to tell her; otherwise, she would think that I went simply to thwart her projects. If I left you to see her, it would appear as if I was afraid or ashamed to — I mean, as if I avoided her."

"I do not wish to interfere with Madame Valfort's projects; on the contrary, I approve of them. But if I should take charge of her projects, would you object?"

"No, and yes."

"Let us see. When does your novitiate begin?" asked Stéphanie, without replying to Rénée's double answer.

"In January."

"That is settled, is it?"

"I had settled it in my own mind. I am afraid Sœur Ursule would not think my going to Spain a very wise idea."

"Since I am to lose you so soon, I think you ought to give me a place in these next three months. That would not be too much to ask would it? But you must decide for yourself; I do not wish to argue with you. If you went to please me simply, you would not enjoy yourself, nor would I either."

"Oh, I want to go, Stéphanie."

"What a silly girl you are! You have actually committed yourself to Madame Valfort's salon against your wish, and yet you hesitate to go with me, although you desire to."

"I have not really committed myself."

"It amounts to the same thing."

"To be frank with you, Stéphanie, I am not afraid of Madame Valfort. It is perfectly evident that she wishes to divert me from what I have in view. If I did exactly what I wished to, I should not accept her invitations; but then, I know that if I do it will not affect me. But I am not so sure of myself with you," she added, playfully, though with an undercurrent of earnestness. "I wish to go with you more than I ought to."

"Why do you wish to?" said Stéphanie. "I am curious to know what these bad motives are that trouble your conscience. Is a little love for me one of them? Because, if it is," she continued in the same earnest pleasantry, " I am in need of some, and you can begin your work of charity without delay."

The undertone of Stéphanie's words did not escape Rénée, in whose memory was still fresh her conversation with her uncle.

"I wish you would promise me something," she said, a little reluctantly.

"What?"

"Not to speak to me of my plans unless I do."

" As a condition of your going?"

Rénée was a little ashamed to say yes, and so remained silent.

" Well, no, my dear child, I will make no such engagement; not because I wish to argue with you or to influence you, but because I do not wish you to distrust me even if I do. You are proposing a truce, as if I were your enemy. Now, if I should happen to differ from you on any point, you must first respect my views, and then you must give me credit for enough delicacy and good sense not to importune or to wound you by forcing them on your notice. That is the condition that

I should propose to you, and the only one under which we can make any progress together."

."Yes, you are right; I know you are," said Rénée, sitting down on the hassock at her feet. "But I was not suspicious, Stéphanie; of you, I mean. And if you only knew," she said, laying her head down in her lap, "it was myself I was doubtful of. I don't know—I am perplexed sometimes—I want to talk with you. I have been thinking of it ever since you went away. Sometimes I feel terribly lonely."

Stéphanie's hand was on her head, and its soft pressure, as it moved over her hair, was a message of love and sympathy.

"We won't talk of these things to-night, Rénée dear. Put them all out of your thoughts, if you can. You are troubled and nervous. We will make our excursion to Spain together, and when you come back it will be like waking from a sleep; you will feel refreshed, and your way will appear clearer to you."

"The only way out of perplexity is decision," said poor Rénée, resolutely.

"Yes, my dear, but our perplexity is often the result of too much thinking. Wait a little, and let your mind rest. Do you accept my plan?"

"It seems a perfect dream to me."

"Well, then, we will realize it. When can you get ready?"

"I am all ready,—that is, there are only a few

little things, — one of them is to tell M. Michel."

"Do his friends come as usual, on Saturday ? "

"I had not thought of it; we are only just arrived; no one knows it."

"If you go, it hardly seems worth the while. Suppose you should suggest to him that he invite those who were at Beauvais, and perhaps one or two more, and wait until you return to commence his usual receptions. I am anxious to go at once. If you send your invitations to-morrow, perhaps we shall be able to start on Monday. I shall take Lizette, and she will answer for both of us. How little luggage can you take? I will show you what restrictions I put upon myself, if you can come to see me to-morrow."

"At what hour ? "

"At any time in the afternoon."

"And what about Madame Valfort ? "

"You will do as you please, of course; but if you ask my advice, it would be to leave it with me. You can hardly see her without raising the very question you wish to avoid, while I can arrange it without her even thinking of it."

"You make all the difficulties vanish," said Rénée, lifting her head and looking up into the face above her.

"Often, dear, they are only imaginary, and sometimes our best road lies round them, not over them."

Just then the library door opened, and M. Michel appeared on the threshold, the gold rim of his spectacles shining in his gray hair.

"Why, sister, is it you?" he said, advancing to greet her; "what a charming tableau!"

Rénée was still sitting at Stéphanie's feet, her elbows in her lap, and her head resting in her hands.

"Baptiste did not tell me you were here."

"No, I did not ask him to. I wished to approach you by a flank movement."

"By a flank movement?" he said, looking from one pair of bright eyes to the other; "I capitulate beforehand."

As, in fact, he did; and when Rénée fell asleep that night, it was to build veritable castles in Spain.

VIII.

STÉPHANIE had not forsaken the pleasant party at Beauvais simply to revisit Kief, and the episode at Aix might have enabled Roger to answer Rénée's question better than M. Michel. While the latter had been writing history, Madame Milevski had had some share in making it, and had narrowly escaped playing therein an important part.

The political situation in France at this time was disturbed and perplexing. The humiliation of a disastrous war, the bitterness of a terrible civil strife, were still fresh in the public mind. The tread of a foreign host had scarcely died upon the ear, and ruins, yet blackened by smoke and torn by shells, met the eye in the very centre of the capital.

Republican for eighty years, France still worked persistently at the gigantic task of organization. But for a moment progress again seemed doomed to another check, and once more France faltered between her traditions and her aspirations.

In the Assembly, factions were numerous. They formed and reformed about important measures, like the battalions of an army about its standards; ever in motion, but without making progress. A vote was the vote of a coalition; a coalition which straightway thereafter fell asunder. There were those who still rallied round the eagles of that great comedian whose feet, from Boulogne to Sedan, were wet with blood; there were still those who uncovered their heads before the recluse of Frohsdorf, and asserted the divine right of kings; there were the personal adherents of the princes and the constitutional monarchy, the fanatical devotees to the radical republic, and that old guard of democratic conservatism, the flower of French politics, which stood firm amid this chaos around the "liberator of the territory."

Fused for a moment by a common hate, all these factions save one had united against the common enemy, the conservative republic, and M. Thiers was overthrown in May by the Assembly which had apotheosized him in March.

In the name of order and public security, evoking the red spectre of revolution before a people which had not yet forgotten the horrors of the Commune, this coalition had called to the presidency a tried soldier, whose disinterestedness and nobility of character were unquestioned. But this coalition, held together only by a common animosity, was destitute of principles, and therefore had no programme. Successful in its attempt to overload the Left Centre with the follies and crimes of the extreme republican wing, it had awakened the fears of the people by the old rallying cry of " social order." But the people asked, What next? Conservatism, on the 24th, meant social order; but on the 25th it might mean the monarchy or the empire. Fused for a day, after the skirmish the coalition segregated about the old centres. The Assembly had adjourned; the people watched and waited.

It was at this time that one, who for years had been forgotten, was remembered, — the First Gentleman of France, — and that words almost lost to memory were repeated on every lip, — the legitimate monarchy and Henri Cinq. This reaction was intensified, after the adjournment, by many favoring influences. The cry, " Beware the Red Spectre ! " had a temporary success ; the horrors of the Commune, the follies of the radicals, the errors of the republic itself, inspired fear ; rumors of another Bonapartist *coup d'état* filled the public heart with uncertainty ; the Orleans princes, representing the constitutional monarchy, had given in their allegiance to their chief. and the royal house of France was again united under its legitimate head ; satisfactory guaranties were rumored abroad, — that the rights acquired by the Revolution would be respected by the throne, — liberty of the press, universal suffrage, the right of assembly ; the fleur-de-lys was to be blazoned on the tri-color of the Revolution ; moreover, it was the season of pilgrimages to Lourdes, to **La Salette**, pilgrimages not altogether destitute of political significance; the *vieille noblesse* emerged from the retirement into which, during the empire, pride and disgust had led them; while lovers of tranquillity, who had money in their stockings, hesitated between the uncertain stability of the republic and these promises of a liberal monarchy.

On the 5th of August took place that interview between the French princes which brought the slowly elaborated plans of the royalists to that point at which they must either succeed or miscarry.

It was the day before Stéphanie Milevski received her summons to Paris. On the 7th, at eleven in the morning, she reached the city, and drove to her hotel in the Boulevard St. Germain; and, still in her traveling dress, without ascending to her own rooms, she entered the door of the salon, where a half score of gentlemen waited to receive her.

During the period of royalist revival there were numerous salons famous as the rendezvous of the monarchical party, and having a certain political significance. They were graced by the presence of party chiefs, of church dignitaries, of the representatives of the old nobility. They were the foci of attraction for all who dared to hope for the king; their themes of conversation were the restoration, the salvation of France, and the triumph of the Church over her enemies. But there was another, frequented by few, unknown to the many, whence had secretly emanated many of those favoring influences which had once more turned the public eye in the direction of Frohsdorf, composed of a small circle of secondary but important personages, inspired by and under the direction of the great chiefs, instruments in their hands, yet not passive ones, in the formation of public opinion and the shaping of public events. It was a small but select circle of men, devoted, intelligent, resolute; it comprised a general of the army, an emissary of the Order of Jesus, deputies of the Assembly, and journalists, — among the latter, M. de Marzac. For more than a year since first the glittering structure of the empire began to give evidence of that rottenness which predetermined its sudden collapse, this company, united by a common aspiration, had planned and waited. Personally known to their chiefs, but acting without compromising mandate or authority, they had gradually passed from the stage of loyal supporters to that of active agents. On the morning of August 7th they had been charged with a special mission; none other than the preparations for the entry of the king into his capital. The hour for action was approaching, and the plan was as follows: —

The king was to proceed incognito to Versailles and remain in seclusion; at a favorable moment, when the tide was highest, he was to gather about him the House of France, and appeal to the nation ; the president was pledged to maintain order and execute the will of the Assembly ; the people wavered between fear of anarchy and love for peace ; it needed only, therefore, that, at such an auspicious moment, the king himself, with his suite and generals, should enter the gates of Paris, that France herself should recognize him as her safety, and resound once more to the echoes of that old cry, " Vive le roi ! "

This plan, fully matured in all its details, was not to be submitted to the approval of the king till the decisive hour had come. Subject to contingencies, it might even be abandoned. This reticence on the part of the conspirators towards the chief actor proceeded from uncertainty as to his own preferences. It was a resource to be held in reserve for the time when, if he had not himself already taken the initiative, there would be no choice save between it and failure. Nothing indeed had been more remarkable in the history of this illustrious exile than the calm assumption of his divine rights and the complete absence of all thirst for power. He had waited, incapable of intrigue ; the king, but never the pretender.

The summer passed in uncertainty and nervousness. The tone of the radical press served to intensify the reaction. Further concessions to the spirit of the Revolution inclined the people still more to listen to the promise of a wise and stable administration. The Assembly was to convene early in the autumn. It seemed best to take the tide at the flood, and to profit alike by the conservative union and the political uncertainties which the opening of the Assembly might dispel. It was decided, therefore, to force the issue and to sound the king through an emissary to Frohsdorf.

" I am going," Stéphanie had written to Rénée, late in September, " to make a little journey. You will soon return to Paris. I also. We will then talk together."

There were reasons, both in the character of the king and in the history of Stéphanie's family, why she, a woman, was selected for this mission. Her mother, Rose de Vigny, was the daughter of a leader in the war of La Vendée, who yielded to none of nobler blood in the fervor of his devotion to the cause in which he at last laid down his life. To Rose his only legacy was his uncompromising character, which she in turn had transmitted to her daughter, purified but unimpaired. Sent into Russia for safety while a child, Rose's only memory of her father was that of his exploits in the field and his last words on the scaffold : " I commit my soul to God, whom I do not fear, and my daughter to the king whom I serve."

But it was an age when royalty was no longer able to pay its debts, and the daughter of De Vigny would have died unremembered had not

M. Michel's father, who had abandoned France on the fall of Charles X., found his fair countrywoman living in poverty with an aged aunt in Kief, where he had taken up his abode. M. Michel married her, — the phrase is apt, — and if she was not altogether happy, it was not his fault, nor hers. Disparity of years is like a grain of sand between the axle and the bed, which, harder than either, cannot be gotten rid of, and scores its furrow in spite of the best lubricants. But God provides a recompense for this, and worse evils; he had given Rose Michel a daughter. Poverty and exile had reduced her life to a cipher; when Stéphanie came, God wrote a figure before it, and gave it value; and in this daughter Rose watched for all those qualities which she associated with the memory of her father, and in this young shoot her hope foresaw the blossom and the fruit of her own barren tree.

Soon after Stéphanie's birth, M. Michel's death left Rose a large fortune. Upon the soil of France she had resolved never again to step; and it was with some reluctance, and no little heroism, that she parted from her daughter, and sent her to Paris, to be educated under the care of her brother.

When, after the completion of her education, Stéphanie was summoned from Paris to Kief, it was for the express purpose of being given away; and all the world admitted that madame, her mother, had made a judicious and fortunate selection. As for the Count Milevski, he had barely been presented to the person thus selected for him unawares before he lost his heart; there were designing matrons to aver that he lost his head at the same time, for Stéphanie Michel was not his peer in lineage. But the count, who was an enthusiast, thought of but one thing at a time, and this young girl, fresh from her Paris convent, with her alternate moods of dignity and radiant comradeship, reduced the diplomacy of match-making to the mere minimum of a presentation.

Father Le Blanc had said of Madame Milevski, when, after an interval of sudden and sharp experience, — marriage, death, and retirement, — she reappeared at Paris: " Whether the sky be clear or full of clouds, the stars continue to rise tranquilly; she is one of them, and has a destiny to accomplish." Father Le Blanc's simile was not an unhappy one; but had he seen her at Kief in those earlier days, how might he have likened her to a very star indeed, when, newborn, its exultant pulse of light throbs in the rose-blue of the twilight sky !

Stéphanie had dreamed some dreams in her convent school at Paris; and, like all first dreams, they contained a supernatural element. In some outward respects tney were surpassed by the reality. The count made a good prince, and the wedding at Kief was a page from the Arabian Nights, even if M. Michel had pronounced it like all others. Her lover had been devoted, her husband generous and kind. Still she was conscious that something was lacking, of falling short of her capacities. One might have enumerated to her all her blessings and privileges, still she would have asked in secret, as if the one essential thing was absent, " Is this then all ? "

Certainly there is this disadvantage in the marriage system to which Stéphanie had been an offering, that it reveals what it does not always give, — love. It is often a stage trick, wherein the only dupe is the chief personage, who believes all is reality, and wakes to find herself also one of the actors in a comedy. What wonder, after having seen all the court assembled, and every puppet in its place go through with its part in the ceremony; what wonder, after having discovered what love might be and found an alien on the throne, this comedy should turn into a tragedy on the arrival of the king who comes to claim his own !

The experiences through which Stéphanie had passed developed her suddenly. There are periods in life when circumstances conspire to a growth rapid as that of a week in May; when influences focus and work sudden transformations. A grief, a disappointment, a success, is a new lens to the eye, changing the entire aspect of nature. The world spoke of Madame Milevski's affliction without in the least understanding it. Conceding the count to have possessed all which should make his loss an irreparable one, it was still true that he personally counted for little in her feelings. We love the virtues, but we do not fall in love with them. They confirm and nurture love, but at Stéphanie's age they do not give it birth. Other mothers than hers have secured in their white-haired years model husbands for their daughters, as if there were no subtler influences in nature than those of sober worthiness and eminent propriety. But if Love is blind, it is because Nature, who will not risk the life of the race on sober second thoughts, is not. We may sip the wine of a forty years' experience and descant wisely the while with Joan, who fortunately possessed the seven cardinal virtues; but Florimel will still sing beneath Phyllis' window panes, and, after leading our Chloe up to the perfect paragon, we discover that she is looking over her shoulder, and that the magnet is in another quarter.

The world pitied Stéphanie as one who had lost the earthly paradise; and not one of all its dupes read aright this serious-eyed woman, who saw beneath the dominos and could not feed on illusions. The show was well enough, the fiction well sustained; the trouble lay in this all too serious spectator, who came like an intruder into the midst of a joyous carnival. The revelers could not gauge the heart of this alien, in which, as the mists of illusion rolled away, there remained the conscious capacity to be and to make the great reality of this caricature.

The death of Madame Michel, occurring shortly after that of her son-in-law, prolonged and deepened Stéphanie's seclusion. This was a real and serious loss, for, though long separated from her by school life in Paris, absence does not strain or sever the bond of a mother's love; and no one shall ever know what sacred communion these two held in those silent days when the house at Kief was closed to visitors and the mother's health was failing. Madame Michel herself could remember spring days, and although she had long since learned to take life as she found it, and had been less rebellious than her child, misgivings arose in these closing hours; there was a resurrection of some forgotten things that had been put away with her wedding slippers, and her last look at the world was through the eyes of her daughter. As she grew more feeble, her anxiety for this child (whom she could not believe to be a woman, and who, alas! if she were, was only one woman, beginning life alone) increased. When the thought first came clearly before her, that she was soon to leave Stéphanie, not for a time, or even a long time, but forever, she was utterly overwhelmed. But before she died this fever of solicitude and apprehension gradually wore away, as she saw the silent development of a self-reliance which had its origin at once in sadness, indifference, and the pride of race. Sitting in her sick-chair at the window, in the summer nights of her last illness, her daughter's hand in hers, Stéphanie's wide eyes fascinated her more than the stars; many a time her own sought them furtively and wonderingly, and they filled her heart with both peace and awe.

At the death of madame, M. Michel had gone to Kief again, and had unhesitatingly urged Stéphanie to return with him to Paris. The thought of leaving her alone in that great house troubled him. He had a vague idea that Paris possessed the balm for all wounds; a curious, almost pathetic compound of his salon, a walk in the Bois, a month of Beauvais' quiet and boxes of bonbons, plus Rénée and himself, constituted the relief in this case, and he shook his head and sighed between Kief and Paris as many times as there were stations, over the refusal of his young stepsister.

But Stéphanie followed her bent. She enjoyed solitude as one who has so many things to think of, so many questions to settle, that it is indispensable. She felt as if she had escaped from the toils of a vast net, from the pressure of a great throng, and, like a planet broken loose from its system and freed from all restraints, she went her way through the immense and lonely spaces of her own thoughts with a sense of independence and freedom.

As the months wore away, however, this unnatural existence stole the color from her cheeks. One day an old physician, who had attended her mother and whom she often met in the visits of charity which occupied much of her time, — one of those homely country practitioners who make up their arrearage in science by a big heart, large sense, and wide experience, — advised her to travel. Madame la Comtesse, as he persisted in calling her notwithstanding the imperial edict, should take her maid and go to Nice, — to a thousand places of which this somewhat rusty old gentleman would not be suspected of knowing. But though he had the appearance of a moss-grown stone which had seen the building of Kief, he had rolled over many lands before gathering his moss, and knew how to open up the horizons of travel to Stéphanie's eyes.

When she yielded, and set out from Kief, she thought to preserve her incognito, and to carry the cloud of solitude with her. But the star was too bright to be so hidden. Moreover, society had not lost sight of her; her name revived the story of her marriage and memories of La Vendée. The circle into which that marriage had introduced her was a large one ; one, too, which does not forget wealth and beauty even in misfortune. No sooner had she set foot within its precincts than it sought to reclaim her. At A—— the wife of M. P—— called upon her; and at B—— her name was added to the invitation list of Madame la Princesse X——. Lizette's duties began to increase, and she sometimes secretly found fault with madame for the indifference she evinced for the flowers laid on her dressing-table.

At Vienna she became acquainted with a French colony of those voluntary exiles to whom France with the empire was not France at all, and with certain pilgrims to the shrine of Frohsdorf. Majesty itself, though fallen from its high estate, had not lost the habit of blessing, and was very gracious to her.

The tranquil atmosphere of this miniature court, its sense of superiority and calm, revived in this heart not yet full grown, stunned but not broken, something of its old faith in the world and its love of life. Kief, which she had thought never to leave, and which she at first kept in mind as a refuge, was less frequently remembered, and, as is often the case, having once fairly broken with her surroundings, she looked back with dread to that silent house, the very memory of which awakened so sad a train of recollections. She had begun to forget them,—and to desire forgetfulness.

Afterwards, on establishing herself in Paris, she fell naturally into the same circle and under the same influences, and when the events which attended the breaking up of the empire and its fall gave shape and life to the long dormant projects for a restoration, she yielded to them with an enthusiasm and interest which at times brought a smile of fine irony to her own face. Perhaps even more than her position, her wealth, her standing at Frohsdorf, and the episode of La Vendée, her peculiar influence and personal magnetism had designated her as a leader in the Paris intrigue, and had led to her selection for the task of persuading the king. This personal power gave her a kind of pleasure. Father Le Blanc was rightly puzzled, for she was at a turning point, when it was a question what things in life were to engross her, what her mission was to be, into what definite and final unit the elements of her character were to group themselves under the forces of experience and circumstance. This was the mystery which had both interested and perplexed him, as also Roger Lande.

The etiquette of Frohsdorf was simple but severe. Its inmate, readily accessible to all Frenchmen, fulfilled to the letter the rôle of king. All were his subjects upon whom he looked, as upon France, with the love and pity of a true monarch. But the granddaughter of De Vigny possessed titles to more than ordinary favor. Young, beautiful, courageous, simple and frank in manner, she had made a deep impression upon him during the sojourn of the previous winter in Vienna, and her reappearance at Frohsdorf awakened emotions plainly visible on the calm but indolent face of the Bourbon. Her eyes, never free from a trace of melancholy, were lighted by an unusual fire.

He addressed her kindly, holding in his hand the papers which she had presented to him. They contained the details of the plan and the assurances of success. They sketched briefly and rapidly the state of affairs, the readiness of the people, the hopes of old France. They contained the prayers of the Church, the oaths of an army, the pledges of the nobility. As opening them he began to read, a shade of annoyance passed over his face, succeeded by a look of mingled pity, weariness, and dignity. Then he laid them on the table, and regarded her with that air of sympathy and authority which he had so often breathed into his letters.

" All this is impossible."

" Sire," said Stéphanie, who misconceived his meaning, " I come to bring you the devotion of faithful servants, and to such nothing is impossible."

" I repeat it, it is impossible," he said; and, taking from the table a letter, he extended it to her. She took it from his hand.

" Read it," he said.

It was that last and famous letter, in which, with the serenity of unalterable conviction, the Count de Chambord ignored the work of the Revolution without deigning to argue, and declared that as there was no other flag than that white one which he had received from the hands of Henry the Fourth, so there was no monarchy beside that which comes not from the people but from God; that letter replete with the pride, not of arrogance but of calm, which caused the royalist camp, so formidable, so gay with hope and promise, to melt away in a day from the political arena, and left its chief, like a feudal castle in the midst of modern civilization, a relic of the past and an object only of curiosity.

"Sire," said Stéphanie, "it is an abdication."

"The monarchy of France," he continued tranquilly, as if not hearing her, "is not only a political institution, it is a religion. The throne is not the gift of the nation nor a prize for the ambitious, and he who ascends it assists, as did my ancestors, at a sacrament of Heaven. France is not yet ready for the king, and the king cannot be controlled. She still suffers from the frenzy and the stupor of the Revolution, when in humiliating so cruelly her appointed head she humiliated herself. To-day, like a drunken man, the fumes of license and scepticism obscure her vision; she still vacillates and suffers. God grant the expiation of her sins may soon be finished! But she is still troubled and agitated. The king is not the head of a privileged class whom you might represent to me, but of France. And France, countess, yet wishes to impose conditions upon her savior. The trust which I received from my ancestors cannot be thus dishonored. When it shall appear sacred to France as to me ; when the illusions of the present shall have disappeared and she perceives the hollowness of all she now invokes, she will herself demand without reserve the régime she has dishonored, and will recognize that only in the stainless standard which I represent can she find true security and true liberty. Do not permit your desires to delude you. Republican institutions cannot take root in a monarchical soil. The marriage of two such principles would be monstrous. Bear to the noble defenders of my cause my profound esteem. I am proud of them, for they are France. In these sad days it is sweet to me to remember their faithfulness, and to assure them of my constant friendship. And if you do not survive these times, when so long you have stood in the breach without truce or repose, God will yet reward you, my child."

Stéphanie listened to these words overwhelmed with dismay and astonishment. Carried away by her hopes, she, with others, had forgotten the unalterable convictions of the king.

" I was not thinking of rewards, but of France, sire."

From this interview she came out as one rudely shaken awakes from a dream. No further illusion was possible. All was over. Yet she could not bring herself to reproach the king. Differing from him in her views as she did profoundly, in this act there was nothing unkingly, and too much self-abnegation for the suspicion of cowardice.

All the way back in her long ride from Vienna, she saw this edifice, so long prepared and so majestic, crumbling again and again before her eyes. Once, two fellow-travelers, conversing over a newspaper, aroused her.

"It seems Henri Cinq has committed suicide," said one.

"Well, what difference does it make!" rejoined the other. "Monks no longer rule the world from monasteries."

She looked from her window upon the shifting landscape, but observed nothing; all seemed a blank. So long intent on one object, her mind possessed no rallying centre of thought when that object was withdrawn: so long filled with one figure, her vision seemed to gaze upon vacancy. She recurred again and again to the old theme, only to find it elude her very thoughts. Yet no deep personal interest underlay her disappointment. This failure did not compromise her, had not ruined her; but it had taken out of her life the one absorbing object of thought and activity which had long occupied it, and as the distance from Vienna increased, she dwelt more and more upon this and less upon the king. A sense of personal isolation took possession of her. Had she lived so much upon this intrigue that the secret of its enjoyment had been self-forgetfulness!

"It would be all the same," she said to herself, "had we succeeded. It was the pleasure of the chase; in either case, success or failure, I should have been left alone at last with myself."

She arrived late in Paris. It was a clear night. The streets were full of people and carriages. The lights of the lamps and the cafés were never brighter. But an aspect of unreality pervaded everything. The carriage taken at the station moved through all these lights and sounds with a horrible slowness. The night was warm, but her hands were cold. She was obliged to wait at the door of her hotel, for the porter did not expect her. There was a carriage before it which she did not notice. To the servant who opened the inner door she said, "Send me Lizette." He followed her as if he had something to say to her, but at the head of the large stairway she stopped, — there was a light in the small salon where she received her intimate friends, and she entered the room.

A man was waiting there, — M. de Marzac.

IX.

"You here!" she said.

There was more of weariness than of surprise in her manner. She sank into a chair, as if no one was there to see her, and, leaning her head upon its back, looked vacantly before her. The light above fell on her bare throat, not whiter than her face which, though bearing traces of fatigue, possessed that beauty of pallor belonging to clearly defined features. It was not a happy face, with its weary, restless eyes; but it was not ennui one saw there, — for ennui results from lack of resources, or their exhaustion, — but restlessness, that restlessness which belongs to desire without an object; and between these two there is the difference of satiety and hunger.

"Yes, I was expecting you," replied her visitor, rising and standing before her. His hands were crossed behind his back, but, if one might read his eyes, they were around her.

"Then you know," she said, without moving except to turn her head till her eyes fell upon him, — "it is all over."

"Yes, I have read the count's letter. All the journals have it."

"I have nothing more to tell you, then," she answered, turning her head away again.

"I did not come to speak of this; it is already an affair of the past." He stood still, but his voice seemed to reach out after her as his hands did.

"You wish to speak of something else? It is late, and I am very tired."

M. de Marzac mistook a warning for an excuse. This woman had puzzled him as she had Father Le Blanc, with this difference, that she had also deceived him. He interpreted the oracle before it had spoken. With his natural vanity and arrogance, he read the puzzle in the light of his own reason, which said, "This woman, beautiful, young, is, to begin with, a woman," and this alpha was also M. de Marzac's omega, and the conclusion of the whole matter.

"Do you wish me to defer it?"

"Oh, no. Since you are here."

"Stéphanie!" he said. At the sound of her name, a little shiver of cold ran through her. "Have you forgotten what day this is?"

A faint flush rose to her cheeks, and she went to the glass and began to remove her hat.

"What day?" she replied, her back towards him. Her manner annoyed him, and a gesture of anger escaped him which she could not see. But he made an effort to control himself and to speak calmly.

"No, you have not forgotten, Stéphanie. Women do not forget such things. Will you not look at me and let me speak to you?"

Still she stood before the mirror; was it his eyes or her own that she wished to avoid? — for hers were not lifted. Her bent head, her downcast eyes, the trembling fingers that wandered over the plume in her hat, did not escape him. "They are all the same," he thought to himself, "in sorrow or danger they will not falter, but when they love " — and he drew a step nearer.

At the sound of his step she suddenly turned full upon him, with that in her eyes and attitude that bade him stop.

"Stéphanie," he began again, pleadingly, " why will you torture me? Have I not waited faithfully? Why should I be here now, at this hour, the first, after so many, in which my lips are unsealed, if — if I did not " — But he could not finish. There was that in her eyes which bade him stop again.

"You are tired," he said, gently. "I am a fool to weary you to-night. No, not a fool" — with a passionate gesture — "a madman! I will come to-morrow."

Still she stood with one hand resting on the mantel, facing him like a statue, silent and immovable. Perhaps he had expected her to say, "Yes, to-morrow, my friend;" perhaps he looked to see her lips tremble, or her eyes turn away;

perhaps that would have satisfied him to-night. But there was no such signal. Her fixed gaze seemed to look him through and through. What she might see there was not a pleasant sight; that mad thirst for possession which he had stifled and crushed down so many times. M. de Marzac called it love, but it was a love not to be laid bare too soon, —'this love of self which to his own eyes could make crimes seem virtues, and has made demons appear martyrs. Whatever he wished to say, prudence would at least have bidden him wait, and prudence was M. de Marzac's guiding star. It was even on the point of triumphing at this moment, when she spoke.

"Well, M. de Marzac, is this all you have to say to me?"

There was a faint smile hovering about her mouth that at once annoyed and allured him. It is at times a disadvantage to be a man of the world, for the experience of such is often at fault, even to the extent of misleading innate judgments. In secret, M. de Marzac always had felt this woman to be mistress of herself and beyond his touch, but there were always at hand those formulæ of his creed which weighed and gauged everything, leaving no unknown quantities, — her with the rest. And, in the light of this creed, that faint smile said to him, " Patience, and perseverance!" and silenced his misgivings. How strong it was, this creed! it had become a second nature. Aye, and strange, too, for while it led M. de Marzac to sneer at woman, it would have led him also, and for no other reason, to sneer at one who did not bear it witness.

"A year ago I told you that I loved you, Sté-phanie. You would not listen; you imposed silence upon me; you asked the greatest thing a woman asks of a man, — how great, you did not know, — and I consented. The rôle was not new to me. The Count Milevski was my friend, and I his," — he said this proudly, — "ask yourself, is it not so? Do you wish to force me to parade that friendship pitiably before your eyes? No! it would then cease to be sacred. You would even revolt against the confession that since I first saw you — But why? Do we command our hearts? No, we can only wall up their cry lest it be heard, or break them. When I brought you back that miniature of yourself which I took from his heart on the way to Siberia, where I accompanied him — oh! then it would have been an outrage! But I felt it next my own, and when I gave it into your hands it seemed as if in that long journey it had become rooted there, and that in giving it to you I gave you my life. I listened to your inquiries, I saw your tears that did not fall, and you did not know that they lay in my heart like drops of burning lead, and that at every sob you repressed I myself shuddered. What miserable friendship? Well, I admit it. One does not dis-

pute with love — one crushes it. And I crushed
it. But tell me, honestly, will you say that of
all those who paid you the cold courtesy of the
world; who left their cards of sympathy at your
door and went to their baccarat without thinking
twice of you, I alone was unworthy because, having the misfortune to love you, I could leave Kief
with my hand at the throat of this love, bidding
it be silent forever? But that is the code of the
world," he said, bitterly ; " the man who does not
tremble is brave, while he who trembles and conquers is a coward."

He turned to the window to hide his emotion.
The smile on Stéphanie's mouth deepened, only,
had M. de Marzac seen it now, he would no longer
have been at a loss as to its meaning.

" Long after," he continued, "chance threw us
together. Confess that I did not seek it — that
I even avoided it. I saw you again — young,
beautiful, unhappy. What reason then prevented
me? The debt to propriety was paid, and I
spoke to you. Why did you exact from me that
promise, that for a year I should not speak to
you again of this? Did you, perchance, imagine
that I was a boy to whom a year sufficed for forgetfulness? Certainly, in fixing that time, you
had some reason; but I did not demand it. I
asked no question. I went back simply as a prisoner returns to the solitude from which for a moment he dared hope to escape, — because you

asked me. I promised, and that promise has been
kept. Day after day I have seen you ; day after
day you whom I loved tempted me by your very
confidence. Ah, Stéphanie, do not believe that a
promise is easy, simply because it is kept."

All the while that smile, half curious, half scorn-
ful, was on her face ; his words struggled with it
as the oar struggles with the current.

"How do you expect one to love you, M. de
Marzac, when one knows you ?"

It was now too late for prudence. Those words
were a challenge. Hate must, indeed, be very
close to love; if M. de Marzac's face at that moment meant anything he was very near wishing
to crush out forever that smile on the lips which
goaded him.

"Insults are not worthy a woman," he said,
hoarsely.

She shrugged her shoulders impatiently.

"M. de Marzac, I would tell you frankly that
I do not love you,"—she said it with a nervous
spasm, as when one swallows an unpleasant
draught, —"if you did not know it already. Your
language bears witness to it. But that does not
appear to satisfy you. You have the weakness to
protest, to demand an explanation. Have you the
courage to wish me good-night ? For, if not, I
shall answer the reproaches you have addressed
to me."

"Let us finish with it, madame," he said, between his teeth, losing sight of his object.

She laughed.

"It is such men as you who give rise to the proverb that the sublime touches the ridiculous. You can stand here before me trembling with indignation, appealing to every noble sentiment, — oh, I give you credit for them! Noble sentiments, M. de Marzac, are so real, they exist so truly, that even you, when you invoke them, acknowledge their power. You have told your story with such vividness that it appals you: for the time you believe it true. You admire and pity yourself even more than you love me. But the clubs are still open. You will yet have your baccarat also to-night. I will even allow that you play to distract yourself, and will give you till to-morrow to lay these ghosts of momentary feeling that have disturbed you."

"If you were a man I should know how to answer you."

"And yet you love me! Doubtless you would tell me that only those whom we love best have the power to render us completely mad. And you are right, M. de Marzac; it is yourself with whom you are most incensed, because it is you who have obliged me to unveil that self which you worship, and to expose its character, which your vanity does not always permit you to recognize. I am not the object of your anger except as I am the spectator of your ignominy. Yes, M. de Marzac, I repeat it," she said, passionately, "your ignominy!

Do you wish me in addition to telling you that I do not love you, to tell you why? That is a question of which lovers like yourself should beware. Well, no, I will not thus degrade myself. Oh, the insolence of some men! whose honor is a little circle of ground traced with the point of a sword, and whose love is that miserable counterfeit which they scatter so freely. Do you wish me to tell you what it is that makes your heart quicken its beat and your brain reel, and which you call love? It is not I, M. de Marzac, but this perfume which lingers in my glove, and which lasts longer than the passion which it inspires."

"For a woman who has discovered the value of perfumes, you set your standards high, madame."

"Yes, M. de Marzac," she replied, calmly, "they are high,—higher than you understand; and when you have learned to respect the shrine without desiring to violate it, you will know how high and —how different. Love does not ask for perfections," she said, turning away from him and addressing herself rather, in a tone from which all anger had vanished, "it asks only for its own. You cannot propitiate it with gifts, nor satisfy it with all the virtues, if you cannot pay it back value for value in its own coin; and if this tribute be paid," and an expression of exaltation irradiated her face, "it will forgive every weakness. You shrug your shoulders, you no longer understand me. Why should you!" she said, striking the bell on the table, "every man measures the world with his own measure."

"You speak with the conviction of experience," he said, with a sneer. "Permit me to congratulate you."

"What we seek we shall find, M. de Marzac, and when we come to our own we shall know each other."

As she spoke, the servant, answering the bell, appeared at the door.

"M. de Marzac's carriage, Jacques," she said, in her usual tone.

"It is ready, monsieur."

At the door M. de Marzac paused, as if about to say something, then left the room abruptly. "Monsieur has forgotten his gloves," said Jacques, following him down the stairs.

"Keep out from under my heels!" was the reply.

"Thanks, monsieur," said Jacques, as he closed the heavy door. "They are perfectly new, and " — drawing them on — "they fit me marvelously well."

X.

M. DE MARZAC drove through life in his carriage. He had in his stables all the virtues, blooded animals of the purest race, and on the driver's seat a whip who knew how to control them, called Selfishness.

With this turnout he gained admission to places from which good honest vices were excluded.

The idea was not altogether original with M. de Marzac, but he had perfected it to a marvelous degree. His appointments were faultless, and his driver understood his business; and no one ever dreamed that it was M. de Marzac himself who sat upon the box, or suspected that the real occupant of the carriage was a lay figure. Nor was M. de Marzac to be blamed for this deception. Nature had endowed him with a strong imagination, and, as is well known, this faculty creates what it imagines.

This method of making the journey of life has so many advantages that it is difficult to enumerate them. Some of his friends, for example, who had boldly harnessed the vices into their equipages, found it difficult at times to prevent them from kicking over the traces. Well-trained and carefully domesticated as were these wild animals, harnessed with the glittering restraints of society, bred for this most civilized Parisian market, groomed till their coats shone soft and glossy as the polish of the society which they drew, their wild instincts often proved ungovernable, and led to a catastrophe on the very highway of social display. How much better these quiet and less fiery virtues, a little slow at times, but which, on the other hand, never committed the impropriety of running away with their owner. Their value to M. de Marzac was, of course, wholly due to the peculiar genius of their driver, who had these docile animals completely under his control. There was no by-way or cul-de-sac into which he would not venture, and where he could not gracefully turn : and between the hypothetical M. de Marzac and the real one, — for he, like every man, was an hypothesis which his neighbor never completely verified, — there was the most perfect understanding. Yet this intimacy was not one of which he even admitted the existence. Perhaps, in the earlier stages of his career, he had been more or less aware of the double rôle he was playing ; but, like all true actors, he had lost himself in his part, till in his eyes, as in those of the spectators, there was no other M. de Marzac than that correct and respectable one constantly before the footlights.

He was thus more than the mere juggler who

deceives the audience, for he deceived also himself. Selfishness, like a robber crab, had taken
complete possession of this shell of propriety in
which, as in a state carriage, he made the journey
of life ; and, at last, he had lost track of his own
identity. He? He was himself this varnished,
satin-lined vehicle of propriety, which had grown
to him like a skin, and the virtues which drew it
coursed with his own blood in his veins!

He had acquired the habit of doing what was
proper, and finally what was right, from mixed
motives. Tolerating at first the mixture, he gradually ignored its unworthy elements, to deny them
at last altogether. The propriety of his acts slowly
overspread the motives also, and a kind of automatic process resulted. It was a mill to which
any grist might be carried; so that when M. de
Marzac, like other honest people, secretly confessed
himself not so good as he ought to be, he was des-
perately worse than he thought he was. He carried with him a reversible glass; in observing
others he used the large end at the eye ; where
self was concerned, the small one. Thus it was
that the whole question of right had resolved itself into one of rights, — that is, the rights of M.
de Marzac.

He was the last of a good family, and, if one
does not mind it one's self, this is rather desirable
than otherwise ; if only for the reason that it is not
generally so regarded, and thus furnishes an oo

casional opportunity for a feeling allusion. If only M. de Marzac could have displayed for the living the affection which he felt for the dead! But this was impossible. All the force of his affection was retroactive. With him it seemed necessary to have lost, to love at all. He had the air of a man solitary and alone; far too sensible to seek an open sympathy, or even to pretend a desire for it, still obtaining it and producing a good effect. For this solitude he consoled himself in various ways. Fortunately for his tranquillity these consolations were more agreeable than that for which they consoled him; but this fact he had forgotten. In his own eyes he was what he ought to have been under the circumstances, and having established this fact he could condone certain efforts to forget this imaginary and unhappy self of his own creation. The transition from indulgence, through compensation, to right, was thus made easy.

It would be no easy matter to explain the intimacy between M. de Marzac and the young Count Milevski. It was one of those things for which there is no *raison d'être*, yet whose existence is beyond question. The theory of the attraction of opposites would not explain it, nor would that of the affinity between similars. It is more convenient to fall back upon some unknown principle, as was the custom of the early physicists, and invoke a sentimental caloric. Otherwise one would never understand how the Count Milevski, young, generous, and enthusiastic, should have threaded his way through all the currents of personal magnetism and attached himself to M. de Marzac.

This attachment began on the occasion of a visit of the count to Paris, during the latter days of the empire. M. de Marzac was then well known through the columns of " L'Univers " as an ardent defender of the monarchy. The articles which appeared over his signature were bold, haughty, and uncompromising; but dignified, fervent, and forceful. He put a certain honest effort into all he wrote, which won respect even where it did not carry conviction, and which was frequently a source of astonishment to himself. He was often surprised at the strength of his own arguments. Behind M. de Marzac's mixed motives was, of course, a mixed character. Did any one ask why he was a royalist, there was, first, the answer that, as a gentleman of fortune and leisure, with great energies and high principles, he must be something; that, as a man of prudence and foresight, he was far too sagacious to take passage in the imperial ship of state, already among the breakers; radical republicanism was a crime, the Left Centre was too prosaic. For M. de Marzac had a vein of romance in his composition; a true Gallic love for glory, external effect, and decorative detail. This element of his character passed for chivalry and fearlessness, whereas it was in reality pure vanity. He had the courage of his convictions, in so far as he was convinced they deified him. Before the altars of great principles he did not bow, — he stood upon them ; they were the pedestals of a statue. He could contemplate heroic deeds; his dreams — for M. de Marzac dreamed — were woven of imaginary exploits which he was ready to execute at the risk of his life, provided that death rendered him immortal. Let us do him justice; he would have led a forlorn hope, only it mattered little on which side, provided he led it, and men marveled. There was thus a real foundation for the admiration he inspired, although the warp of good and the woof of evil would have taxed Minos to unravel. Habit had fused them into one solid texture, to analyze and separate which one would have to follow the method of Solomon's famous judgment, and cut the whole asunder with the sword, — and, with a like result, it would have destroyed M. de Marzac.

The count had exacted from him the promise to return his visit at Kief, and, on the eve of the former's marriage, he was urgently reminded of it ; so that when M. de Marzac first saw Stéphanie Michel, it was just as she was about to wear the orange blossoms.

He did not escape the fever of admiration for the young bride which swept over the circle of the count's friends. She bewildered them all. Some glances, and some words even, were dropped at her feet which a coquette might have dallied with; but all this admiration was to Stéphanie a part of the pageant. She was bewildered herself.

The ceremonies terminated with a ball, at which M. de Marzac was, of course, present. As he drives away from the fête in his carriage, a conscience long since subdued, the very clank of whose fetters has become applause, sets his mind at peace with all the world. Once thoroughly mastered, there is no better slave; for none knows better the rough places that need smoothing and the sore spots that need balm. It was a pleasure in which he often indulged, to go on the witness-stand before this conscience, to play the criminal in order to be acquitted; and, on his way home, he amused himself with this game of solitaire.

"Well," he thought, "Mademoiselle Michel is now the Countess Milevski." She had made a wonderful bride; not the least overdressed, — for M. de Marzac was a man of faultless taste, — and her lithe figure reappeared before him in the dark-ness of his carriage as he had seen it under the lights of the ball-room. Oh, yes! he admired her, as must all men who saw her. A few glasses of champagne, the glitter and perfume of the ball, a clinging fold of lace or the contours of a piece of satin, lustrous and soft as what it covers, — what an empire they have! and M. de Marzac smiled. The count, his friend, was a happy man, and deserved to be; a man of promise, — perhaps a little enthusiastic, a little extreme in his views, as the young are apt to be. This " Young Russia " had a great work and a great future before it, — if it did not go too far. Parties acquire so terrible a momentum! and, if anything, the count was certainly a little too radical, a little over zealous. Patience is a very difficult virtue. It was a pity that he should be so rash in his utterances; for words and actions, when unripe, destroy one's legitimate influence. But then, conservatism comes with age. Did she love him? Why not! All these accessories of wealth and position, his youth and devotedness, might well turn the head of one just out from the walls of the convent school of Notre Dame. It was so easy for M. de Marzac himself to fall in love, that he might have been pardoned for drawing a hasty inference. But he was a shrewd observer, and had discovered that a woman's first love does not require such bait, and is an altogether irrational and capricious passion, which sometimes tears usages and conventional proprieties into tatters! How beautiful she was! What depths there were in her eyes, — how placid and serious they were! The fire was there, but it had not been lighted; he had not seen a single one of those glances which betray love, — and, in the corner of his carriage, M. de Marzac indulged in a long reverie. What wild, improbable thoughts, or hopes, flitted through his mind! Whatever they were, let us not laugh at them, for are not bold thoughts and hopes, oftener than is supposed, the only parents of great successes?

Envy? Jealousy? M. de Marzac never descended so low. His passions were too shallow. If fate had not predestined the Count Milevski to wake this slumbering princess, why should any one wonder? The law of chances was against it. Still, she was his; this, at least, was a fact. What an absurd machinery society had invented for pairing the race! It was a matter of pure luck whether or no the parts fitted. Inclinations — important elements — were like friction, lost sight of till it began its work of bringing the machine to rest. Envy? Nonsense! To think of the good fortune of one's friend is not a crime! And as for what he said to M. Z——, whom he had known at Paris, where the latter had been intrusted with certain delicate matters of the secret political service of the Russian Empire, and with whom he chatted for a moment before leaving the ball-room, what folly! He had said nothing which compromised the count. Did not Milevski talk freely with every one? a little too freely, possibly: but never in confidence. He could not flatter himself that he had been to any degree his confidant; on the contrary, the hint he had dropped in the ear of M. Z—— might reach the count, and prove a useful check; he had himself warned him to be more prudent.

Do not imagine that M. de Marzac would have permitted another to ask these self-imposed questions. So imprudent an intruder upon the domain of private rights would have received a peremptory challenge, and, on the way to the ground, M. de Marzac would have said to his second, " Bah ! what object could I have ? It is folly to imagine it ! A mere pretext for a quarrel."

From Kief he went to St. Petersburg, where he soon heard with astonishment of the count's arrest and exile. Ah ! well, then, he was right ; his friend had gone too far, and the police must have had this matter in hand for a long time. He would appeal to M. Z——, who, of course, knew nothing and could do nothing, as he, in fact, told him over coffee and cognac. Could he not obtain a pass for him to accompany the count over the Ural Mountains to Tobolsk, or at least to Perm ? He desired to travel in Russia, and might thus also console a friend.

In the subjugation of conscience, M. de Marzac wore gloves and avoided brutality. His was the instinct of perversion, not of murder. Instead of slaying that inward monitor outright, he confronted it with expediency, and taught it to doubt its own dictates. He thus managed to preserve the fountain of fine emotions and noble sentiments, although the waters were soon contaminated and polluted. He was ever looking abroad, and ran the impulses of his better nature into the mould of expediency. He walked on the sands, where footprints never linger long, so that when any one said to him, "See! this is the way you must have passed," he could answer simply, "Show me the proofs; there are none, and you are mistaken."

When, with his passport duly signed, he joined the escort of the count, there was in his heart a spark of real pity and sympathy, and the capacity, — oh, only the capacity! — for an equally real treachery.

He had no plan; M. de Marzac never had any; his theory of life did not include the creation of opportunities. Events, like torrents, rushed down the slope of time under laws beyond his control; man was the leaf in the stream, fortunate indeed if he desired to go whither he was perforce obliged to. This did not prevent him from acting at times in his own behalf, prudently and deliberately, as every struggling swimmer would, who was bound to make the best of his situation. But, weighed in the force of the torrent, what mattered in the long run such insignificant efforts? Life was a vast machine, intricate, delicate in its infinite details, but ponderous and remorseless; a machine altogether out of joint, for which he was not accountable; with which a thousand busybodies were forever interfering, and of which he was an irresponsible part; irresponsible, not because he could not do his part well, but because the whole affair was in such a chaotic jungle of cross purposes that it made no difference.

The count would have gone to destruction entirely independent of M. de Marzac; and if, in the loneliness and privations of Siberia, a wife was made a widow — it was not an unreasonable supposition. God forbid it should come to pass! Madame could not have learned to love her husband very deeply, — a mere child out of a convent, — and, moreover, not a woman who was owned simply because she had been bought. What compensations life brought! And M. de Marzac fell asleep in the wagon beside his friend, whose buoyant nature had been crushed at the first blow, and who made the entire journey in a stupor.

All that is known of that journey is what M. de Marzac told on his return; and while he came back with the prestige of faithfulness to a friend in disgrace, and devotion at the couch of a malignant fever, he was — to his annoyance, strangely enough — taken at his own price, granted a painful half-hour with the countess and her mother, and dismissed with the latter's blessing.

He returned to Paris to resume control of L'Univers;" to fill its feuilleton with brilliant sketches of life in Russia, to wage a literary war on the empire, and to defend the Church against the radicals. He illustrated the saying, " The nearer the throne, the farther from royalty; the nearer the Church, the farther from God "

When, later, his ability, prudence, and pen designated him as one of the "petite société" of the hôtel in the Boulevard St. Germain, he was astonished to find its mistress and his coadjutor none other than the woman whom he had left at Kief, and whom he had forgotten — as a dog sleeps, with one eye open — till it should be worth while to remember her.

Clearly it was Fate that had thrown this woman, free and alone, in all the splendor of matured beauty, across his path. For the first time he now really began to love her, although he could afterwards say to her as he did, and believe it, that he had loved her all the while. M. de Marzac must have played baccarat well, if he shuffled cards as he did words. He had indeed desired her from the first; and between now and then the difference in the possibilities of success was the only difference. In weighing these possibilities, he had this excuse, that with him Stéphanie was really provocative. It was not long before she read both his passion and his nature. Her insight was keen, and this, with her tact, made her at times appear to him reckless, or at least daring, when in reality she was so sure of herself and so indifferent to him that he counted for nothing. In exacting from him the promise of a year's silence, after his offer, she gave some ground for the reproaches he made her the night of her return from Frohsdorf. Waiting always taxes patience, and he had been waiting to no purpose. Had he not composed himself, like a fox in the sun, under the fruit that is destined to fall in due season? But Stéphanie felt an instinctive aversion to him. If there was any bitterness in her nature, he excited it. The honey of his words and the gilt of his exterior was a perpetual reminder of what she was endeavoring to forget; he stood for her as the symbol of what she despised, and she could not forbear to play with him. To this little comedy she consented as the lioness, sleeping disdainfully with half-closed eyes, consents to the gambols of a mouse in her cage.

M. de Marzac had not thus lived in vain,— since he extracted and conveyed away the gall and bitterness of a great nature.

XI.

Madame Valfort had resigned her claims over Rénée, as Stéphanie had prophesied.

"I am very glad that you are to remain near her," she had said to Stéphanie, "and that she will have your experience to direct her. You can oversee and counsel her so much better than I, and with so much more propriety. I really owe you an apology for venturing to intrude at all; but M. Michel did not seem to realize that she might be making a great mistake, and it seemed to me that before so young a girl takes a step as decisive as that she had in mind, her knowledge and her vision of life ought to be enlarged and widened. This journey with you will be admirable for her in every way, and I congratulate you on the thought of it, as I shall do her on the delightful prospect before her."

"You must not congratulate her too warmly," Stéphanie said, quietly.

"Oh, I fancy she has read me already. She is very quick and clear-sighted, — that is, as far as she sees, — and I had no idea of deceiving her. Indeed, I did not rely upon myself at all. I simply wanted her to meet people, — in short, to come out of herself, — and, if these influences had failed to divert her, I could have used no others."

Rénée had followed Stéphanie's suggestion, and, beside the party which was at Beauvais, only the Baron Scherer and Madame Valfort had been invited to the Rue du Bac. But for an unexpected incident, this last gathering before her departure would have been a reunion *en famille*. But M. Lande had met M. de Marzac the night before, and, in the innocence of his heart, had imparted to him the information that M. Michel had returned, and would receive the next evening as usual.

It might be supposed that M. de Marzac would not care to go where he was quite sure to meet the woman who had so cruelly repulsed him. The rebuff had been so unexpected, so full of scorn, that many a man in his place would have avoided the encounter. But in defeat pride is the backbone of courage. The salon of M. Michel was not one of those crowded ones, in the perpetual coming and going of whose guests his absence would have been unnoticed. Its habitués were few and constant, and in the eyes of one woman at least his absence might be construed in a manner mortifying to his vanity.

And then M. de Marzac's emotional nature resembled somewhat India-rubber, which, after receiving a deep impression, regains its form readily. When the first smart of his interview had passed he began to reproach himself angrily for his lack of restraint and loss of temper. He had thrown the game away; and he felt now more keenly this his own folly than the caustic words of Stéphanie. He had chosen the very day on which his probation ended, partly because he was impatient, but mainly because it was a day of defeat and disappointment, and he had calculated the effect of failure and despair upon this mind, so long occupied with a great ambition. When the storms blow about the great peaks of achievement and ambition, the heart seeks shelter in the green valleys of affection which lie at their base. It were a fit time, indeed, for the lover to open his arms; but a lover who is not loved is no better than a statue; and when he made this discovery, instead of offering that mute sympathy which inspires gratitude, that disinterested love which may yet win something by resigning everything, he had pressed his own interests, and a moment of impatience had destroyed the work of a whole year. It was the mistake of a tyro to allow a look, a word, to overcome prudence and to convert him into a madman consumed by his own passion. To a sense of the ignominy of his defeat succeeded an angry self-exasperation for the folly which had contributed to it, and the desire to retrieve himself. Pride, more than love, had been outraged, and wounded pride is like a general who sacks the city he cannot keep.

But M. de Marzac had not yet wholly given himself over to thoughts of revenge. He still hoped. The picture of himself which Stéphanie had so mercilessly unveiled had become indistinct. He thought less and less of himself as she painted him, and more and more of her. He remembered that if he had lost his self-control, she had also. " In anger, divide by two," he thought. " Women are so intense! A little heat, and directly they are sublimated ! " By dint of repeating this he succeeded in dulling the sense of certain words of hers which he could not altogether forget. And that which made these lame excuses walk, and gave body to this thin argument, was the thought of *her*, — his love for her he would have said; and it is a word to which he has the right, as have other people, — the thought of her as he had seen her so many times in the year just passed. On the sensitive plate of his senses all these images were stamped indelibly, and they drew him back to her, and asserted their power over him, as on that evening when he stood in her presence. That very presence which filled his eyes had been more potent than the words which rung in his ears.

M. de Marzac was hungry ! He had been starving for a whole year.

There were times, it is true, when the recollection of that evening was so vivid that it seemed he must admit that his theory of woman, based though it was upon some actual experiences in

which a stormy and protracted contest had terminated in capitulation, had its exceptions. But
in M. de Marzac's theory there were no exceptions,
and what seemed to be such fortified the rule.
There was another lover!

Who was he? It was not the first time M. de
Marzac had thought of such a contingency; but
this thought now possessed a new force, and on
his way to M. Michel's he searched the list of his
acquaintances, — but in vain. Madame Milevski's
name was not one of those which circulate at the
club, between a smile and an innuendo, — not the
less understood because it lacks precision. Still,
the lover must exist. The logic of his theory was
irresistible. If he failed, it was because another
succeeded. Well, then, perseverance, or revenge!

As he entered the room, a rapid glance assured
him that she had not yet come.

Renée received him with her usual grace and
simple-hearted cordiality. She was not yet old
enough to know the wolf from the lamb, except as
each wore his own skin. She was looking remark-
ably well that evening. The prospect of so sudden and complete a change, as her journey with
Stéphanie involved, added to her face what it had
to her thoughts, anticipation and exhilaration.

"Mademoiselle has been so improved by her
summer at Beauvais," old M. Lande had said as
he greeted her that evening, "I can hardly recognize her. That is a compliment not very well

turned, but I was not thinking of paying you one."

Rénée was none the less pleased with it, however. She had not reached that period which comes to a woman, when every line and contour of the face is known by heart; and, before her dressing-table that evening, the tall candles had shown her in the glass a face which was a veritable surprise; and M. Lande's expression of pleasure was no more sincere or harmless than her own had been, when, standing before the long mirror, a figure she had never before seen stepped out from its dark background, fastening about its neck the pearls M. Michel had given her that very afternoon. This was a custom he had observed ever since she was a little girl, — to bring her Saturday evening some gift, — a book, a box of bonbons, a plant for her window, or a flower only. It was, perhaps, his way of making good a conscious deficiency in attention to his niece, or, perhaps, it was, constitutionally, the only way in which he could evince a secret tenderness for her. Many a nature which, like his, seems sealed to the ordinary observer, has these back windows which it opens shyly now and then to a few privileged ones, disclosing the same heart which others, with equal naturalness, wear on their sleeve. Usually, on Saturday evening, M. Michel brought his offering in person : but these pearls he had quietly placed on Rénée's table, where she found them on going to dress; and no one will ever know whether this bashfulness was due to the unusual magnitude of the gift, or whether both the gift and the giving were the confession of an affection which insisted upon escaping restraint now that its object was about to take wing.

Yes, she looked really charming to-night. Her beauty had suddenly assumed a value which it had not before possessed, as when a statue, seen in some new or stronger light, seems all at once to breathe; and it caused M. de Marzac to say to Madame Valfort, —

" Mademoiselle Michel is no longer a child; she is a woman."

" And that surprises you? "

" The transformation is common enough, to be sure, but it is not always so ravishing."

" You are late in discovering it."

" I ? late ? "

" Yes, late, as usual; but not you particularly. You gentlemen see only what is thrust under your very eyes."

" There is not sun or light enough in the Rue du Bac for such a flower," said M. de Marzac, following Rénée with his eyes.

" She will find enough of both in Spain."

" In Spain ? " he said, looking up with surprise.

" Do you not know she is going to Spain? She leaves next week, with Madame Milevski." And while Madame Valfort was confiding to M. de Marzac the history of this proposed journey, the door opened, and Roger entered.

On coming back from Beauvais, Roger had endeavored to persuade himself that he had been dreaming. The realities of life, and his work, seemed on his return more than ever attractive; for he had really been in need of rest, and he came back with that zest and elasticity which an active man always experiences after a temporary relaxation. When a vision of that wooden seat by the water's edge under the rocks of Mont St. Jean came to him, he put it away with thoughts of the long row of cots at the Hôtel-Dieu St. Luc, the lecture he was to deliver, or the appointments which filled his calendar. And yet, when first he saw the black figure of Sœur Ursule again, he started, as if he expected to see Rénée's face under its black veil; and when the day, with its absorbing work, was over, and night came with its moments of quiet loneliness or weariness, it required sometimes the hurried ring of his door-bell to banish a pair of gray eyes and drown the tones of a sweet voice.

M. Lande had not expected so ready an acquiescence when he called at his son's room to urge his acceptance of M. Michel's invitation. He was accustomed to meet with an excuse and a refusal. But men of strong will and firm purposes make sudden changes which are thoroughly in keeping with their character. Inflexible as they are, for this very reason when they yield, it is like a brittle bar which snaps, but does not bend. They give none of the external signs of resistance; all their tension is within. When M. Lande announced Rénée's departure for Spain, Roger laid down his book and promised to follow him. He was on the watershed of resolution, and this single remark, accidental and trivial as the stone which, in the path of the current, determines its direction, had decided him. The pros and cons are often so evenly balanced in our lives that the decision depends upon whether the next event be odd or even. M. Lande was pleased. This man was still "his little Roger." He was always delighted to accompany him anywhere, for he was proud of him, and at such times had the air of saying, "This great man is my son." But, besides this pardonable vanity, the fact that Roger appeared in the least to be letting go some theories and views of life he had always combated gave him the greater pleasure, and he went away saying to himself, "After all, it is not what he does, but what he says only, which troubles me."

Roger thought Rénée received him coolly. As if the phases of our feelings always matched! Or, were this the case with Rénée, as if she would have permitted him to know it! There was no lack of warmth in the greeting he received from M. Michel or from Father Le Blanc, neither of whom he had seen since his return ; but the conversation into which he was drawn — for the gentlemen were discussing the political events of the day — failed to interest him. He looked over constantly to the corner where Rénée had joined Madame Valfort and was chatting with M. de Marzac, — to no purpose, however, for M. Scherer was speaking, and, like an ancient oracle, must be listened to with respect.

" No," he was saying, " even if the monarchy had been restored, it would have had a brief day. The chiefs shook hands, to be sure, but the armies never united."

" Then you were not deceived by all these pourparlers," said M. Lande.

" Not in the least."

" I am glad of it. I do not like to wake in the morning to find I have changed my domicile. Last night I lived in the Rue du Deux Décembre, this morning in the Rue du Quatre Septembre, and I was afraid to-morrow it would be Rue Henri Cinq."

" We make history so fast in our dear France," said Father Le Blanc.

" Too fast ! too fast ! One is obliged to ask like Greuze, ' And who is king to-day ? ' "

" The monarchy of Henri V., messieurs, is to-day an impossibility," continued M. Scherer. "The alliance between the count and the princes was a mere formality, — as one pauses at a door to say, 'You first, monsieur,' and then enters. I have known the count too long to share the belief, so seriously entertained, that he was about to give France a liberal monarchy. It seemed for a time, perhaps, that he was about to yield," he said with a shrug, "but those who assumed to speak for him did not comprehend him. In the hope of success, they promised too much, and in the end would themselves have been no less royal than the king. In politics, temperament is stronger than promises, and outlives them."

"And principles are stronger than temperament," said Father Le Blanc.

"Principles regulate governments, but do not determine them. Governments are like garments; we outgrow them and seek new ones."

"Exactly," said the priest; "and I, who always wear the same one, quarrel with the fashion."

"You make my comparison go on all fours," said M. Scherer, with a deprecatory gesture. "Humanity is the determining factor; the government follows where it leads. If you wish permanence in this form and society which envelops man, arrest his development. One is only the expression of the other. Between the two there is the sign of equality; or, if not," with another shrug, "why, then, revolution restores the equilibrium. I hold to my simile in its original sense. The nation is a growing child; if his government does not fit him, he will burst the seams, and the only remedy is to give him a new one, or, like the Bonapartists, put him in a strait jacket."

The door opened again, and Stéphanie entered. There was a hush as if by magic. M. de Marzac, who had been waiting for this moment, with eyes riveted upon her face, watched her every movement, as he would scrutinize an adversary at a distance, before advancing to engage his sword. Rénée went forward to meet her eagerly. He felt her eyes as, in their survey of the guests, they passed over him without recognition, and saw them rest for a moment upon Roger Lande. Was it only his jealous fancy? Or did they rest there as on the person for whom they were searching?

Roger profited by this interruption to approach Rénée; and Stéphanie, after exchanging a few words with the gentlemen who had come forward to meet her, advanced straight to the sofa where Madame Valfort was sitting with M. de Marzac.

"Quelle diable de femme!" thought the latter. But he was a man of self-possession. The swords were crossed, and he felt the nerve which the duelist gains when he feels the strength of his opponent's wrist.

"M. de Marzac has been amusing me by relating the discoveries which he has made," said Madame Valfort.

"He has been entertaining me in a similar manner. What is this new one which you find so amusing?"

" He has just found out that our little Rénée is
adorable."

" You give me a credit which I see does not belong to me only," replied M. de Marzac. " Look!
It would seem that M. Lande has also made this
discovery."   He was still watching Stéphanie's
eyes, and, although they neither met his nor
avoided them, he was confident that he had made
a second discovery of far more importance.

" Really," said Madame Valfort, looking at the
two young people, who were in a most earnest
conversation, " it seems so. What Argus eyes you
have ! " and, turning to Stéphanie, " Your voyage
to Spain may not prove necessary."

" Or more than ever so," said M. de Marzac.

" Why so? You have accorded to mademoiselle beauty, and you must admit M. Lande has
talent.   It would be an admirable match."

" Shall I offer you a glass of Malaga, madame ? "
said M. de Marzac to Stéphanie, taking the silver
flagon from the tray which Baptiste presented
him.

" Ask M. Michel what vintage it is," she replied,
coolly. " New Malaga is intolerable."

M. de Marzac flushed. This question, so impossible for a guest to ask of his host, was an
intimation he could but accept. But he did not
flinch, and, appearing to accept the mission as
naturally as it had been given to him, bowed and
retired.

"Ma chère, vous êtes un peu mordante," said Madame Valfort, laughing. "But the temptation excuses you. And the wonder is he will value you none the less for it. By being too good one becomes actually stupid."

But Stéphanie scarcely heard her. On M. de Marzac's withdrawal she had for the first time looked over at Rénée.

"So you are going away, to leave us, made-moiselle," Roger was saying to her.

"I can hardly do one and not the other," she replied. "And it takes away from my pleasure in going to think that my uncle will miss me. He does not say so, but I know he will."

"And so shall I."

"You! M. Lande?"

"Why not?" he said, gently. "Am I to be the exception to all your friends? You will not deny my claim to the title, will you, mademoiselle?"

Words are nothing, save as *we* dwell in them. The same sentence may be a sword of flame or of steel, as we ourselves are cold or hot, or, if indifferent, as we often are in going through the sham fights and parades of society, a stage weapon with neither edge, point, nor weight. Any of Rénée's acquaintances might thus have claimed admission to the circle of her friendship, or expressed a regret at her departure, in those self-same words, without sending the blood up where the pearls lay about her throat. In Roger's question, simple as it was, and quietly asked, there was a meaning which lay neither in its form or its tone, and it pressed like a strong arm against the door of her heart.

And Father Le Blanc, who at that moment happened to be looking at Madame Milevski, — for her face always attracted him, — discovered a sadness in it he had not seen before. Was it only that, being supposed to have had her day, the scene which was passing under her eyes, and which Father Le Blanc saw also, made her realize it? But she seemed herself too young, and too beautiful, to have had all her day. Or was there something in that past of hers, thought he, which dragged upon her even more heavily as she looked at Rénée? Time, it is true, covers over our pains and our sorrows; experience overlies them in layers; but they are there, even when forgotten; and we drag them after us as weights, or carry them as scars, no matter how easily Time may bribe Memory. "A woman begins to grow old as soon as her dream is over," he thought. "But then," said this shrewd old observer to himself, looking from Roger to Stéphanie again, "one may grow sad because a dream just begun cannot be realized! It is quite possible; they would be worthy of each other. Bah! This wise Nature of whom we hear so much nowadays sows at random, with her eyes shut!"

Roger was unconscious of both Stéphanie's gaze

and the priest's reflections; as also of Baptiste, who had brought a message, and was finally obliged to say, " Monsieur ! " aloud, to make known his presence.

" Say that I cannot go," said Roger, on hearing it ; " that I will come to-morrow."

" The messenger says that it is urgent, and that his master will take no refusal."

Roger's eyebrows contracted, but he said nothing, and Baptiste retired.

" I wish you would go, M. Lande," said Rénée, timidly.

" Why ? " he said, surprised. " If I were to obey every call, I should neither eat nor sleep."

" But the call of distress. I could never accustom myself to it, and, after refusing it, could neither eat nor sleep. Time, monsieur, is so precious to the sick and to the dying."

Her earnestness disconcerted him.

" If you should regret it, — if, on my account " —

" I do not refuse on your account. I stay to please myself. But," he added, for he saw Rénée was in earnest, " I will go — to please you."

" You make me appear unreasonable, whereas " —

" No! on the contrary," he interrupted again, " it is I who appear selfish, for it will give me more pleasure to go, now, than to stay. Goodby," he said, rising. " I shall not see you again."

"Good-by," she said.

That was all. But she was conscious for the first time of a sovereignty, and the sense of pleasure in her heart escaped to her face. He saw it there as she looked up, and it repaid him.

He made his excuses to M. Michel, and then crossed the room to say good-by to Stéphanie. He felt towards her that sympathy which we have for the woman who knows our secret and has thus become our confidante. But she did not take up the conversation where it had been left that summer night on the ride back from the Château ot Beauvais. She seemed a little *railleuse;* why, he did not know; and, as he left, this provoked him to say : —

"I gave your message to my friend."

"Ah!" she replied. "I hope he proved rational."

"Would you consider him irrational if he differed from you ? "

"Why make needless suppositions ? "

"To see what you would say."

"I should say nothing."

"Yet you once gave him advice."

"Only to take counsel with himself, which is very simple if one is honest."

"Will you permit me to ask you a question ? " he said, bluntly.

"A second one ? Certainly."

"Are you taking Mademoiselle Rénée to Spain because of me ? "

"I might say ' yes,' and not be your enemy," she replied.

He hesitated a moment, and their eyes met. He thought of what Father Le Blanc had said. "One never sees the bottom." But this did not inspire distrust. The light of those eyes was as pure and steadfast as that of a planet. If he had been in doubt as to her meaning, that look scattered every misgiving.

"Madame, it is impossible for you to deceive me !"

She misunderstood him willfully.

"I think you could be deceived very easily, M. Lande."

"Not by you. You are incapable of it."

"On the contrary, I am deceiving you this instant."

She laughed nervously, and he regretted the directness of his compliment.

"And yet I am content. Well, I wish you a pleasant journey. Good-night," he said, reluctantly. He wished the wall were broken down.

"Good-by," she replied.

XII.

On the afternoon of the day preceding that of Madame Milevski's departure with Rénée, Father Le Blanc set out from his lodgings in the Rue Tiquetonne, and crossing the Rue de Montmartre which led to St. Eustache, turned into the Rue J. J. Rousseau. This was a sign that he was going out for a promenade, wherein he always blended pleasure with duty ; and Stéphanie, in her account of the manner in which he surveyed the view from the château at Beauvais, had exactly described the manner in which he took his enjoyment.

For all the many times he had passed down the Rue J. J. Rousseau, he had by no means exhausted its resources. He stopped before every window, in which he was ever discovering something new, and he kept up a running commentary upon all he saw, mingled with a soliloquy on things human and divine. At the corner of the Rue Coquillière he hesitated, as usual : he was making up his mind whether he should turn to the right and pass by the Palais Royal through the Place du Carrousel, or to the left over the Pont au Change. The former route would have led him to the bookstalls on the Quai Voltaire, the latter through the Ile du Palais, both of which places possessed for him a strong attraction. He decided on the first, and entered the Palais Royal by the Rue Baillif. Here it was not so much the glittering shops which interested him, as the garden with its children and shaded seats; nevertheless, with his hands crossed behind his back, he never failed to examine the brilliant display of wares multiplied by the reflecting mirrors, or to stand for a moment, as if he saw it for the first time, before the glass dial plate over whose transparent face the skeleton hands moved mysteriously, urged by an invisible power.

But Father Le Blanc used his eyes judiciously For certain windows he had a supreme contempt. Paste diamonds failed to hold him for a moment; he had no love for vases simply because they were made by an Arab in Tangiers, or for sleepy-looking women, sitting tranquilly upon nothing, simply because they were painted in Japan. The novel and the bizarre never blinded his keen eye for the beautiful, and he did not tarry long before objects whose claims to consideration rested only on their being old, or from over-seas. If one would know what retained him longest, search for that which, with age, possessed beauty also; with intrinsic worth, old associations. Before a bronze lamp, with fragile silver chains, before a reliquary from the hands of the Flemish goldsmith, he would linger a good half hour; for they led him back to the charming villas of Rome or to the vast world of Gothic manner and adventure.

Many a child in the garden knew this venerable face, and could distinguish this portly figure and somewhat slow step from among the crowds which thronged the corridors; and many of them had felt the kindly pressure of his heavy hand upon their heads.

After a half-hour's rest, he passed out by the front entrance and traversed the Place du Carrousel, in the middle of which he might be seen stopping now and then, like some stranger, with eyes fixed meditatively upon the pile which surrounded him, as though he were reading that history, sombre and momentous, which belongs to the palace of the French kings. Another halting-place was on the bridge beyond, from whose life and movement he betook himself to the musty but beloved bookstalls of the Quai Voltaire.

But to-day, as he crossed the bridge, he was thinking of other things. He was wondering why Madame Milevski should suddenly carry off Rénée to Spain. "It is restlessness," he said to himself; then, as his thoughts recurred to what he had seen in M. Michel's salon, he sighed. "Bah!" he continued half aloud, with the air of one who wishes to persuade himself against his fears, "I am imagining a tragedy. And yet, if it be true — Well, I believe in her! She is capable of this heroism. — What paths God traces out for us! If only we know that it is He who leads us, we can follow."

Father Le Blanc had a profound belief in human agencies. He loved to play the ministering angel, for his heart was a well of sympathy. There was even a latent chiding of Providence at the bottom of this well sometimes, when the sight of the poor and the suffering stirred its depths with pity for those lonely wayfarers who, neglected by this world, seem forgotten also of God. This was but one of those many themes which this mind, at once simple, honest, and profound, turned over and over reflectively, never seeing its one aspect except as on the way to the other. "The difficulty does not lie in believing the truths of the Church," he once said, "but in those other things which we must believe also." Or again, "Belief is an edifice never completed, because we do not yet comprehend its plan, and every day some workman brings a new stone from the quarry." So that while Father Le Blanc was very devout, he was not a devotee. He flavored his religious belief with the salt of a good sense, against which he endeavored to be on his guard, as he was even against his charity and compassion. The vision of Milton's fallen Spirit, beating its wings vainly in a non-resisting air, drew from his heart a profound sigh.

His thoughts turned very naturally to Stéphanie and her journey, that day, for he was on the way to secure the nineteenth volume of the " Viaje de España," of Pontz, for which he had been long on the search, and which awaited him at last on the Quai Voltaire. Those old books which filled the shelves of his room in the Rue Tiquetonne had left his purse a light one. "But," said Father Le Blanc, "I am not poor, since I have what I want."

After possessing himself of his coveted book, he took up his way along the quai, with his treasure under his arm. " I have a mind to call on her," he said, still thinking of Stéphanie. " The art of knowing when one is needed is more difficult than that of helping ; " and he paused on the curbstone to watch a company of the line, coming from the caserne of the Cité. A carriage, arrested a moment by the passage of the troops, approached the spot where he was standing, and he recognized M. de Marzac. The priest was evidently sauntering, and M. de Marzac called to his driver to stop.

" I see you are out for a promenade," he said. " Accept this seat beside me, and take a turn with me in the Bois."

Father Le Blanc was not in his second childhood, for he had not yet outgrown his first ; consequently the temptation was a strong one. But M. de Marzac was no favorite of his, and not even the fine day, nor this opportunity to enjoy it, could counterbalance M. de Marzac's company. Dislike at first sight is more common than love, as discord is more common than harmony. So he excused himself as about to make a visit. "Well, then, that decides it," he said to himself, as he trudged down the quai with the gait of a man with an object in view. "Now I must go."

At the door of the hôtel in the Boulevard St. Germain he stopped a moment, before entering, and took a deep inspiration. To tell the truth, the day was so fine he regretted going indoors. "I feel that I have a pair of lungs," he said, as he rang the porter's bell.

Stéphanie was not expecting a visit from Father Le Blanc, yet was glad to see him. She was in that period which lies after decision and before action, when, having made all her preparations for an early start in the express of the next morning, there was nothing to be done but sit down and wait for the hour of departure.

"The air is so pure that I feared to find you were out. And you go to-morrow!"

"Yes," Stéphanie said, "*Si Dios quiere*, as the Spaniards say."

"But I shall be there before you. I leave this evening."

"This evening!"

"And without fatigue," said the priest, mysteriously, drawing his volume from under his arm. It is my nineteenth journey."

"You have been to Spain?" said Stéphanie, taking the book, but still perplexed.

"Oh, never! except in those leaves which you are turning; and for two reasons," he added, laughingly; "the guide-books tell us that there are in Spain priests by the thousand, but not a single cook! Still, you perceive that I am about to follow you, and who knows! shall, perhaps, lodge at the same inn. That is a country in which nothing becomes obsolete, and I have no doubt but that, if you inquire for it, they will show you in Toboso the very *fonda* at which Don Quixote dismounted."

Stéphanie thought she heard in this pleasantry something more than was said. Certainly Father Le Blanc had not even whispered, " Though you are going away, my child, I shall follow you in my thoughts and in my prayers : " and yet, that is what she heard. Some of his most common-place sentences were so many half-hidden channels, such as the brooks make under the grass of the meadows, into which overflowed the currents of his sympathy and kindliness. In spite of a strong natural reserve, an invincible trust in this homely face, crowned with white hairs, mastered her.

"You are very good to think of me, father," she said, in a voice so full that it brought straight from his heart the message he had come to deliver.

" All who suffer are my children ; and you suffer, — and that grieves me. The Master who took upon himself the sorrows of the world, bade his followers imitate him. Why will you not lean a little upon me, daughter? I am an old man who has traveled the path before you."

She turned her eyes upon him, and they said, " I do not speak, but read, and comfort me."

"Sorrow is a very real thing," he continued in a voice full of sweetness and authority. " It is neither a morbid nor an unhealthy state. When it seems deepest; when, after the world has failed us, self also proves insufficient, it may even be a blessed one. I do not chide, I even agree with you. But I wish you also to agree with me. Be our life wide or narrow, whether we live humbly or sit on a throne, whether we dwell in our own thoughts, in the midst of action or in the search of pleasure, we come to the verdict of the Hebrew king, — that verdict which I read in your face and which broods over your life. All is emptiness and vanity! It is not the range but the depth of our experience which convinces us, and from the first we apprehend this truth dimly. We own this sad statue of Sorrow in the block from the outset, before experience chisels it out for us ; and in our first search for happiness, when we look on the splendors of the young world for what they do not contain, it is this intimation of what they cannot yield, and the capacity of our own natures, which both allure and deceive us."

She seemed to be listening to the story of her **own life.**

"And, as we live on, this conviction deepens. The voices without echo and reinforce those within. We are ever looking to something better than we have or are, and whether we attain it or lose it, there is no rest for our feet. It is the man who is fooled and deluded that is to be pitied. He who finds life and self sufficient is either a monster or a caricature. Do you not see that I do not argue with your tears? But do not think to dry them in Spain, my child. Sorrow is the handmaid of God, not of Satan. She would lead us, as she did the Psalmist, to say, 'Who will show us any good?' that, after having said this, we may also say with him, 'Lord, lift thou the light of *thy* countenance upon us.'"

"All else is a broken cistern," said Father Le Blanc, taking up his thoughts after a pause. "See how time deceives us! He covers the sore, he even heals the wound, but he gives no immunity from a fresh one." Stéphanie's eyes fell. "God only renders us superior to calamity. Honestly," said he, lifting his hands as if he appealed to his own conscience, "priest of God though I am, in understanding I am as a child. I cannot explain, — I testify. I witness to you this mystery, that out of the very hurt which brings me low, the spiritual life is developed. And," he added, as he would the benediction to a discourse at St. Eustache, "Blessed are the poor in spirit, blessed are they which mourn, blessed are they which hunger and thirst, for *these* are they which shall be filled, for *theirs* is the kingdom of heaven."

How much soever of gratefulness she felt for these words, she could not answer them. Had he held her hand, her answer would have been a pressure. But Father Le Blanc was not hurt by her silence. Though words bubbled easily over his lips, none better knew the difficulty of sometimes saying, " Thank you." He sat quietly, smoothing the wrinkles of his soutane over his broad knee, with his eyes on the floor.

" When you return," he said at last, looking up, " I shall ask you all the questions which are not answered in my nineteen volumes. Think of it, at my age ! never to have seen the sea. Yet I have lain stretched out on its yellow sands, in the sun, listening to the music of its blue waves — in the Rue Tiquetonne ! And when I go to my window at night, it is to stand on the summit of some high cliff, and the roar of the city is that of the sea at its base. Chained as we are to our little patrimony in the Rue Tiquetonne, the imagination is a free rover in space and time. I wager you are surprised to hear an old man talk of imagination," he said, taking her share of the conversation, and putting in her mouth the replies which he wished to answer, — " imagination, which is supposed to belong only to youth. I say rather youth belongs to imagination, which is then a wild Barbary colt, and carries one wherever it wills;

but at my age it has become domesticated, and it is on its back that I have ridden, as did Sancho on that of his patient donkey, over all the by-ways of Spain. And when you see some worthy colleague of mine on his ass, plodding before you with a shovel hat on his head a metre in length, you will say to yourself, ' There is my friend ahead of me.' "

Her hands crossed on her knees, plunged in a delicious revery which this voice penetrated without disturbing, Stéphanie raised her eyes to his face and smiled.

He took his book from the table where she had laid it, and put it under his arm again. He had dropped his few seeds of comfort, and was ready to permit God to water them. So he sought an excuse to go.

" I am like a school-boy," he said, tapping the volume, " with a new copy-book, who cannot rest till he has written something on the first page. What a good friend this book will be! I count upon him in advance," — and his eyes spoke to hers, — " he will not speak unless I question him ; we shall, perchance, differ profoundly, but he will not reproach me ; I shall rifle his pockets and put him aside at my pleasure, yet he will not feel neglected. I shall invite him to-night to a *tête-a-tête* before my fire, and fall asleep while he is doing his best to entertain me ; but when I awake, his countenance will be unruffled. Doubtless because all the while he is aware that I still prize him. What strange things we do to those whom we love! Absolutely, madame," said Father Le Blanc, rising, and with a self-accusing gesture, " I am an inveterate sermonizer, and I have not given you even the opportunity to interrupt me."

Stéphanie followed him to the door of the room, and at the threshold put her hand softly upon his arm.

" Thanks, father, for this visit," she said. Her voice was low ; it was all she said, but her look, and that gesture, were more eloquent than words.

" I say to you as they will say to you in Spain," replied Father Le Blanc, " go your way with God, my daughter."

When he had gone, she went to the window and watched him as he crossed the court-yard, following him out through the gates, where he stopped to say something to the porter, who touched his hat to him. She seated herself there in the wide open window which projected over the area, as did its counterpart at the other end of the room over the garden in the rear. Flanked by two long and narrow projections, this court-yard with its large paving-blocks of stone was not very inviting in its aspect. It was in the other window, overhanging the garden, whose casement the trees brushed, over which the vines swayed with the wind, that she loved to sit. But her thoughts were far away.

It was still early in the afternoon, but the sun went slowly down behind the tall roofs of the neighboring houses before she rose to do what greatly surprised Lizette, who thought madame altogether too much of a saint for a woman who neglected mass and confession. When madame was dressed, and Lizette had taken her place beside her in the carriage, she wondered at the route taken by the coachman, whose instructions she had not overheard. She supposed they were going to the Bois, or the Parc Monceau. And still greater was her surprise when she found herself a little later in St. Eustache, placing a chair for madame at the vesper service.

It was nearly over. Father Le Blanc himself in the pulpit was finishing his exhortation. Here the day had almost gone. The shafts of the columns rose into the shadows, which had begun to gather overhead, like massive trunks which lose themselves in the sombre foliage of the forest. The lamp, suspended by a black line which vanished in the darkness above, hung like a star on the horizon. All these people about her were silent, and the words of the preacher gathered force from the immense space in which they were uttered; from those dim, aspiring vaults into which they were gathered, and where they died away without a confusing murmur.

Break your theological rocks, O ritual-hating brother, on the King's highway, and worship Him after your own fashion. For every way-faring heart over-fed upon these symbols, you shall show us one starved on your formulæ. Not only for thy weaker brother, to whom God has not given the brains of the doctors in the Temple, shall these vaults of stone be the very arches of heaven; not only for thy frailer sister, in the keeping of whose warm heart God has placed the sacred things of this life, shall the incense of this swinging censer be the very fragrance of celestial fields; but unto many of thine own dignity, also, shall this star above the altar be the very star of Bethlehem.

Stéphanie sat in the outer circle of the congregation. Directly in front of her was an old woman with thin white hair straggling out from beneath her cap; close beside the rich fold of her dress she saw a plain, blue-and-white checked apron. She listened.

"My children," Father Le Blanc was saying, "you put all your treasures into earthen vessels. Your aspirations, so noble, soar upward like the branches of the tree, but your roots are in the earth that you must certainly leave. All your faith which will not take denial; all your hopes which will not be gainsaid; all your wide-embracing affections, you place in humanity, — in a few frail hearts which cannot meet the infinity of your need and of your desire. And all these things which must fail you and pass away, which you have, perchance, already gauged and found wanting, why will you put them in the place of heaven, to which you go to live forever; in the place of God, whose love knows no variableness nor shadow of turning? It is not I who undervalue them; it is you who overestimate them. Measure them rightly, and I shall no longer be to you a prophet of woe, or a sorrowful comforter. Love them without sacrificing yourself to them. Make them the rivers that water your life, and also the rivers that bear you to the infinite sea into which they shall be merged. Then shall this life cease to be for you a vale of tears walled about with tombs, and become the pathway to your abiding country. Its beauties shall not satiate, if you see behind them the world of spiritual beauty. What will it matter to you that its fetters chafe, that the soul discovers it is imprisoned, when that end, in which every beauty of flesh and color is engulfed, is not an end but a beginning? Verily, verily, I say unto you, whoso loseth his life for my sake, shall find it!"

"For my sake," thought Stéphanie.

And Father Le Blanc, who had not seen this listener, — who, having sown the seed, had left it humbly to God, — was thus himself permitted to water it.

The candles were lighted in the parlor when Stéphanie returned. She extinguished half of them and sat down in the recess over the garden. Presently Lizette entered.

Lizette was not wanting in assurance; still she advanced hesitatingly. The darkness was unusual and made her timid; moreover, madame had not called her, and yet it was time for her dinner toilette.

"Pardon, madame," she said. "Madame does not dress for dinner?"

"No, I dine as I am. Mademoiselle Rénée dines with me, and she will sleep here also. Have the room next to mine ready for her. We shall start from here early in the morning. Is everything ready?"

"Yes, madame. Does madame require me this evening?"

"No, not till I retire. Do you wish to go out?"

"Before leaving for so long, — I have a visit to make."

"Well, make your visit; and, as you go out, tell Jacques that, when mademoiselle comes, I shall be here."

"Merci, madame."

And Lizette that night told her lover, with whom she went to the Cirque, that madame, who she thought was recovering her gayety, was again as she used to be at Kief.

"This time, at last, she has a lover," said Lizette's companion.

"Idiot!" she replied, with ineffable scorn, "you think she is no better than myself?"

"Allons donc! perhaps she is not a woman," was the incredulous reply. "Elle a ses nerfs alors."

"Her nerves are stronger than yours," rejoined Lizette, tartly; and this episode nearly spoiled her evening. Her thoughts reverted again and again to her mistress, whom she had left in the twilight of the great salon, and she thought, "I am glad Mademoiselle Rénée is coming."

Stéphanie was waiting for her. All the light had faded out of the sky. The window had become a black surface in which she saw her own outline and the slender flames of the candles. Suddenly another form appeared in this mirror. She turned with a cry of pleasure. But it was not Rénée.

It was M. de Marzac.

Accustomed to admit M. de Marzac so frequently, Jacques had not even followed him up the stairs. He knew madame was in the salon waiting for Mademoiselle Rénée, and M. de Marzac glided up the stairway as if he had an appointment. In reality, the latter had not lingered lest he should hear Jacques transmit the orders which his mistress had very probably given him. As he ascended the staircase he expected to hear the formula, "Madame ne reçoit pas, monsieur;" but Stéphanie had not thought of it. The reappearance of M. de Marzac for a *tête-à-tête* was inconceivable, and he had dropped out of her thoughts. When, expecting to see Rénée, she turned to find him standing so near to her, he was as it were an apparition.

He had a sentence prepared, but the cry of pleasure which escaped her disconcerted him. For a moment he appropriated it to himself.

"It seems the dead come to life, monsieur," she said, coldly.

"It is said so, madame, when they die with a fault on their conscience."

"M. de Marzac," she said, looking at him steadily, "why do you persist in playing a comedy with me?"

Her words were like ice. If they swept away the hope that always rose in his heart when he was near her, they also confirmed him in his suspicions, and the tide of his anger rose to his very throat. It was indeed a comedy, which, persisted in, would become a farce. But M. de Marzac was cool: he had his reserves, and the savage pleasure of destruction slaked his passion. He no longer felt impotent.

"Have patience, madame; the comedy is over. We will now have a little tragedy."

The tone of his voice struck her. It was quite natural, and he laughed composedly.

"So you go to Spain," he said, seating himself, quietly. "What an original idea! Spain is such an interesting country. It lies between France and Africa, as it does between civilization and barbarism."

Stéphanie was self-possessed, and she did not yet understand him. But this swift change of base disturbed her. She felt a vague sense of coming peril.

"And you have so charming a companion," pursued M. de Marzac, playing with the ivory paper-cutter on the table. "Really, I congratulate you."

"It seems we are still in the last act of the comedy," she said, with an effort to appear calm, "and I am tired of it."

"Do you think so?" he replied, with a smile fine as that of a mask. "Shall we make Mademoiselle Michel, whom you are waiting for, the judge?"

"Whom I am waiting for!" repeated Stéphanie, carried away by surprise. Then, with a quiver of indignation, "You employ spies, monsieur."

"Yes, two, madame; and they are looking at you. You do not comprehend me," he said, still smiling. "You are too impatient. We are only in the first act. Your plan is so ingenious, — this little journey to Spain! There is nothing like absence, spiced with a little novelty, to wean a young girl from her lover."

"M. de Marzac!"

"What! She does not love him?" he asked, in a tone of well-feigned incredulity, affecting to misunderstand her. "You do not believe, me?

Well, it is not pleasant to admit it-- I do not blame you — that she should love this maker of pills, the son of a music-teacher. It is ridiculous!"

The very walls seemed to reel as she listened to him.

"Come," said M. de Marzac, clapping his hands softly, "you are admirable; in the first act, too! But if you are surprised at what I am telling you," he pursued, confidentially, "we will ask mademoiselle, when she comes. She is very frank, and very — innocent. I am confident she will avow it. That would afford an excellent opportunity to furnish mademoiselle a little surprise in her turn, also. If, for example, I should admit her into our secret, and explain to her this excursion to Spain, which has for its object to make her forget one whom another will remember."

"It is a lie!" cried Stéphanie, white as death, springing to her feet, overborne by terror and indignation.

"At all events, it is a lie in which you appear marvelously interested. But I lack precision; let us be more definite. Is it, then, a lie that Madame Milevski loves M. Lande? And to think that you call this a comedy! A comedy of errors, truly! One which would doubtless prove as surprising to M. Lande as to Mademoiselle Michel, if I should perchance change my mind, and admit him into our confidence."

"You would not dare to," she said. The attack was so sudden, surprise and terror benumbed her.

"Pouf! Dead men have no fears," replied M. de Marzac, tranquilly.

He rose and walked the length of the room, stopping before the mirror to adjust his cravat. He was quite content with himself. He had taken her unawares, and was now sure of what he had only suspected. The game was a risky one, but it had succeeded beyond his expectations.

"So you imagined that, having rung the bell for Jacques, our affair was well settled. Your rôle was a very pretty one — to insult a gentleman while you rely on his remaining one to follow your servant's heels meekly out of the door. What a pity that you could not call a brother, or a husband, — or even a lover," he added with a sneer; "some one whom I should have the pleasure to run through with my sword, — as I may yet do for a certain doctor. Think how many resources I have," he said, coming back to where she stood.

This allusion to her defenseless position was a masterstroke. It brought the tears to her eyes. He saw them glisten, and for an instant he pitied her. Without a doubt, he would have thrown himself at the feet of this woman if she would have permitted him.

Rudely and suddenly shaken as she had been, she began to collect her thoughts. This insult gave her strength.

"M. de Marzac," she said, slowly, "you are a coward."

"We are a pair of them," he laughed. "But calm yourself, madame, for I, at least, am a reasonable one. It is not necessary that I should consult the physician to-night, or even make friends with Mademoiselle Michel. We have plenty of time before us. We might wait until Mademoiselle Rénée becomes Madame Lande, — that is, if you will permit it. To-night you fear the denouement; but I can conceive that you may in time welcome, even pray for it, — after a long suspense, for example. You will make your excursion to Spain, and I — I will wait here in Paris. It is not I who am impatient. Having practised patience for a whole year, I have become an adept."

"You are more than a coward," she said, as if she did not hear him, "for you think to trade on cowardice."

"On yours, or mine, madame? Explain yourself. Nothing is changed since yesterday, and yesterday, when I saw you, you did not seem to be afraid. Ah! to be sure, at that time we were ignorant that we were discovered. That makes a difference. As to trading on anything, what have I to gain? Absolutely nothing. Divest yourself, I beg of you, of all thoughts of me. I have no longer any interest, except that of the spectator. But observe the proprieties! The mise-en-scène is changed. Scorn became you very well the other night; you chose a good weapon, and you used it admirably. But to-day it is different. Does what I say displease you? Very likely! I have had the misfortune to displease you once already; but I was appealing then to a heart of stone, — to day I address one of flesh and blood. That makes a difference again, — whether one invokes a love that does not exist, or one that does. And therefore it is that I say scorn does not become you to-night. Against calumny I would not dispute your right to it, — but against the truth " — and M. de Marzac indulged again in his fine smile.

While she heard every word of this reasoning which was the very perversion of reason, Stéphanie could think of Father Le Blanc, who so short a time ago had been seated in the very chair before her. She had even time to wonder at herself, to wonder that, as she looked at this man, at his pale, aristocratic face and faultless dress, no detail of which escaped her, her mind could thus wander back to St. Eustache, and that before her eyes should appear the blue and white checked apron of the bourgeoise who sat beside her.

"You have nothing to say?" said M. de Marzac. "Parbleu! and yet it is worth the trouble of a denial. Let us recapitulate. First, a young girl and her lover, indispensable to every piece. Second, a woman who loves — the latter. The characters are few, the plot is simple, but amusing. For this woman has lofty ideas! She indulges in lectures on the morals of love. One wonders what she will do. Ah! I forget! there is also the rejected lover to whom she delivers these lectures, and whom she thought herself well rid of. As to the denouement, that is undecided, and we will not yet hasten it; that would be to diminish the interest; one can only conjecture. Love may prove stronger than morals, in which case, this poor lover, who profits by his instruction, interferes in the name of society and virtue; or this woman conquers her love and makes a sublime sacrifice, — there is again this poor lover, who looks on and applauds. In any event, she suffers, in any event he is rewarded; her sufferings avenge him. Whatever she does, he is a witness. And if this little piece, which you deign to dignify with the title of comedy, moves too slowly, if the scenes are delayed, he reserves the right to hasten the action, and to ring the bell for the finale."

M. de Marzac had not prepared any definite plan, and, for this reason, this impromptu scene did him the more credit. He had no idea what he should do. He had made a discovery which so burned in his heart that he could not wait to deliberate; he could not resist trying a little, *à l'improviste*, the edge of this weapon which fate had given him. He had dealt his blow and had enjoyed its effect; but he saw that it was time to go. He did not propose to repeat his former mistake, and to wait again for Jacques to hand him his gloves. Like the lion-tamer when the performance is over, he cast an uneasy thought in the direction of the door.

He rose quickly, made a sudden movement as if he would approach her, then turned abruptly, and before she could have prevented him, had she desired to, was gone.

XIII.

Two things in life are absolutely certain,—Death and Sorrow; and these two, about which there is nothing contingent, alone possess the power to surprise us. All that is problematical we are ready for, and accept without lifting our eyebrows; but this figure of Sorrow, whose shadow falls athwart our path a few days' journey ahead, and Death, who waits at its end without clamor, since he is sure of us, — to these we say, "It cannot be! it is impossible!" We count upon the uncertain; the inevitable surprises us.

After the echoes of M. de Marzac's footsteps had died away, after the great door below was closed, and silence had settled down upon the room again, it all seemed a dream; and, of that afternoon, only the voice and face of Father Le Blanc and the incense of St. Eustache were the realities. M. de Marzac was a phantom, which in vanishing had carried away the only proofs of its brief existence. No! there was the dull monotone of her own heart; there were his words, still ringing in her ears, and there was that from which those words had torn away the veil. Why should she feel surprise? M. de Marzac had not created this love, which till now had been a delicious dream, like the mother's hope ere she feels the strong, new life at the very core of her own.

M. de Marzac had but brought the vague image into the focus. He was not a friend to paint a fancy portrait and deal in flesh tints, but the enemy who goes deeper and hits upon the joints of the skeleton that is within. Before this thought her first indignation and outraged pride lapsed into a stupor, in the thick of which, nevertheless, her mind thought on, as her heart beat on, like a galley-slave in chains.

Suddenly Rénée, whom she had forgotten, came; the freshness of an autumn evening in her hair, the light of expectation in the depths of her gray eyes, and the matin song of happiness in her heart. Ah, si jeunesse savait! says the poet.

Stéphanie was not yet mistress of herself, and the less so because she knew it. She was perpetually rousing herself from her thoughts, to see Rénée and fall back again. At dinner she alternated between silence and a forced gayety. Her eyes had the dry brilliancy of anxiety.

Rénée, who had a good appetite and was full of anticipation, chatted away innocently. She had never before possessed a friend like Stéphanie; of her own sex, one for whom she felt just that modicum of awe which dignifies love without chilling it; and she reveled in the possession. Somehow, she found it very easy to talk to her. How sur

prised M. Michel would have been to hear her!
She asked a hundred questions about their journey, for which Stéphanie thanked her. Twenty
times the latter glanced at her furtively, unper-
ceived. How unconsciously pretty she was! She
gave no support to the satirist who said, "Il faut
souffrir pour être belle." There were no mys-
teries in her toilette which were not innocent, for
Nature was her maid. She had fairly startled
the solemn Jacques that evening, though he had
been her usher times enough before. As she
looked at her, Stéphanie felt to a certain degree
responsible both for her beauty and her happiness. She noticed that some of her suggestions,
made during the week's preparations, in the matter of this very travelling dress which she wore,
for example, had been followed. She had vetoed
some ideas of the modiste, who can more easily
spoil a good subject than remedy the defects of a
poor one, though the latter is her trade. In more
senses than one, she had begun the task of bringing Rénée out. Since that conversation at Beauvais, Rénée had leaned upon her with a somewhat
shy but happy confidence which touched her; and
the mere fact that she was about to exchange the
quiet and solitary life of the Rue du Bac for one
so new and strange as that into which the journey to Spain ushered her, deepened this relation
of wardship which had insensibly grown up between them. It was manifest in Rénée's manner,

in the questions which she asked, and the expectant curiosity of inexperience which they revealed. From the moment she entered the room, she had been unconsciously exerting on Stéphanie that immense influence which lies in the faith of the child who, with his hand in his father's, laughs in the face of danger.

And this was why, after dinner, Stéphanie, with a sudden impulsiveness, went up behind Rénée's chair, and with her arms about her neck, said, —

"Do you promise to obey me, little daughter, in everything, if I take you with me?"

And Rénée, who could not see her face, replied, in mock gravity: —

"Absolument! ma petite mère."

"Well, then, if you mean it, since we are both tired to-night, — or, rather, since we must make an early start, — go up to my room, take off your dress, — Lizette is out, but you will find my dressing-gown and a fire. Sit down before it, take a book, and wait for me. I have some affairs to arrange, and will join you in a half hour. Have you all your instructions fast?"

It seemed to Stéphanie that she must have this half hour's breathing time; that before going upstairs with Rénée, some resolution should take shape out of the chaos into which M. de Marzac's sudden threat had thrown her. She felt that need of putting her hand on the lever of events, and arresting their progress till she had looked them and herself in the face. 'Making up one's mind,' even if it can only be to meet what comes courageously, is the secret of 'taking heart.'

What would she not have given for a friend! Not for sympathy, not for words, not for comforting assurances; not to sit down with her in sackcloth like those of Job; but one of flesh and blood, who should rise up and smite the Sabeans, even as they had smitten, with the sword of a righteous indignation. Father Le Blanc's voice still lingered in her ears, but it sounded afar off, as in a dream, and stood her in no help. There are times when we seem to have more need of ourselves than of God; when life is too real and too short for the measuring rod of eternity; when the soul scorns a far-away retribution equally with revenge; and will not even own that Justice, having permitted injustice, can restore equilibrium by rebalancing her scales. What coin is there in the mint that shall pay back the debt of a great wrong! She had gotten so near to the brutal facts, that the language of the spiritual world was a pure mysticism. Sorrow is often misquoted. It is only one step in a long journey, one stage in a long growth. It is the furnace from which the steel emerges hard; another process softens it. Many a brave soul finds itself first, God afterwards.

She sat down on the low causeuse in the window; on her hot brow the cool pane against which it pressed was like ice. She tried to think; but her mind, so prompt, so energetic, seemed paralyzed. Like the deer which, dozing in the shade of the wood, hears suddenly the bay of hounds, and does not know whither to turn, but only that it must flee, she felt at once a feverish impatience for action and the indecision of sudden terror; terror, not of M. de Marzac, but of those mighty energies of her own heart which, so long crushed, had been ripening silently, till she felt their power as that of a clutched hand on her conscience. How could she shut the door against herself! Yet that door must be shut, and soon. Amid the alternate pleadings and commands of her heart, she heard the voice of this conscience, saying to her, "Soon! soon! soon!" All the present was a whirl of conflict which blinded her eyes and hid the future; but the past was brilliant with a supernatural light. It defiled before her with all its half-forgotten scenes like the platoons of an army which emerge from the darkness of some obscure street to pass in review before its chief in the blaze of a lighted square, and vanish again into obscurity. She saw again those sun-kissed heights of dream on which her child's eyes had gazed. How bright they were then! What hopes blossom there where the sun shines forever and capacities bear their fruit! Something of the old splendor yet lingered about those peaks which her young imagination had piled to the very gates of heaven, glimpses of which had grown so rare to her from the lonely path which a miscarried life follows in the sombre forests. As she sat lost in that past, the bells of St. Séverin struck the hour. They brought back to her the prayers of her mother, the sweet faces of the Convent of Notre Dame, and the words of Father Le Blanc; and, for an instant, she longed to throw herself upon her knees. But her pride revolted.

She rose from her seat and went to the mirror above the fireplace. The candles burned brightly upon the mantel, and she looked at the face they revealed in the glass as though it were that of another person which she could analyze curiously. She saw its beauty; not a line that an artist would have seen was unnoticed: she saw its trouble and anxiety; not a sign that a friend would have detected escaped her; and, as she looked, she felt the warm flood of tears rising to her eyes. If she had buried her head in her hands, they would have vanquished her. But the sight of this weakness turned pity into a scorn that froze them at their very sources, and fired the eyes into which she gazed with a light of defiance. There was almost a sneer in the smile of self-contempt which swept her face as she turned away, and when she opened the door of her room where Rénée waited her, it had settled into the cold expression of self-mastery and resolute determination.

14

Patience, good father! this strength is the sign of the steel. Have no fear for the temper!

Wrapped in blue cashmere, her head thrown back on the cushion of the chair and her book on the floor, Rénée had fallen asleep. Stéphanie stood for a moment silently in the open door. This picture of loveliness and happiness made her both cold and hot, hard and pitiful. Under the arm that guards there must always be that which is guarded; beside the watcher who waits, the sleeper who dreams. What! could ye not watch with me one hour!

"How unjust I am," she said to herself, thinking of the resolute gray eyes under the fallen lids. "She does not dream of it."

Though she closed the door noiselessly, Rénée awoke.

"What, are you here!" she said, rousing herself. "When did you come? How long have I been asleep?"

"Just now," said Stéphanie, sitting down beside her.

"A fire always makes one dozy," Rénée said, apologetically.

"Or a book, sometimes," suggested Stéphanie, looking at the one on the floor.

"No, I was reading something which interested me intensely," replied Rénée, stooping to pick up the book. "I did not fall asleep reading it, but in thinking of it afterwards."

"What was it about?" asked Stéphanie, holding out her hand for the book. "Pliny! and Latin! Where did you get it, pray?"

"Why, I found it here on the table, with the leaf turned down."

"With the leaf turned down?"

"Yes. Were you not reading it?—this page —I mean the letter about Arria?"

"No, my little blue-stocking; I cannot read Latin," looking at the book curiously. It was small and thin; well-worn, but it had no name on the fly-leaf to tell its owner.

"Read me the story which interested you. I am going to take down my hair, but I shall hear you."

"I will tell it to you," Rénée said. "Arria was the wife of the Consul Pætus, who took sides with — I have forgotten the name — but he was defeated and made prisoner, and sent to Rome. Arria went with him" —

"With whom?"

"With her husband, whom the Emperor Claudius condemned to die — by his own hand. But Pætus had not the courage to kill himself; till one day, to give him courage, Arria snatched the poniard he wore from his side, and plunged it in her own breast. And then, O Stéphanie, think of it!—drawing it out, she gave it to him, saying, 'It does not hurt, Pætus.' I see the very smile with which she said it."

Stéphanie, taking out the pins from her hair, kept her face turned away.

"I do not believe there are such women to-day," said Rénée.

"Could you not do it?" asked Stéphanie, after a pause.

"Only to read of it makes me think I could. It would inspire a coward, as it did. But without the example — I don't know. It is so much easier to follow an example than to set one. I should have tried to save him."

"But suppose that were impossible."

"How can you ask me, Stéphanie! I should not like to have been Pætus," she added, thoughtfully. "No one has a right to such a sacrifice."

"Perhaps you would not be consulted."

"After all," said Rénée, breaking an interval of silence, "how many heroic deeds are done that we never know of, even to-day, — and greater ones than Arria's."

"What ones?"

"Those that are inspired by duty, instead of affection. For how Arria must have loved Pætus! It was her love which made it easy. When I think of that, her death does not seem a sacrifice, but a consummation. I was thinking of it when I fell asleep. If you read the whole story, Stéphanie, how she followed him to Rome, submitting to hardships and degradation to be near him, and remember how she loved him, she does not surprise you when she says, 'It does not hurt, Pætus;' her death is like the crown on the head of a great king — it dazzles you, but you expect to see it there."

"You will not always find what you look for, even in kings."

"I should in Arria, because she loved. She was born to do this thing. Besides, she had no motive to live; her husband's doom was her own. She had the motive to die; and when she struck the blow, she lived most and best, and knew it. Before you came up-stairs, I was wondering whether she thought of it beforehand, whether she had to make up her mind to it. I do not believe she did. It was a burst of love, not of courage. I do not want to think the less of her, but would it not have been harder for her to see Pætus die — and live — than to die with him? Do you understand me, Stéphanie?"

"Yes, I understand you."

"Arria did not have to endure. She reached the mark with one act; all her heroism was concentrated in a single moment of time. That makes it more brilliant, perhaps" —

"More brilliant than what?"

"Than that lonely courage which has to endure," said Rénée, sitting up and speaking very earnestly, "that cannot reach the mark with one burst only, but has to keep steadily there; that does not give a life which has become worthless,

but one which is precious.   I am sure I could do
greater things out of my love for you, Stéphanie,
than out of my duty to you.   Love earns its reward so quickly, — it is its own reward.   But
that of duty, — sometimes only faith can see any
reward at all.   Don't you think so?"

"Yes."

"That was what I meant by greater deeds than
Arria's.   Her love inspired her and satisfied her
at the same time; and she had Pætus' knowledge
of it besides.   But is there not heroism which
must be lonely, — that is fit for an example, but,
because unknown, can never be one, — would, perhaps, cease to be such, if known?   One does not
think of Arria's life as cut short, like a broken
column; her death was the capital which made
it perfect and complete.   But there must be lives
which love and duty deform instead of crown, —
destroy all their happiness, I mean.   Don't you
know Arria was happy in dying?   I think it was
the happiest moment in her life.   But oh, Stéphanie!" and in her earnestness Rénée came over
to the dressing-table and sat down beside her,
"think of those lives whose whole mission is to
hide, and yield their place; to surrender not mere
living, but all life's opportunities, — and yet live
on when rightful happiness is gone, while the capacity for it remains.   There must be such lives,
which cannot achieve all by ending all, as Arria
did; which have no choice but to endure.   For

these, Arria's poniard would be cowardice, or flight."

She sought Stéphanie's face as she spoke, but the hand, unfastening the coils of hair, hid it.

"You discriminate like a professor giving a lesson," said Stéphanie, with that rashness which had sometimes disconcerted M. de Marzac.

"You have not answered me at all," replied Rénée. Her enthusiasm was a little dampened by Stéphanie's manner. "But you agree with me; I know you do."

"I admit that, though a little pitcher, you are running over."

Rénée laughed, and went back to her chair, putting out her feet to the warmth of the coals.

"I have ever so many things I want to talk over with you. I have been 'stopping to think' ever since I can remember. Where shall we be at this time to-morrow night, Stéphanie?"

"At Lyons."

"And the next night?"

"On the Mediterranean."

That word plunged her in a revery from which she did not wake till Lizette came to show her to her room, unfasten her traveling-bag, — for the heavy luggage was already at the station, — and make ready her chamber for the night.

"You may go to madame; I do not need you," she said to Lizette, after the latter had completed these preparations.

"Very well, mademoiselle. When you are ready I will come in and put out the candles."

Presently Rénée appeared at the door between the two chambers.

"Stéphanie, my prayer-book is in my trunk. May I have yours to-night?"

"Here it is, mademoiselle," said Lizette, adroitly taking her own from her pocket.

Lizette ought to have known better; but she was quick-witted, and in the emergency — for she knew well enough that her mistress had none — her instincts naturally went to the front.

"Who taught you to answer for your mistress, mademoiselle?" said Stéphanie, when Rénée had closed the door.

"Madame," stammered Lizette. Older than Stéphanie by ten years, she nevertheless stood in awe of her.

Stéphanie laughed impatiently.

"You are too zealous. There are worse faults, but it will be worth while to conquer this one."

Lizette took up her brush and resumed her work over her mistress' hair, nervously.

"Who left the book on my table, Lizette?"

"Madame," said Lizette, expecting a second reproof, "I " —

"Well, what is the matter? It was Father Le Blanc, was it not?"

"Yes, madame, he told me to place it there."

"When?"

"This evening, as I was going out."

"Well, you did rightly. What is the matter?"

"Ah! Madame, you startled me. You asked me so suddenly."

"Why should I startle you? He did not forbid you to say that it was he, I presume."

"No, madame. But when I asked if I should say who sent it, he said, 'If she does not know, there is no need to tell her.'"

"And that perplexed you?"

"Yes, madame; I confess it."

"No wonder," said Stéphanie, tranquilly.

And Lizette, though she took the first occasion to scrutinize this mysterious book, delivered a message which she does not to this day understand.

XIV.

EIGHT o'clock of the next morning found our travelers comfortably ensconced by themselves in a compartment of the Marseilles express.

The shrill " En voiture, messieurs!" of the guards, the shutting of doors, the first Titan breathings of the locomotive as the train drew slowly out of the station, had drowned the voice of M. Michel. There was only to be seen his benevolent face and the glitter of his spectacles, a last wave of the hand, somewhat disconsolate, and the platform on which he stood slid away with all its bustle like a river.

M. Michel had provided Rénée with a guidebook, between which and the two windows she was in perpetual trouble. Like an ill-matched pair of horses, the château out of the window and its description in the book were never together.

" Give it to Lizette, and let her read aloud," suggested Stéphanie, as a compromise.

So Lizette read volubly, undaunted by statistics, omitting not a line, beginning with the Lunatic Asylum and the Forts of Charenton, much concerned over the names of certain worthies unknown to her, — Monaldeschi, Queen Christina, Dukes of

Burgundy, and Cæsar's Commentaries, — noting with gravity that the viaduct of Avon, passed some time before, was thirty-three feet wide, and that at Fontainbleau the Hôtel de France was clean, comfortable, and moderate.

Rénée gave Stéphanie an amused glance, whereupon Lizette was released from her task, not a little proud of her success as a reader, and quite satisfied with having so well gotten over the pitfalls of pronunciation.

"It is useless," Rénée whispered, despairingly. "I shall keep the left side till we come back, and sit down with you at your window, and enjoy myself in my own fashion."

Down the yellow Seine crept the barges; the walls and roofs of Thoméry, covered with vines, swept past the window; a peasant, standing in the road with a basket of grapes packed in heather, caught Rénée's eye for an instant; village and town succeeded each other swiftly; till, at last, the plain of Dijon unrolled like a mantle, fringed with the faint blue outlines of the Jura, — the city, with its frowning palace and churches, lying, a strong black shadow, in the foreground.

Stéphanie could but tease Rénée a little at the dinner-table of the Dijon station, where, as Rénée said, nothing was lacking but time. Neither Chambertin nor Romanée were needed to quicken her appetite.

"Between hunger and the desire to appear at

least decently," she whispered to Stéphanie, as they were hurried back to their carriage, "I am half starved."

Out of the dark station, through the straggling skirts of the town, they rushed on, among those rich terraces of the Côte d'Or, long coveted by France of the Dukes of Burgundy, where the vines left scarce a glimpse of the yellow-red soil; the clustering villages, thickly sown as the almond trees that dot its fields, fled past the window; the tops of the tall chimneys of the iron works of Creuzot blazed with blue and red fires in the face of the sun; Macon came and vanished; sunset touched the hills of Charolois and reddened the white châteaux of thé Saône, which narrowed to a ribbon's width under the wooded heights of the Mont d'Or; then, with a shriek, the train plunged into the tunnel of Notre Dame, that announces the approach to Lyons.

Stéphanie had planned to break the long ride at Lyons, passing the night there, and taking the train on the following morning, so as to reach Marseilles in season to embark on the Spanish steamer sailing in the late afternoon. In this way, also, the scenery along their route was all passed in the daytime, which has both its advantages and its drawbacks. It at once surfeits and tantalizes. Against the former, to close one's eyes is but a poor relief; while against the latter there is none whatever. The rigid rails which

permit no wandering, the iron steed which brooks
no dallying, how sorely would they have tried the
spirit of Montaigne, who said, "If the way is bad
on my right hand, I turn on my left; if I find
myself unfit to ride, I stay where I am; have I
left anything behind me unseen, I go back to see
it; 't is still my way; I trace no certain line,
either straight or crooked."

Still, Rénée stored away many a fresh and
pleasant picture; of the turbulent Rhone, braid-
ing its yellow strand of waters from the torrents
of Drôme and Ardèche, to unweave it again
among the gravel beds and salt lagoons of Ca-
margue; now broad as a sash on the wide plains
lined with avenues of poplar and willow, now
narrowed and pushed aside by naked cliffs, girdled
with hamlets all but lost in the shade of the mul-
berry, and crowned by roofless gables and towers;
of the valley of the Isère, cradled among the Alps
of Dauphiné, which, in the distance, buttress the
white peak of Mont Blanc; of Avignon's spires
and Papal towers; and last, but not least, of that
first evening on the Mediterranean, in the twilight an indigo sea, when, walking the deck of the
steamer with Stéphanie, she breathed for the first
time that indescribable freshness of the night peculiar to those countries which border this sea,
and watched under the stars the receding lights on
the mole and quays of Marseilles.

XV.

Hugging the sides of the buildings in the short shadows of ten o'clock, Antonio, el Moro, guide and courier de place, might have been seen on his way to the Hôtel of the Alameda, to meet the two French ladies to whom he was engaged. In any other land than Spain this curious figure would have attracted attention. Beardless, yet always unshaven, gaunt, but with an air of ruggedness, he pursued his way leisurely, with that shiftless gait of the Spaniard, who has always the day before him, and religiously employs it in doing nothing. His garments were a peculiar mixture of Barbary and Spain, loose, awkward, and ill-fitting, and had the appearance of being conscious that they were despised by their owner, and tolerated only from necessity. No one knew whether the stoop of his shoulders was due to age or weariness, any more than whether this alien to the brotherhood of guides was in reality a Moor, as he was called, or a Spaniard: solemn, not to say cadaverous, taciturn, and dignified, he little resembled the type of his genus, so generally full of yarns, ditties, loquacity, and lies.

Sitting in the shade, on the wooden bench outside the door of the hotel, mine host of the Alameda saluted him effusively, receiving a nod of recognition in return. Although making his headquarters in Granada, Antonio was known to every man, woman, and child in Andalusia. He took a seat gravely by the innkeeper's side, and rolled the cigarette offered him between a thumb and finger yellow as parchment.

"You come from Granada?" inquired mine host.

"Last night," replied Antonio, with a puff of smoke from his nostrils resembling the breath of a laboring horse on a cold day, — an act of energy forming a solitary exception to the usual air of tranquillity and repose.

"You go back again soon?"

"That depends."

"Ah, dolt that I am! you have come for the two French ladies who arrived in the steamer of yesterday."

If silence gives assent, Antonio's answer was affirmative.

"Jesus! Would they were to remain with me! I should have all the gallants of Malaga for company."

Antonio made a grimace; possibly at the thought of having them all at his heels.

"Which way do you go? Granada, I suppose."

"God knows," was the reply, and it would have been difficult to tell whether this proverbial expression betokened in his case indifference or Christian resignation.

From the open balcony directly above him Rénée was looking out through the narrow vista at the end of the Alameda, on the sea, which melted into the sky in a band of azure mist scarcely definable. In this belt of soft color the white sail of a fishing-boat caught the sunlight, and shone like the under side of a bird's wing in the clouds.

The conversation below had not troubled her, inasmuch as she had not understood it; but the strange sounds of another tongue were in themselves an attraction, to say nothing of Antonio's pointed hat with broad velvet rim, which, from above, completely concealed all but his legs.

Breakfast was just finished, and Stéphanie had sent to inquire if this guide, well recommended and reliable, had yet arrived. When, then, this pointed hat and pair of leathern leggings vanished, to reappear at the door of the room, it seemed to Rénée as if she were at the opera, and one of the actors had just entered from the flies.

Wherever he went, Antonio carried with him an air which had the effect of an interrogation point. He might have been some decayed Castilian gentleman whom reverses had driven from home, and who in vain sought to accommodate himself to the gaudier dress and livelier manners of the Southern province ; or some professor of languages in reduced circumstances, wearing the badges of his

unworthy calling with an ill-disguised awkward-
ness ; or a very Moor indeed, the sad relic of
other days, of which he was always thinking.

" At your service, señor-itas," he said, removing
his opera hat, and changing the termination of the
word during the instant that he glanced at the
young faces of the French ladies. " Here are two
fillies who will lead me a pretty jig ! " he thought
beneath his grizzled pate.

During the settlement of the preliminaries with
Stéphanie, Rénée gazed at this specimen of di-
lapidated dignity with wonder. Left to herself, it
is quite likely he would have overawed her ; from
the mere fact that he said nothing, he claimed respect and excited curiosity ; and, at the same
time, like a prickly pear, which, for all its needles, has within what is not bad eating, his manner seemed to say, " Provided you handle me
carefully, I am not such a bad fellow."

Stéphanie encountered this rough surface at the
outset. They were to go to Granada that night
by diligence. Antonio suggested the hiring of a
calesa ; he had relations, doubtless, with the ven-
dor of these vehicles, and had a thought to his
pocket, which was ever empty, — " because it is so
capacious," he said. But the pleasure and novelty
of a diligence ride over the Sierras was precisely
one of those experiences which Stéphanie had no
mind to forego.

" You fancy the springs of a diligence are tempered in Toledo," said Antonio, determined not to begin by submitting to a caprice. "I promise you your bones will ache for a month."

"Secure us seats just the same," replied Stéphanie, laughing in spite of his brusqueness.

"It will consume twice the time; and if it rains "—

"We will not go."

"But I assure you "—

"Antonio!" said Stéphanie, quietly, "am I to travel with you, or are you to travel with me?"

"Better be a fool than obstinate," grumbled Antonio, as he went out; though, in reality, she had risen immeasurably in his estimation by this display of decision. Grim, singular, and opinionated as he was, like any lonely old eccentric long lost to settled moorings, he knew the real metal when he found it, and had himself a mellow, kindly side which his new mistresses were not long in discovering.

It will be many a year before Rénée forgets this her first ride in one of the last strongholds of picturesque Europe. How many illusions a journey dispels, in this century, before whose wire and rails and press variety gives way to uniformity; which has a universal solvent for all the picturesque remnants of older civilizations, and which pushes persistently and relentlessly into the past all those figures and images which once delighted us, — the fluted cap and gold plate of the

Friesland peasant, the conical hats and bright hues of the cantonal costumes, the spurs, leggings, and sheepskin of the herdsman.

To Rénée, especially, it was a land of enchantment. That lumbering old vehicle, with its faded colors and dusty coat; its leathern baggage-cover, pulled down like a cap over the eyes; with its half-dozen pairs of mules, whose trappings were covered with innumerable little tufts of red wool and silk, interspersed with bells, — was the very coach of Cinderella; the driver coming out from the stone archway of the stables, with his peaked and tasseled hat, broad red sash, and broidered jacket, was the prince of the opera.

As they climbed the outlying hills, not a single shaft of palm or bristling leaf of aloe escaped her eye. Up from the fertile valleys, amid the green, flat foliage of the cactus, twisted and misshapen, into the defiles of the ashen and desolate mountains, she seemed about to enter the land of Doré.

Despite the predictions of Antonio, she at last fell asleep with her head on Stéphanie's shoulder; but it was long after the night had let loose its leash of stars.

When, with a mellow note upon the horn, this vehicle drew up, after midnight, at a relay station, where supper might be had, and, on its stoppage, all the noises attendant upon its motion — creakings, groanings, and tinkling of bells — ceased also, it was as if the world had been arrested in its flight. When one goes to sleep to a motion that is positively infernal in its ingenuity, sudden peace is a nightmare. The ladies did not alight, but Antonio brought them some white bread, with creamy cheese of goat's milk, burnt almonds fresh from the fire, muscatels from Malaga, and pomegranates from Granada.

" I wish we might live in the Alhambra itself," said Rénée, in the morning, when Antonio, appearing mysteriously at the window while the coach was at a full gallop, pointed out the vermilion towers.

" The señorita can do so if she wishes. I have a friend who keeps an inn by the Torre de los Siete Suelos; it is as good as being in the palace."

" What sort of an inn is it, Antonio?" asked Stéphanie.

" An inn without fleas, and God wot there be few such in Spain, señora."

" Then you counsel our going there."

" After I have first arranged for you. Things do not go there on a grand scale," he said, rolling the *r* in a way which conveyed an impression of unparalleled magnificence. " Pears do not grow on elms; but you will be comfortable."

So that night found them installed under the shadow of the Torre de los Siete Suelos.

Although the diligence ride had been fatiguing, they were both ready to listen to the proposition of Antonio, seconded by the allurements of a moonlight night, to cross the dark forest of oaks to the Torre de la Vela. For a long two hours they sat on the top of this old Moorish watch-tower, which stands on the crest of the hill of the Alhambra, and almost throws its shadow on the city below. Decked with a thousand lights, this city glittered like a fairy one at their feet; faintly to their ears came up the tinkle of mule-bells and the twang of guitars from the gypsy caves of the Darro; fresh from their sources in the snowy Sierras, the twin rivers, mingled in the Vega beyond, ran till, a silver thread, they were lost to view among its rich and level gardens. Behind them, in the yellow light of the moon, slept the Alhambra and palace of Charles V.; over the gorge of Los Molinos, the white walls of the Generalife shone in their dark setting of orchards; and round about this Paradise stood the mountains, a girdle of safety. What might not these silent witnesses tell of what they had seen on this plain, once the battle-field of two faiths! How might they not recall the time when the ruins which are now its chief attraction were mosque and palace and bridge, thronged with life; when this capital vied with the opulent cities of Italy; when its waters flowed through a thousand irrigating channels; when the Arabian was the teacher of Europe? Who can wander now over that plain, still a garden basking in the same soft climate, but from which the bloom of its once varied husbandry is gone, or look upon that decimated city on which has fallen the lethargy of idleness and poverty, without a vain regret for the splendor and prosperity of the Mohammedan rule? Rome, as head of the Church and capital of the State, still possesses elements of greatness, and, in presence of the Forum or Coliseum, the dominant feeling is one of solemnity and awe; but in Granada there is room only for sadness. What sounds float up from this summer palace of the Moor! of cymbals that reverberate in its domes, and of fountains that plash in its open courts. Listen, Rénée! you will hear the stately tread of silver-bearded men; Linderaxas is singing in the gardens of the Generalife, — Zara dallies with her earrings at the well, — and, over all, a voice is crying, " Allah is great! there is no conqueror but God!"

It was a scene which Stéphanie could not take in as rapidly as that from the château at Beauvais, if only because of the recollections lingering here like the fragrance of fallen flowers. Rénée responded to it as the instrument does to the hand of the player; but Stéphanie was out of tune.

She had looked forward to this journey with pleasure. After the failure of those projects in which for a time she had immersed herself, that secret restlestness, only temporarily appeased, tugged again at her heartstrings. Like Hippomenes, who heard behind him the steps of the swift-footed Atalanta, she knew the approach of this enemy, and like him, also, she had thrown to it the golden apples of a momentary diversion. But M. de Marzac's visit had put on this voyage à deux a new face. Whatever her feelings for Roger had been, or her attitude in regard to his relations to Rénée, up to that time she had floated purposelessly. Perhaps she had M. de Marzac to thank. In Roger's presence she had at least begun to dream, — to taste a draught so refreshing, so delicious to her thirsty lips, that it would perhaps have mastered her, as the wine that quickens the admonishing pulse also clouds the brain.

She really loved Rénée. The bond of their affection was a strand of common nobility and purity of character; even of common weakness. Some friends are such through mutual balance; what one lacks the other has to offer; when one needs restraint or urging, the other is there with the curb or the spur. By this opposition of influences, they maintain a truce which passes for peace, — a sort of statical equilibrium which has more of rest in it than of progress. But Rénée and Stéphanie journeyed in the same direction, saw with the same eyes, and were wrought out of the same stuff. The equilibrium was dynamical.

Under ordinary circumstances, these two women, climbing the same height, might have reached the summit by a common path. But this path had suddenly narrowed; there was room for one only to pass, — one must go first, the other follow.

To Stéphanie's decisive and resolute nature uncertainty and delay was not easy to endure. Even heroism, when it has once chosen, prefers a sharp axe and a sure, quick hand. A comforter who should have essayed with her what the priest does, when he drowns the voice of the headsman with exhortations and hides the scaffold with the crucifix, would have been a long way out of his road. Her mind was intent upon the thing in hand. She could think with a heart full of bitterness of the cruel destiny which had marked her for its own, dwelling upon the things that could not be, except at the price of her own shame and treachery to Rénée, only to set her face the more resolutely and with the cold pleasure of pride against that dream which could never be realized. She had struck its death-blow with her own hand, and found a cruel joy in her own strength. She could meet the world with a laugh on her lips, though her heart was full of tears, as can many a one who lives, and yet stands upon the sod which overlies a grave. How many are those secret burials of hopes and early ventures, which come back to us after their short flight, bruised and dying, and are laid away without other service or hymn than the moan of our own hearts.

But she was not alone. As she laid her treasure away she heard the laugh of her enemy foreboding she knew not what of evil, " I shall be there, to take my revenge!" What would he do?

What might he not do, to betray her, to drag into the light of the world's eyes what she had hidden from her own, to poison the lives of those most dear to her, and to make unavailing a costly sacrifice?

Antonio, who had sat quietly in a corner, wrapped in his cloak, while the ladies enjoyed the view, but who knew the dangers of the night air, had whispered a word to the custodian and returned to the inn for " more clothes," as he said to Lizette, who had appeared to him a very fit subject for mild persecution.

" The moon laughs at you," he said to Stéphanie, apologetically, as he presented her a shawl.

" It is late ; we must go, Rénée," said her companion, rising.

Rénée's answer was a long sigh, " Deep as Boabdil's," she said ; adding, laughingly, " only it is not my last."

On the way down, Antonio showed them the bell which once gave warning to the irrigators on the plain below.

" If you strike it you will see how sweet a tongue it has," he said to Rénée, with a peculiar gesture to the custodian.

" Shall I, Stéphanie ? "

" Why, yes, if you wish to."

The sound was silvery, and seemed to give Antonio especial satisfaction.

" I can hear that bell yet in my ears," said Rénée, as they passed out the gateway.

"It is a good sign," said Antonio from behind; "to the maiden who strikes it, God sends a good husband."

Stéphanie, who was leading, turned and gave a quick glance at Rénée, whose eyes halted midway between a frown and a smile, the latter at last coming off victor. It is so easy to smile when one is happy.

"Antonio," she said, as they reached the wood again, "you must show us a ghost before we go, a real Moor with a turban and scimitar."

Antonio shot a swift glance at her from under his eyebrows.

"You have seen them, — have you not, Antonio?"

"They say so," he replied, cautiously.

"Surely you believe in ghosts, here in the Alhambra!"

"Every hair casts a shadow, señorita," was the laconic answer.

They were crossing an open space in the moonlight. A rude cross under a tree caught the light on its naked arms, and Antonio crossed himself piously.

"Why is it here, Antonio?" asked Rénée.

"A man was killed there, señorita."

They found Lizette waiting. She was not wholly at ease in that lonely inn. She had already made up her mind as to this land of diligences, mules, and garlic, as one fit only for bar barians. Not unlike her class, she could be more difficult to please than her mistress. Descending to the kitchen that night on some errand, she found Antonio relating to his friend, mine host, how the young French lady had struck the bell with the silver tongue. Spanish was for Lizette a jargon to be held in contempt by all civilized people ; and in conversing with Antonio, who spoke French fairly well, she dealt him out a patois of short phrases and ellipses, such as one uses with babies.

Antonio repeated the incident of the bell for her benefit in French.

" So your women have need of charmed bells to get married," said Lizette. " No wonder ! "

" The bell is a good one ; still, it will not work miracles," replied Antonio, pointedly.

" A silver tongue, truly ! it has more need of a golden one."

" True," replied he, with a shrug. " But what will you have ? Fools are not so plenty in Spain, and they are more wary than those of France."

" Rubbish ! " retorted Lizette, tartly.

" At our age you may well say so," Antonio answered, with a well-feigned sigh, a parting shot which Lizette did not deign to answer.

" She is hot as pepper," said mine host, with a grin as if his mouth was full of that article, when she had gone.

" Ay, and spiced with spleen," said Antonio, relapsing into smoke and silence.

XVI.

M. Michel had received a letter from Rénée, written on her arrival at Malaga. A few days later came another, which Father Le Blanc read in this wise.

He was sitting one evening in his easy chair, — for he did not despise comfort, — so deep in the delights of his book that he did not even lift his eyes from the page on hearing the timid knock which he knew so well. As the door opened softly, in his mind's eye there stood on the threshold a short little figure clothed in blue serge, and wearing a tight-fitting cap about a face brown as a walnut and wrinkled as the sea. If the two small round eyes of this face were closed, it contained no suggestion of vitality; when open, however, their perpetual sparkle, sharp as the sword of Saladin, was the evidence of a wiry constitution which had survived unimpaired the wreck of its external trappings. For whatever may have been true in the past, Rosalie had certainly outgrown her name.

Every want and way of her master, this intendant knew by heart, and every detail of the simple ménage was intrusted to her care; a fact which did not in the least prevent her from knocking timidly at his door, nor from laying before him her plans for a *gigot à la jardinière*, as if she expected a veto in respect to this his favorite dish.

This apparent timidity on the part of Rosalie was half real, and grew out of a habit of deference to all her superiors which was natural to her as a servant of the old régime, and was kept alive further by her profound respect for her master, not only as such but as priest and man. But for this she would have been an autocrat of the most pronounced type. When, at the close of these rather one-sided consultations, Father Le Blanc said, "C'est parfait!" Rosalie was as satisfied and delighted as though he had not said it a hundred times before in the very same tone; and Father Le Blanc had grown so familiar with the nature of these councils that he had contracted the habit of not listening; he continued whatever he happened to be doing at the time, and had only to ratify with his customary phrase the propositions submitted by Rosalie, when the cessation of her voice announced that the sitting was over.

In response to his "Entrez!" the door opened, but, in front of Rosalie's blue serge, Father Le Blanc on raising his eyes perceived the figure of M. Michel.

He brought a letter from Rénée, written the day following that of their arrival in Granada.

"We reached here yesterday. I should write you of our ride from Malaga, but for graver events.

"Last evening we were tempted out by a beautiful night, and were probably too lightly clad. This morning we thought to take a day of rest before attempting any sight-seeing or excursions, and walked down to the Zacatin only, to make a few purchases. Stéphanie seemed unusually tired. She lay down in the afternoon, and woke with a chill which frightened me. She has forbidden me to mention it in my letter, but she is more restless and feverish, and I feel such a sense of helplessness and responsibility that I could not promise her I would not do so.

"We have sent for an English doctor, and are comfortably located, — and our guide is very faithful. Still, I wish we were among friends.

" RÉNÉE.

"Antonio takes this at the last moment to the post. The doctor has been here. He says her symptoms indicate a fever, but he cannot yet say much. What he says is not reassuring."

"I think I ought to go," said M. Michel, as Father Le Blanc looked up from the letter. He stood holding it in his hand, thinking. "It may prove to be nothing," continued M. Michel. "On the other hand, if it be serious" —

Father Le Blanc, lost in reflection, made no

reply. M. Michel took the letter again and re-read it.

"I have a better plan," said the priest at length.

"What one?"

"Let us send M. Lande."

He watched the effect of this proposition, but M. Michel's face betrayed nothing unusual.

"The son? He would not go," he replied, emphatically. "Think of it! So far, — and with his engagements."

"But if he would?"

"Ah, if he would! I do not say."

"You do not object."

"On the contrary. But " —

"Well, then, leave that to me. I answer for him."

"You think so?"

"I am sure of it. I will go this instant and bring you his consent to-night."

He put on his hat and cloak, and descended with M. Michel. Rosalie, at the door, followed him out the entrance way. Never before to her remembrance had he gone out without speaking to her, or saying at what hour he would return; and she trudged back over the wooden stairs somewhat bewildered at this sudden depart-ure, and set to work knitting vigorously. Her needles were the thermometer of her feelings. When lying idle in her lap they indicated the zero point of mental energy, and at every degree of rise in her mental activity she added a stitch to the number per minute.

"You see no objection," repeated Father Le Blanc, as they walked down the Rue Tiquetonne. He saw that M. Michel did not comprehend him, so he added: "Nothing could be better, it is true. You have entire confidence in the doctor: he would do all you could, and much more. But it is a young man we are sending to care for two young women."

Father Le Blanc spoke bluntly, first, because it was his proposition, and he felt the responsibility of it; and, second, because he knew there were some things which M. Michel never perceived without assistance.

"I do not see things as you do," replied M. Michel. "M. Lande goes as the physician of the family. But I will go also."

"That seems to me unnecessary," said his friend; "at least for the present."

After crossing the Seine, M. Michel offered to accompany him to M. Lande's.

"No, it is needless. I carry your entreaty with me, and on my return I will pass by the Rue du Bac and inform you of my success."

"Très bien! très bien," said M. Michel, as he went his way much relieved; for with all his readiness to go to Spain, he none the less dreaded so long a journey.

"Yes, M. le Docteur was at home," said the servant in reply to Father Le Blanc's query. The latter gave a sigh of relief, and followed him up the polished stairs.

To Roger's greeting he replied by handing to him Rénée's letter.

"M. Michel proposes to go to Granada," he said, when Roger reached the last line. "It is a long journey for him, and it is doubtful how he would bear it; especially if there were trouble in store for him at its end."

Roger looked at him inquiringly.

"You are the family physician" —

"Not of very long standing," interposed the other.

"True. Fortunately there has been little need of one in the past. But no one knows what kind of services can be had in Granada, and if things go badly with Madame Milevski, there would be Mademoiselle Rénée also in a sad plight." Father Le Blanc was a little embarrassed by the force of his own logic, and went to the window, where he stood looking out into the street with his back to Roger.

"You mean, then, that I should go," said the latter, after a pause.

"That is what I propose."

Roger looked at Father Le Blanc's back, which at that instant was quite as expressive as his face.

"Monsieur, let us be frank with one another. Does M. Michel propose this?"

"He sends me to you," said the priest, turning quickly.

"And does he know, — what you do, — that I love Rénée?"

"Faith, I did not know it myself," said Father Le Blanc, laughing. All his embarrassment had vanished.

"You may call this accidental; the sickness of Madame Milevski *is* accidental, and you come to me in my capacity of physician. That is natural. But, at the same time, you throw upon my protection and into my care the woman whom I love."

"You express word for word my own thoughts," said Father Le Blanc. "Some one must love her," he added, apologetically, shrugging his shoulders.

Roger walked the room agitatedly. All this was a dream, with a possibly bad as well as alluring side.

"When will you go? To-morrow, I suppose."

"I wish you to see M. Michel," said Roger, at length. "Tell him what you please; but if I do not see you again before the express of to-morrow morning, I shall go in it. Meanwhile I shall have much to do. I must see my assistant, and make my preparations."

"I promise to see him; and," added Father Le Blanc, with his hand on the door, "say to Mademoiselle Rénée that M. Michel sent you, and to Madame Milevski, that it was I."

Roger scanned the priest's face, perplexed.

"Ingrate!" said Father Le Blanc, at the door. "Do as I bid you. Believe less in accidents, and have more respect for Providence;" and, before the door was closed these two men exchanged a handshake which meant so many things that it is useless to attempt to tell them.

The priest returned, as he had promised, by the Rue du Bac.

"He goes," he said, as soon as the door was closed.

"I feel an immense relief," replied M. Michel, with a long breath which bore witness to his veracity. "He will not only give help, but confidence, which is the best of help."

"And you are not solicitous for — for what I said to you? Perhaps you would not thank me for this suggestion which I have carried out, if M. Lande, finding Madame Milevski recovered, should steal from us Rénée."

"Do you speak seriously, my friend?"

"Why not?"

"Why not! Because you know very well Rénée's projects."

"The convent?"

"Yes, certainly, the convent."

"She is not yet in it," said Father Le Blanc.

M. Michel took off his spectacles and rubbed them meditatively.

" You begin to regret the step we have taken ? "
he asked.

" Not in the least ! " exclaimed Father Le Blanc,
warmly.

" Let us say no more about it, then. For my
part, I believe Rénée altogether too seriously inclined."

" Love is a serious business," replied the priest,
" and God has steeped our hearts in it."

" And God be thanked," said M. Michel.

" He does not in the least know what he is
talking about," Father Le Blanc said to himself ;
and on his way home he was well nigh forgetting
his own instrumentality in the thought of a Providence that had given to an uncle a niece need-
ing so little the safeguards which this uncle did
not know of, and had sent her a lover who had
no need of them either.

The next morning came, but Father Le Blanc
did not appear, and the Marseilles express carried
off with it Roger Lande.

On that same day Stéphanie entered the crisis
of a fever. Rénée's apprehensions had proved
well grounded ; and, as usual, hers, beside the
couch, were graver and more poignant than those
of Stéphanie, who lay stretched upon it.

At a sudden summons we are led out of the
sun and air to the edge of that narrow opening
into which this warm and living body is to be
laid, covered up forever and forgotten in damp-

ness and night. No man has ever come up from that place; eye nor ear has ever detected faintest sound or lightest stir of life after the last reluctant breath is gone out from the home, so long tenanted, into space; in all the universe no flower, or seed, or fruit that has come up from the chambers of decay is that one which was sown; and we, entering them also, carry no hope, however life has answered it, which has not beaten echoless against the gates of death. Yet on the brink of this grave, we neither shrink nor struggle. In the full tide of life's current we move too swiftly to realize this absolute rest, and as we enter the swirl of the vortex the swirl mounts to the brain.

As Rénée had written, on their return from the Zacatin Stéphanie only felt more than usually tired, and resorted to the usual remedy. On waking, she had a chill.

"It is nothing," she said to Rénée, whose first thought was for the physician; against which Stéphanie protested. But as the afternoon wore away, bringing headache and thirst, Rénée had her way.

The next morning matters were no better.

"An inflammatory fever," said the English doctor, "with possibilities of something worse," he added, bluntly. "We must have a good nurse," and he suggested to Rénée a Sister of Charity, mentioning a French one whom he could recommend.

Rénée saw that Stéphanie was really sick, and looked the situation in the face with misgiving. But there was a kindly interest and hopeful inspiration in this Englishman which gave her courage.

"You must not worry," he had said to her. "Keep a good heart. In sickness we are all of the same country."

She was not conscious of his large hand patting her back cheerily, but she was conscious of his sympathy, though it had an accent and lived behind a rather cold exterior.

Meanwhile Stéphanie had a word with Lizette. She felt a great lassitude conquering her, and it began to blur the issues and interests of life, over which she had been so anxious.

"Lizette."

"Yes, madame."

She was sitting at the bedside. Antonio was probably right as to the spleen; still she loved her mistress with that love peculiar to those of widely different ranks and conditions, — the love which the dog knows for its master who falls sick, when it whines at the door without need of the chain or thought of its dinner.

"If I should be sick"—it evidently cost her an effort to say this—"I might be—light-headed. You understand me," she said, looking at Lizette, who understood, but did not know what to say.

" Yes, madame."

" She must not hear anything," she said, glancing at the door at which Rénée had gone out with the doctor.

" I promise you, madame."

" Manage it — somehow," she said, turning restlessly and closing her eyes.

A little after, Rénée, opening the door, waked her from a light sleep into which she had fallen.

" Remember ! " she said to Lizette, and Lizette's intelligent eyes answered significantly, —

" I promise."

XVII.

IMPATIENT with the steamer which for a week had been creeping along the Spanish coast, Roger experienced a delight as he stepped into the *calesa* he had hired to convey him from Malaga to Granada. Here, at last, was something whose velocity he could to some extent control.

More than a week had elapsed since he left Paris, more than two since the letter he carried in his pocket had been written; time enough for how much to have happened!

On arriving at Granada, he stopped at the hotel long enough only to deposit his baggage and to learn the address of the English doctor. He found the latter a tall, large-featured man, with iron-gray side whiskers, whose look seemed to say to him, "Well, and what malady have you!"

"I have just arrived from Paris in behalf of M. Michel, the brother of Madame Milevski. My last information dates from the evening of your first summons," and Roger presented his card.

The Englishman's face and manner relaxed as Roger introduced himself.

"I shall be very glad to surrender the case into your hands, monsieur, — especially now that madame is better."

"She is better, then?"

"Decidedly so; but the road up the hill is the longest."

"But all danger is over?"

"Entirely, — without accidents. The crisis was passed several days ago," and he detailed at length the progress of the fever and the treatment he had pursued.

"And now, monsieur," he said, when he had finished, "I am happy to express my pleasure at your coming, and to resign madame to your care."

"On the contrary," said Roger, "you are to do me the favor to continue your visits as if I had not come. In what time do you think madame might travel?".

"In two weeks she might begin to think of it."

"She sits up at present?"

"To-day, a half hour, for the first time."

"And mademoiselle?"

"Is perfectly well, — a little tired, but that soon passes."

"These ladies, in a strange land, owe much to you," said Roger, warmly; "but it is a debt which I, and many others, share with them, and which I acknowledge in their behalf. And now, if you please, their address."

"I am just about to make my morning visit; if you will permit me, I will conduct you."

They passed together out the Puerta de las Granadas, following the path which ascends the hill under the lofty trees. Nestling close to the walls, the inn seemed asleep in the delicious coolness of the forest. A wide-thatched roof extended like an awning in front of and on either side of the door, encircling some of the nearest trees, which, with a few slender posts, formed its supports. Under this covering were scattered some tables, at one of which Antonio was sitting, contemplating another twenty-four hours of idleness with profound satisfaction. On another Lizette had laid a white cloth, and was making ready a breakfast. Beside Antonio, whose somewhat picturesque costume suffered on a close examination, and who appeared asleep, — although, like a dog, with one eye open, — this brisk figure of Lizette, with fresh white cap, formed the contrast of two races. She had in her hair a red blossom of the rose bay, and was arranging a basket of fresh figs with their own shiny leaves ; an occupation which did not prevent her from observing with curiosity the stranger approaching with the doctor, whose air and dress announced to her some one who did not belong to Granada.

When, as he drew nearer, she recognized him, the pyramid of figs she had been constructing suddenly gave way ; at which Antonio laughed. On his part, this laugh was a challenge. He laughed at an adversary whom he wished to provoke, as the lackeys of Verona bit their thumbs at one another. But Lizette was far too agitated to notice this provocation. Roger had recognized her, and had made her a sign.

"Oblige me by entering as usual," he said to the doctor; "but say nothing of me, if you please. I will wait here till you return." He wanted the pleasure of a surprise. "Your mistress is better, Lizette."

"Dieu merci, oui, monsieur."

"And you are preparing a breakfast for some one?"

"For mademoiselle, monsieur."

"Go ask her if she will permit a hungry traveler to share it with her. And Lizette," he said, calling to her, as she hurried away so full of her errand she could hardly wait to deliver it, "say nothing to madame."

At the door she met Rénée, who was in the habit of waiting here for the doctor, when he came out from the sick chamber.

It was the last thing she had thought of, to see Roger Lande, sitting at this table where she was to breakfast, under the oak trees of the Alhambra. But Lizette had no need to hurry or to explain, as Rénée had no need to scrutinize this stranger now advancing to meet her. Had she been alone she would instinctively have put her hand on her heart. A week ago, when Stéphanie hovered between life and death, this self-same place was lonely and desolate to her, and she would have welcomed this face from home with

intense thankfulness, but with scarcely any other
emotion, — as one leans, in faintness, on one does
not know what.   But now that danger was over,
this lovely spot, filled with the freshness of morning, not only regained in her eyes its true value,
but by contrast an additional one; and, as she
came to the door, the sunshine filtering through
the leaves was not brighter or warmer than that
which filled her heart.   After all, why should not
Roger Lande be there!   When the heart is full
nothing surprises.

"Oh, Monsieur Lande, I am so glad to see
you!" she exclaimed.

The color mounted to her face.   It was because
sne felt it there that she stopped short in a pretty
confusion.   She knew it now, — this joy which, at
the first encounter, had won a victory over her
self-control, which surged, like a flood let loose,
from her heart, in every vein, and swelled exult-
ingly in her throat.   Refuse it belief, argue with
it, disown it and laugh at it now, Rénée, if you
can!   Nothing is left but to be angry and to conceal it.   But this effort at concealment was not
very successful.   It was well enough for the eyes
of a lover who sees nothing, but not for those of
Antonio, though he had but one open.   What
wonder!   It is so easy to be natural when one
does not desire to, — that is, when one has no
reason to be otherwise.

They sat down together at one of the tables in

the shade.   After the first surprise was over, she had so much to tell, of those first days of apprehension and the hours of suspense and uncertainty which had succeeded them ; of the turn in the tide ; of how much better Stéphanie now was each day ; of how kind the doctor had been ; and of faithful Antonio even.

" Then I have nothing to do but to return to Paris."

Lovers court rebuffs as heroes do danger.

" You must consult Stéphanie," said Rénée, demurely.

" I certainly shall not think of it until I can report to M. Michel that she has passed all the turning points and is on the highway again ; " and he told her of her uncle's anxiety, and how, within twelve hours after receiving her letter, he was in the train.

" But when did you arrive ? "

" This moment.   I came over the mountains in the night."

" And you have not breakfasted ? "

" No, nor dined," said Roger, laughing.   " I confess I am hungry."

And with that Rénée disappeared in the door way.   How pleasant it was to wait her return, to be conscious she was to return, and to hear her say, --

" I have ordered you a breakfast."

In a short half-hour a cover was laid at a table

near hers; but they were lost in conversation, and Roger had forgotten his appetite.

"It is all ready," mine host said to Antonio. His *puchero* was steaming, and he was solicitous that it should be eaten hot.

"So you have not even visited the Alhambra," Roger was saying.

"Pardon, señor," said Antonio, taking off his hat and pointing to the table; "in soups and love the first is the best."

The imperturbable gravity of Antonio's countenance disarmed criticism, and he retreated in good order, under cover of the doctor, who had returned from the sick chamber.

"Better, always better," he said in reply to Rénée. "At this rate she will soon eat her breakfast here with you."

"I am going to see her," Rénée said to Roger. "Monsieur," she explained, pointing to the doctor, "is very rigid, and he has a subaltern in the nurse he sent us, who carries out his orders. I am allowed only so many minutes in the room. I shall tell her you are here."

But Lizette was before her. The doctor had not taken three steps down the stairs before she had glided into the room.

What a bright and cheerful aspect this room had! The morning toilette was over, the window was open to the sun and air, and Stéphanie, pale but with the signs of returning strength, was

propped up in a reclining chair which the doctor
had sent from the city. The chamber itself, so
long filled with a heavy atmosphere and oppres-
sive silence, and which, as if instinct with apprehension and sympathy for the being who occupied
it, had so long worn that aspect of dread expectancy which has so sinister a meaning, had become
transformed. Through the window came the
myriad sounds of life; of waters trickling among
the moss and roots of the forest, the hum of in-
sects, and the song of birds. The very sunlight
danced for joy on the wooden floor among the
shadows of the leaves, and played over the gray
dress of Sœur Marie as she sat reading her prayers;
for Sœur Marie was never idle, — when her hands
or feet were not busy, her eyes were fixed on God.
Stéphanie often wondered, as she lay in the
dreamy quiescence of convalescence, too weak for
aught beyond a passive surrender to that sense of
peace which the slow incoming tide of life brings
with it, whether or no Sœur Marie had ever
dreamed.

Lizette took her seat quietly beside her mistress. She had kept the promise whose import
had been but vaguely comprehended when it was
given; but it had not proved unnecessary, and she
knew its meaning now. So did Sœur Marie, as
any one who could have heard her prayers would
know. Those prayers of hers ran over her lips
continuously, like the water over a dam, and, like

it also, set in motion all the machinery of her life, which thus became itself a prayer.

"He is here, madame," said Lizette in a whisper.

Lizette was a good maid, who loved her mistress. But this did not prevent her from feeling a certain importance as the confidante of madame and the possessor of an important secret. In the first surprise of Lizette's announcement, the thought of this humiliation was more to Stéphanie than the fact of Roger's arrival. The sense of danger under which she had spoken, when the dizziness and confusion of fever began to master her will and rob her of self-control, had all passed away. Her pride leaped out like a sword from its scabbard, with the words, "What is that to thee! I know not this man." But Lizette was quick-witted, and the tact which had once led her to offer her own prayer-book to Rénée, led her now, having forewarned her mistress, discreetly to withdraw.

It was a few minutes before Rénée came in, and in those few moments Stéphanie abandoned herself to a dream. It was a wild, foolish dream, and she knew it, — but it was a sweet one. Strange! though side by side with this dream the reality was also present, she found a keen pleasure in this moment of surrender to it, as returning health itself seemed doubly sweet to her after the fever.

So close is the alliance between pain and pleasure! Each is the true child only of the other.

"Stéphanie," said Rénée, who had stolen in unnoticed, and, standing behind her chair, had stooped over and kissed her hair, "you do not know how happy I am to think you are getting better."

Leaning over the back of the chair, she had put her arms about her, and Stéphanie took in her own one of the hands crossed on her breast.

"Who do you think my uncle has sent to bring you home?"

"Baptiste!"

"What an idea! Try again. But you will never guess."

"Tell me, then."

"I want the pleasure of telling you after you have made a dozen trials."

"I shall deprive you of the whole of it by guessing rightly the first time."

"Try! I defy you."

"Roger Lande."

"How did you know, Stéphanie?"

"You told me."

"You are getting well, for you are trying to tease me," said Rénée, kissing her hair; "but I submit to it on that condition."

"It was a needless journey. He must be disappointed."

"Stéphanie! you are positively wicked."

"Have you seen him?"

"Yes, just now."

"Does he return directly?"

"I suppose he will, if you wish him to; but if he thought that he could be of service to you I think he would stay."

Of service to her? Why not? Fortune had thrown this opportunity into her hands, if she had only the courage to take it. Were there not yet before her long days of weakness and waiting, in which, if Rénée loved him,— ah! if Rénée loved him! All this battle had been fought once, and in a decision once made there is a tremendous inertia, although it has practically to be made over again a second time. Why should he not stay? or why should she hesitate at this which she had desired?

"Yes, he ought to, if he can,—at least, till I am a little stronger. Say to him that I wish it."

"You will not see him?"

"No," said Stéphanie, letting go of Rénée's hand.

"You must not talk to madame too long," said Sœur Marie.

"No, I am going."

"Rénée," said Stéphanie, "you must take Antonio with M. Lande, and see Granada while I am getting better. You have had anxiety for an excuse long enough," she said, smiling faintly, "but you have it no longer. It is absurd for you to stay here at my door all the day long. You must recover lost time, and compensate M. Lande for his journey. Antonio must be fairly rusting away."

"Madame, je vous en prie," said Sœur Marie. "See, mademoiselle, how pale her face is."

This second warning set Rénée in motion. Stéphanie watched her as she went, and it seemed to be her own self she saw standing in the doorway with a happy smile on its face, sending her a bright glance of good-by. "If I were dying," she thought, with a bitter irony in her heart, "but I am getting better."

When Stéphanie advised Rénée to make good the time lost during her sickness, she knew she was giving, not advice, but a permission; and when Roger came, as he did every morning, to inquire for Stéphanie, he had no need to give Rénée formal invitations. Did not everything invite them on those mornings? In a week they had explored every nook of the palace, and knew every path on the hill of the Alhambra. If Madame Valfort would have protested against the freedom of Beauvais, that of Granada certainly would have rendered her mute. Even Antonio seemed in league with the rest, and, finding his services in no great demand, preferred the siestas and cigarettes of the Posada of the Siete Suelos to walks and excursions in which he might have been cicerone had he been asked.

In these rambles Roger found a pleasure apart from that of being with Rénée — the pleasure of peace and restfulness, so deep and tranquil that he was content simply to enjoy it. Could Rénée have been transferred to Paris and surrounded with society, this charm would have vanished. Here were no prior engagements, no disappointments, no division of favors. From the time he first found her in her fresh white morning dress under the trees, she was his for all the day. These were days to hurry which would have been a crime. Why are we in such a fever to finish! There was no press of society and contention of aspirants, no jealousies, no heart-burnings, no annoyances. Rénée knew that Roger loved her. If she did not fully know also that she loved him, it was because as yet nothing had forced her to answer this question ; so that she still preserved the subtle pleasure of reluctance, which, once abandoned, cannot be recalled. It was this reluctance which told her most she was loved. She knew the path, though she had never seen it ; and she followed it with her eyes half shut, in a blessed awe, holding back for very happiness against the hand which drew her on, and finding, in the very sense of being led, that happiness.

When she followed with him the road which wound up the ravine of Los Molinos, it was in reality this other road she traversed, leading to other gardens than those of the Generalife. Was it not fortunate that Antonio was not with them ? For his instinct would have gotten the better of

his tact, and he would have made Rénée start as
from a dream by saying, under the cypress-tree
of the Generalife, " This, mademoiselle, was the
trysting-place of Zoraya." What a revealer is
love. Does the heart open to its influences, as the
flower opens to the sun, to yield its treasures to a
wind that steals and scatters them forever? So,
too, like the flower, it opens its eye then, for the
first time, upon the wide world, — and sees the
mystery of life and death and destiny.

But this was a lesson which both read, Roger
not less than Rénée. She had the instinctive faculty of revelation. She reached the heart of
things by a feminine apprehension so delicate and
so natural that she might almost seem herself to
dwell there. She saw in everything something he
had not seen; for him she was the interpreter.
There were problems and questions before which
he had planted his siege batteries of heavy artil-
lery, to conquer by the parallels and approaches
of a regular investment, — which, if she had not
always the key to them, she could illuminate with
a word, or rob them of all importance.

How many times this young heart, so keenly
susceptible to good impressions, received them
from that which had passed him by, to reflect
them, with the added grace of her own sweet nature, upon his. She was ever a little grave, and
more sedate than most are, and this inheritance of
the Rue du Bac never wholly forsook her. But

in the unrestraint of the present, amid the freshness of all that surrounded her and the novelty of her situation, the deeper impulses of her nature pushed up as flowers through the sod, and these impulses, springing from the woman's heart, how often they outran the calculations of the man.

More things than were dreamt of in his philosophy she showed him, — from the white star of the jessamine in the path they trod, up to the finer aspirations of his own soul, which ambition had well-nigh choked with its thorns.

She was at her best, for she was happy. While not forgetting the convent or Sœur Ursule, she had the feeling that everything was right. Once, in the city, a file of nuns, moving two by two down a narrow street, obliged her to wait with Roger in a doorway until they had passed; and for the moment it seemed to her there was a reproach in their grave averted eyes. Sometimes, too, after Roger had gone, when, in the quiet of her own room, she opened the clasped prayer-book Sœur Ursule had given her, she lapsed between the prayers into reverie, with the book open on her lap. No, she had not forgotten. Sœur Marie, going about her daily round of duties, was a constant reminder. But her doubts were fugitive, like birds of passage. Was it that, on the threshold of love, she saw within the portal such possibilities as made the monotonous, almost menial, life of Sœur Marie seem unworthy? Possibly it was Sœur Ursule's poverty of experience that had led her to overestimate the ease with which Rénée should conquer nature. For before this portal hung with orange blossoms, timorous, shy, ignorant, she nevertheless stood knocking, drawn thitherward, yet gladly, — too happy for doubts or fears, rather than happy because she had none.

Stéphanie did not verify the doctor's prediction that she would breakfast with Rénée under the trees in a week; but one morning Lizette was told to order the table laid for déjeuner in the garden.

Every morning M. Lande had sent fresh flowers, which were placed on a stand beside Stéphanie; and to-day Lizette would have had her mistress wear one, but did not dare suggest it. This was her only grievance, that madame never consulted her. She would have counselled her appearance several days ago, — the traces of sickness were well-nigh gone, and that this was what she was waiting for Lizette was confident, — but madame had not asked her opinion. Lizette had had mistresses whom she feared without loving, and even despised; whom she knew better than their courtiers did; who did not attempt to impose upon her with those artifices to which they resorted with others through fear of being understood. But madame had no artifices. It disturbed Lizette much, in the early period of her service, that she could never take Stéphanie by surprise; but she had at last realized that there might be a difference between maid and mistress, due neither to rank, wealth, nor education, — accidental differences which she scorned, because generally her own shrewdness and her mistress' weaknesses enabled her to surmount them, — a difference of nature, which seems always to render its possessor superior to her company.

And yet Lizette was quite likely right; for after she had gone, Stéphanie took up the hand-glass, and searched it as for something lost.

It must have been through a mere sense of duty that observant Sœur Marie said gently, "What matters it?" for the image in the glass called neither for condolence nor resignation.

"Nothing, ma sœur," said Stéphanie, and she thought of the flowers on her dressing-table, which the evening before had closed and this morning had opened, as if the scissors of the gardener had not cut them off from the sources of life.

Her sudden determination had taken every one by surprise. Rénée had gone down to the Zacatin with Antonio, and M. Lande had not yet come up from the city. Only a flower-girl, on whose brown cheek flamed a color vivid as those of her wares, disputed the solitude with a little beggar-boy coiled up asleep in his shady ambuscade like a bent wire. From the trees festoons of creepers hung drowsily in a delicious air; a faint breeze lifted at intervals the frondage scaling the tower wall, to die away in the effort. The long aisles under the elms, into which, now and then, sunbeams ventured, to vanish on the instant like fear-stricken intruders, opened vistas over terraces of orange and cypress upon the Vega glistening with intersecting waters. Sœur Marie had followed Stéphanie, and sat quietly by her side during breakfast. The nun's pale face and thin lips seemed strangely out of place. The natural product of that air and sky was the little flower-girl, whose brown skin was lustrous as the bloom of the Andalusian grape, and in whose dark eye shone the dangerous fires of its wine.

"How beautiful the world is!" said Stéphanie.

In the cant of the convent, "the world" meant only one thing to Sœur Marie.

"The world, always the world," she said, with a little smile and *moue.* Despite her gravity, she had naturally a playful way, which, overlaid as it was by the serenity of her calling, gave a charm even to her reproofs.

"What do you know of it, little sister?" said Stéphanie, amused at her superficial wisdom.

"I have seen a great deal of it," replied Sœur Marie, with a sigh of conviction.

"From the outside. Moreover," after a pause, "seeing is not knowing."

"It is a prison, but no home. It is full of pleasures which, like sweet wine, double the thirst but never satisfy; oftenest not really such pleasures, only the hope of them fleeing before like to-morrow. The world is a garden full of sweet poisons, without a single antidote."

" There are moments of pleasure worth a life-time, my sister."

" Life-time means eternity," replied Sœur Marie.

The flower-girl had approached them with her tray full of what might be had for the picking in this garden of nature, "ambient in perfume, exquisite in fruits." But begging in Spain wears all masks, even that of flowers. Standing with pleading attitude and beseeching eyes, she was a true child of the south, — bare, dirty feet and cheeks of velvet; lazy limbs and blood of fire; tattered rags over the contours of a model.

" You love flowers, sister," said Stéphanie.

" Our Lady loves them."

" Don't you love them for themselves, of your own accord? "

" Ah! madame, what is sweeter than to love what our blessed Mother loves? "

" Why does she love them, sister ? "

" Por el amor de Dios," chimed in the flower-girl.

Stéphanie bought a spray of mimosa, woven in with myrtle and roses.

" Let us take a walk. I feel it will do me good," she said to Sœur Marie.

" I am afraid you are not strong enough."

" Yes, a little way. This air is an elixir."

They passed down the avenue, under the mystic hand and key of the great gate, through the Court of Myrtles, into the Hall of Ambassadors, and seated themselves in its alcoved window.

"You are tired; you have come too far," said her companion.

"No, I feel stronger than you think. Everything refreshes me."

She leaned over the window and looked into the green depths below, a mass of vegetation; of orange, pomegranate, and cypress, amid which the waters of the Darro hastened; of myrtle, laurel, fire-plant, and rose bay, scaling the walls guarding the river, climbing the very battlements of the fortress, — an army of luxuriant verdure, a mosaic of moisture and sunlight, dark shadow and blossoming flame.

Looking at this view, she forgot Sœur Marie, who, left to herself, reopened her prayer-book. What a companion Father Le Blanc would have been for her in this recessed window! Looking up from the gray dress and pale moving lips of the sister, into the roof, whose gorgeous hues had been to its inmates an undying remembrance of the flowers on the upper plains of Arabia, was like taking an upward flight from a narrow self-denial and fruitless obedience into a region of freedom and splendid achievement. This dome was the symbol of brilliant audacity and tender phantasy. Where was duty? Did it overarch her simple companion with a radiance too bright for her eyes, or had she it fast between the dingy covers of her book?

Suddenly the book was closed. Footsteps were heard in the Court of Myrtles, then a voice, singularly clear and sweet, which made her start.

XVIII.

M. LANDE was that morning writing his letters in the café of the hotel. He had begun seriously to ask himself why Madame Milevski, who was now so much better, had not permitted him to see her. His position embarrassed him. He could neither go, nor remain. Two weeks had flown by like a dream, and he felt that with regard to Rénée he owed a duty to madame which her seclusion would not allow him to discharge. Letters and telegrams afforded him ample excuse to return to Paris, but to leave without speaking to Rénée was impossible, and this step delicacy forbade him to take, notwithstanding his warning to Father Le Blanc, without the authority of Rénée's present protectress.

His letters finished, he took his way up the hill, preoccupied with these thoughts. He was almost inclined to classify Madame Milevski among the eccentrics, and to demand an audience. Walking rapidly, as was his wont, he overtook a priest following leisurely the same path. A priest was no unusual sight in Spain, nor would this one have attracted his attention but for certain peculiarities in his walk and bearing not characteristic of the

Spanish monk. It seemed to him that he had somewhere seen this figure before.

What are those nameless accents, so distinct and yet so difficult to define, which mark off the individual from the million, even at a distance?

As he approached, the priest turned and saluted him. It was the face he had seen at Aix in the garden of the Hôtel du Nord with Madame Milevski.

" Good morning, señor," he said in Spanish, lifting his hat.

Roger answered in French, in which language the conversation was continued.

The priest's face was an attractive one, although composed of discordant elements. It was not thin, yet clear cut, wearing in repose a high and noble expression which, when he spoke, produced an effect of authority, without the least pretension. On removing his hat, as he did later in the shaded walk which they traversed, the tonsured head together with the straight lines of his robe heightened an air of resolve peculiar to his face. Its predominant trait was a marked intellectuality, never indeed wholly absent, yet at times so transfigured by a persuasive sweetness as to destroy any impression of coldness which might first have been made. So the soft lights of a crystal hide its angles without causing us to forget its hardness.

They fell into a conversation upon the many events suggested by the place. Perhaps the penetration of Father Roche detected in his companion a spirit of criticism, or regret, which in this tomb of Moorish splendor is not uncommon to the traveler. He replied for a time in monosyllables, not distinctly of assent, yet placing no check upon his companion's utterance. He had a way of making one feel at one's best and of opening the lips of another without opening his own.

" History," said he at last, " is the most important and the most dangerous of studies. The zealot and the liberal alike find in its pages their arguments, while the inquirer sees at first only a vast flux without apparent order or stability. Out of it theorists gather what they need, or construct what they desire, and the evil-minded find there every excuse at hand. The most enthusiastic and conscientious student will rise from its study only with weariness and disappointment, if not disgust for all those party strifes undertaken in the name of God and truth, but embittered by selfishness and ambition, for all those creeds whose very loftiness is the proof of man's need and misery, if he does not bring to that study the maturity of an experience which has outgrown the illusions of youth, and a faith which enables him to see the Divine purpose. History is not an ice-floe of fragments, which clash aimlessly and melt away, to him who discovers the drift of the current; it is rather a ladder upon which one may ascend into the council chamber of God. Yes, it is easier to prophesy the future than to interpret the past."

They passed some curious plants by the wayside, which Father Roche paused to examine, and on which he made some observations surprising to Roger.

" You have studied botany, monsieur?" he asked.

" A little," replied the priest, modestly. " I love much the sciences."

" Then you do not fear them?"

" Those who fear science live in ruts so deep that they cannot see over them."

" And yet Religion to-day is losing treasures which she must regret, and of which Science alone despoils her. Like the foolish virgin of the parable, she wakes from dreams to find that her companion has bought oil and kept her lamp trimmed, while she was lost in visions."

Father Roche made no reply, and they walked on for a time in silence.

" I do not say," continued Roger, " that science destroys religion, that it even affects those great focal lines of probability which converge towards one centre. But those poems on which the world has fed, so full of mystery and promise, those dreams in which everything appeared great because we were children, — does it give you no pain to see them fade away? Science has no quarrel with religion, but with religions. Aspiration cannot live upon generalities; it defines and specifies; it clothes itself with the creations of its own enthusiasm and revery, and transmutes each hint and hope into a certainty. Have you no fear of that colder, rational method which checks every conjecture by a thousand experiments, and confronts, not the native desires of the soul, but the creed into which they have crystallized, with the spectre of verification?"

"There are the phenomena of spiritual experience."

"A sea on which the wind blows," replied Roger. "I cannot there watch your experiment, or repeat it myself under like conditions."

"Therefore you suppress those phenomena altogether," said Father Roche, smiling.

"No, I do not deny them; experience is not limited to sensation, and science herself raises the questions which she cannot answer. But, within her province, verification justifies induction and furnishes a unit of certainty. In that very tumult of opinion and change, with which men reproach her, goes on, as in the alembic of the chemist, a constant precipitation which increases her capital. Without, there is inference, but no verification; motion, but no progress. The questions remain, for the answers never emerge from the region of hypothesis. It is the wheel of Ixion."

Father Roche made no answer, though he did

not have the air of one who was silenced. He walked slowly, with his hands behind his back and his eyes on the ground. They were close to the inn when, as if there had not been an interval of five minutes' silence, he said, quietly, " You were speaking of religion. Philosophy is not religion."

Roger thought of Rénée, at this reply.

His curiosity was excited by the recollection of the circumstances under which he had first seen his companion. He was not, therefore, surprised to hear him inquire for Madame Milevski, though he was not a little astonished to hear that the latter was walking in the Alhambra.

"Since we are seeking the same person, with your permission I will accompany you," said Roger. The priest bowed, and they followed together the path already taken by Stéphanie. It was the voice of Father Roche in the Court of Myrtles which had caused her to start.

Despite the emotion with which she had anticipated this meeting with Roger, her interest seemed altogether absorbed by the priest, who, on the other hand, after saluting her and inquiring after the state of her health, addressed himself to Sœur Marie. Stéphanie began to speak before Roger had time to address her.

" You were very kind to come so far, M. Lande, — and very considerate. M. Michel is so easily alarmed for others."

"I came very gladly. After danger is over, it is easy to smile at our fears, but when mademoiselle's letter reached M. Michel" —

"Yes, I know. I forbade her to write. I knew it would alarm him. He thinks so little for himself, and is so readily made anxious about others. He was your real patient all the while."

"I should have been glad to have rendered *you* a service, madame," said Roger. "In coming to Spain, to be honest, M. Michel did not enter my thoughts."

"Do you regret I was not at death's door?" she said, with a smile.

"I merely wished to say — what I did," he replied, a little haughtily, "that to have assisted you would have given me pleasure, more even than to have pacified the alarm of M. Michel." Feeling is contagious.

"Oh, doubtless you were entirely disinterested," she replied. She was sorry for these words, even while uttering them.

"No, I was not wholly disinterested. I had something in mind."

She stood in the recess looking over towards the caves of the gypsies in the opposite hill, without appearing in the least to understand him. Her reserve piqued him. Certainly she knew what he meant. Did she really wish to make a nun of Rénée? He was on the point of speaking, when she turned abruptly and put her hand on his arm.

"Do you really wish to do me a service?"

She spoke with so much earnestness that she startled him. It was not a question, but a proposition.

"Go back to Paris," she said, rapidly, — "to-morrow."

The thought that in some way the presence of Father Roche concerned Rénée flashed through his mind, but it was only a flash. Stéphanie's eyes were full upon him. Their very appeal inspired trust. For some reason which he could not fathom, she seemed to be throwing herself upon his generosity.

"I do not in the least understand you, but I will go," he said. "Only, I shall see Rénée before going."

"I shall give you no reason but a woman's whim," she said, with an attempt at levity, and not noticing his last words.

"I have asked for none." He did not know whether, as she turned away, the light in her eyes signified triumph or gratitude.

"Father, will you give me your arm," she said to the priest; and the four left the room.

Father Roche had not seen Madame Milevski since her journey to Frohsdorf, and the failure of those projects in which he also had taken an active part. So thoroughly had she entered into the hopes of the hour that he was not prepared to find her indifferent to the new plans which were ever forming in his busy brain. But he betrayed no surprise. In the interview which he had with her that afternoon, his chagrin (for he had come expressly from Madrid without doubting the success of what he had in view) was not apparent. He was very skillful in adapting himself to a new situation. He had definite purposes, but, when once moulded, he never allowed them to harden beyond the point of readjustment. In this respect he possessed a quality of mind the lack of which has brought ruin on otherwise great strategists; a quality which enabled him not only to seize the essential and disembarrass himself of all those trivialities which perplex the action and obscure the judgment, but to make his often devious way through those contingencies which beset the wisest plans, and, if they be too rigidly set, destroy them altogether. He made what was to have been a communication to an associate, a confidence to a friend; and although sincerity had dropped out of this confidence, it was none the less a tribute to the good faith of his listener. He consulted her judgment, her opinion of men, her knowledge of the world, and he showed that interest in herself which a man accustomed to society knows so well how to offer without intrusion or indiscretion.

Stéphanie was not blind to his ways, yet she enjoyed his visit. Much that gives pleasure is only that exterior with which intelligence and good breeding disguise the unreal. There was a refinement in this intriguer, a fascination in this mixture of the courtier and the priest who, if not so honest as Father Le Blanc, was less gross, precisely because he was less natural.

"No one is better fitted than you are," he said to Stéphanie, "to take part in this work in which I am engaged, but I should do you wrong to urge upon you a course-you are not inclined to follow. Few of those who labor with us are free from motives of self-interest and ambition. Some seek position and favor, some are happy only in satisfying the spirit of adventure, others risk their fortunes and their lives through their pride in the hierarchy, an instinct of birth and caste. They believe they have renounced self, whereas it is encased in that very pride to which they sacrifice fortune. But towards the Divine purpose, all contribute. He who will not ride in His chariot, drags it in chains."

She had said that she could be of no assistance to him.

"It were possible for you to be of the greatest," he replied. "Not in your present state of mind, but in one to which I would lead you."

Stéphanie raised her eyes and looked at him.

"We wish above all to be happy. Does he who embraces the highest cause, for what it brings, attain happiness? No, not so long as there exists

In the motive which animates him the slightest alloy of selfishness. In the pure gold of God's furnace there is no trace of it. The fruit of happiness comes only of that which dies to itself. I have seen those who in disappointment and misfortune have entered the path of sacrifice and devotion to some great principle, when in the very desire to forget self, selfishness was supreme. Set happiness before you as an end, no matter in what guise of wealth, or fame, or oblivion even, — you will not attain it. Renounce it, seek the pleasure of God, and that instant is the birth of your own. But I have seen men seek the pleasure of God as they seek that of kings."

"It seems I am very transparent," said Stéphanie.

Had not Father Roche, during all his life-time, analyzed the heart of woman? Had she not herself bared the springs of life to the eye of his confessional? How many interests are there to snare the soul of a man! But with woman, — he had only to look at this one in her youth, her beauty, to put his finger on the hurt.

"Pardon me," he said. And then, after a while, "Can you not forget the man in the priest? To the one, confession may outrage pride and endanger self-respect, but to the other " —

"They are never separate, father."

"Seek God, then," he answered, gently.

"Do you go to Frohsdorf?" she asked, after

another pause. Yes, he was going, and they began to talk of those whom she knew there, the ladies-in-waiting of the queen, as she was called.

When he went away, she descended the stairs with him. In the garden it was already dark. Coming from the lighted room, the warm air, the perfume of flowers, and, above all, the mysterious potency of night, overpowered her. They filled her senses and swept her away as in a current.

"You are still weak; you must go no farther," said Father Roche. She stopped, leaning upon one of the trees. He would have supported her, but she recovered herself, and with one of those impulses which sometimes broke down her reserve, she said : —

"What you said to me is true. Pray for me, and remember, even in the death of the body, the heart stops last."

Long after she had gone, Father Roche stood meditatively in the place whence she had vanished, then walked slowly down the hill under the lofty trees, and disappeared in the darkness as he came. He never saw her but once again.

XIX.

ANTONIO had evidently taken a great fancy to Rénée. His natural antipathy to all exertion vanished at the sound of her voice. He accompanied her with the solemn dignity of a mastiff guarding a treasure, consenting even to walk in the sun when she led the way. Lizette had dubbed him " Monsieur l'ange tutélaire." Mine host of the Siete Suelos, who seemed Antonio's especial friend, evidently knew more than he cared to tell, for on one occasion, when Lizette was making fun of his friend, he explained that Antonio had once a daughter of Rénée's age ; but, to Lizette's question what had become of her, he answered only, " Eso va largo " (that 's a long story).

> " By the porch of the cathedral
> I dare not pass to-day ;
> I see my mother's face,
> Tears fall apace ;
> I pass some other way."

Rénée wished to buy a fan, that " second tongue " of the Andalusian, and had set out with Antonio, on the morning of Father Roche's visit, to purchase one. It was her second search after that ideal which always haunts the mind of the feminine shopper, the first having proved fruit-less.

Did the señorita desire one of sandal-wood? Here was a marvel, with rice paper from Japan, enlivened with spangles. Or did she prefer ivory, delicately carved? Ah, here now was the paragon of fans! of tortoise-shell, painted in water-colors, with gold mountings of filagree work.

But no, the señorita was not easily satisfied, and abandoned the quest for another day. In the mean time Antonio had not been idle. Had one been able to look in upon him at night when the rest of the household were asleep, he might have been seen taking from a small black box, containing apparently other treasures, an object which he handled with reverence. It was a long time before he closed the box, but, when he did so, he had not replaced what he took from it. It was a small fan of exquisite workmanship in mother-of-pearl, covered with vellum on which was painted a landscape which might have been a scene from the isle of Cythera or the gardens of Calypso.

The next day he took it to the bazaar, and requested that, when Rénée came again, it should be shown her.

"Not at first," he said, significantly. "Show it last of all."

"Jesus! que lindeza!" exclaimed the shop-keeper. "It is worth at least a hundred pesetas."

" Ask what you will," said Antonio.

" I will give you that myself," replied the dealer, examining it.

" No, it is for the señorita."

" And how much do you give me?"

" At a hundred pesetas, five," replied Antonio.

" It is not much, but to oblige you " — and, folding the fan, he found for it a case of scented leather. " With the case, ten pesetas," he said, holding it out in his hand.

" Corriente," said Antonio.

This time, the extravagant praises with which the " most beautiful thing in all Andalusia " was produced were not belied by the dainty fan as it was drawn from its leathern case.

Antonio's eyes shone with pleasure at Rénée's rapture. He took his pesetas when her back was turned, but it was the full hundred that he dropped in the box under the plaster Virgin of the Plaza de Vivarambla.

" Do you give alms to the Church, Antonio? " asked Rénée, in surprise. Antonio passed for a heretic ; some even said that he was a Jew.

" A cuarto for a blessing on my lottery ticket."

Rénée looked at him wonderingly. Did he really thus buy the blessing of Heaven on his gambling venture? Or was he more devout than his detractors would have him? She inclined to believe the latter.

On the way home she could not refrain from

examining again her purchase. She drew it from its hiding-place, and spread it wide open.

"We saw nothing like it before, Antonio. It is a gem, so strong, and yet so delicate." She turned it over, and held it out at arm's length. "The case is certainly a new one, but the fan looks old," she said. "See! is it not worn a little on the folds?" and she held it up.

"Yes, señorita. They do not make such fans nowadays."

"I like it the better for that. It must have belonged to some one, I wish I knew to whom. It is smaller than most, — is it not, Antonio?"

"A little, señorita."

"Is it Spanish? The painting looks French. How fresh the colors are!"

"Spanish, señorita."

"I shall always wonder whose hand once held it, and believe that it has a history. Why will you not invent one, Antonio? I will tell it to its admirers in Paris."

She laughed, — a silvery little laugh, Antonio looked so perplexed. It was wicked to tease him, that good old Antonio!

"Do you never grow tired of your life, Antonio?" asked Rénée, at the fountain where she lingered to rest and to drink some of the cool water. "I should think you would, going the same round and showing the same things over and over to so many."

"First of all, one must eat," said Antonio. It embarrassed him when any one spoke of himself.

"I suppose you have very little love for us French, who have done you so much injury," she continued, looking down into the well. She little thought what chords she was touching. "Soult was a monster!" she added, energetically.

When they reached the inn, Lizette was at the door.

"I have bought the loveliest fan, Lizette," said Rénée. "I am going to show it to my aunt."

"Madame is asleep, mademoiselle," said Lizette. "She has been taking a walk" —

"A walk! What a surprise! When did she go?"

"This morning, and she took her breakfast here."

"I never once thought of it, or I should not have gone out. Let me know when she wakes, Lizette. I am going to dress for dinner."

"M. Lande has been here, mademoiselle," said Lizette.

"Ah," said Rénée, nonchalantly. "I was out."

"He wished to know where you had gone. He returns to Paris to-morrow."

Rénée's heart gave a bound. "What surprises!" she said. She thought Lizette was looking at her. She was not in the least afraid of her, and had no fault to find with her; still, she never wholly liked her.

She went to her room, and began her toilette. From being perfectly happy, she had suddenly become nervous, and she knew it. She took out her fan again, but it did not interest her. There were some things she was trying not to think of. She was a very orderly little being, and usually dressed very leisurely; but she put on her dinner dress hurriedly, and slipped the yellow Christ Sœur Ursule had given her in her bosom. She had not worn it for days.

When she came down again, Sœur Marie said Stéphanie would dine in her chamber; she was tired after her walk. Rénée said she would go to her.

"Madame has a visitor," replied Sœur Marie.

Who? A priest, from Paris. Rénée remembered to have seen him sitting outside the door when she returned with Antonio. When dinner was served he had not gone, and Rénée ate hers alone, Lizette waiting upon her. After it was finished, she wandered out into the gallery in the rear of the house where Sœur Marie was reading. She did not wish to be alone.

For a long time she sat quietly by the sister's side, watching a little fountain whose water, after falling noisily into an upper shallow basin, dripped softly into a black pool below.

Presently Antonio brought a cup of chocolate, which she sipped silently while Sœur Marie read on in her book.

She wanted to see Stéphanie, to talk with some one, to divert herself, but Father Roche was still there. The minutes slipped away, and the sun crept slowly towards the white horizon lines of the mountains. In an hour only the snow-peak of the Mulahacen would emerge from the shadows, and mine host would then light the lamps that hung in the gallery.

" Read aloud to me, sister, please," said Rénée.

" ' And the three Marys brought precious spices to anoint our Lord. Take good heed now, my dear sisters : these three Marys denote three bitternesses, as the name signifieth. The first bitterness is remorse and making amends for sin, and this is the first Mary, Mary Magdalene, for she in great bitterness of heart left off her sins and turned to our Lord. The second bitterness is in wrestling and struggling against temptation, and this is that other Mary, the mother of Jacob, which meaneth wrestling. This wrestling is very bitter to many who are well advanced in the way to heaven, for they still waver in temptation. And the third bitterness consists in longing for heaven and weariness of this world, when one is of such piety that his heart is at rest with the war of vice, and is as it were in the gates of heaven, where all worldly things seem bitter to him. And this bitterness is to be understood by the third Mary, Mary Salome, which signifieth peace.' "

Sœur Marie bent her head over her book as she read. All her thoughts were there; one might know from the tones of her voice that, though she read aloud, she was reading to herself. For her it was as if there were no fountain splashing cheerily in the *patio*, or any snow dyed with sunset colors on the mountains. Rénée heard the words, but her thoughts struggled up and mingled with their meanings till the trickling waters of the fountain and the reader's voice blended in a confused murmur.

"'But now observe here, my dear sisters, how after bitterness cometh sweetness. Bitterness buyeth it, for, as the Gospel saith, these three Marys brought sweet-smelling spices to anoint our Lord. By spices, which are sweet, is to be understood the sweetness of a devout heart. These three Marys buy it, that is, through bitterness we arrive at sweetness. So saith God's dear spouse, I will go to the hill of frankincense by the mountain of myrrh. Observe: which is the way to the sweetness of frankincense? By the myrrh of bitterness'"—

"It is growing too dark, it pains my eyes," said Sœur Marie at length, closing her book. "I will go and see whether madame is alone."

Rénée sat for a while with her hands in her lap, then she took the cross from her bosom; its weight seemed to oppress her. By and by she rose and stepped out from under the gallery into the *patio.*

Just beyond the fountain, beneath a cluster of bays, a little path led round to the ruined tower. She followed it mechanically until she came to the loose stones which, fallen from above, and now overgrown with moss and creepers, formed so many rough-hewn seats at the base of the wall. She had been used to come here in the early days of Stéphanie's sickness, when she longed for air and space, yet did not dare to go far from her chamber.

How long she sat there she could not have told, if indeed she knew she was there at all till his footsteps roused her. Had she not listened for them all that afternoon ? And yet now, after the first leap of her heart, she was perfectly calm. When they stopped close beside her she looked up into Roger's face.

It was the last of the twilight, yet at that distance one could see distinctly. She was sitting on a fragment of stone, with the cross of Sœur Ursule in her hands. Roger saw its gilt image, which still reflected the faint light. Her eyes looked into his without shrinking, — they were wet with tears that had not fallen.

" Rénée, there is nothing in all this wide world which can keep you from me, — if you love me."

She did not answer; he bent over and took her

hand. She did not resist him; then he took her in his arms. She lay there quietly, her eyes closed. He drew her closer to him and kissed her lips. She opened her eyes and smiled.

Then suddenly, springing to her feet, her hand still in his, she cried, —

"**Kneel down and pray with me!**"

XX.

WHEN Roger left the tavern of the Siete Suelos that evening he would have given his purse to a bandit, and said, " Thank you!" He had lingered for a while about the place, with the reluctance of a true lover. Philosophy and reason, what had they to do with instinct and sentiment!

He would have returned by that path under the rose bays, to that place at the thought of which every other forsook him, had not mine host intercepted him with many bows and apologies.

" Did the señor go to Malaga the next morning? He had some business there. That rascal Villegas! who failed to send him his *janqueta* — white bait — and who owed him sixty duros. The diligence was full, every place was taken. What luck! it burns the blood! Would the señor permit his unworthy servant to occupy the seat beside him? A thousand thanks; he threw himself at the feet of the señor; all that he possessed was his."

Mine host, who took tithes from travelers, under the name of Matías, proved no disagreeable companion for the twelve hours' ride. He had been a muleteer before the days of his prosperity, and had slept on his mule-cloth in every market-place in Andalusia. A cigar opened the heart of this Spanish Gascon, full of childish good-humor, vivacity, boasting, credulity, and wit. The sun under which he lived, and which had made his skin into a tawny leather, had also volatilized his nature and painted his apparel. He shone in velvet and buttons as he stepped into the *calesa*. He had a story for every turn in the road, and at every *venta* a jest for its landlord, a compliment for its maid, and a tip for its hostler.

From some of Matías' adventures, related *in loco*, Roger inferred that he had once relieved travelers of their duros in a less legitimate fashion than at present. This was, however, an unworthy suspicion. The contrabandista is no footpad. It is the exciseman that is the robber and defrauds the people. The smuggler is at the worst but a venial sinner whom the padre absolves almost as readily as the bright eyes for whom he brings his calico or the dandy whom he keeps in cigars.

From Alhama, where the horses were baited, they followed the bed of the Marchan, white with rage over the obstacles in its rocky descent; on the ledges above clung the houses, embowered in vines and gardens, making more striking the ragged rent swept by the torrent and the barren desolation of the mountains. As they passed over a bridge where the noise of the waters drowned the voice, Matías touched his companion with a significant look ; and afterwards, — divested of many exclamations as well as gestures, with which he garnished his narratives, — this is the story, in substance, which he told as they climbed the pass.

He and Antonio were at Ronda. They were associates in business. Those were good days, though pocket and stomach were often both empty. They lived at Granada, he and Antonio, with the latter's daughter. It was said her mother was a gypsy who had paid with her life for this *liaison* with one outside of her tribe. God only knew, — one might as well try to open the teeth of a donkey as the mouth of Antonio. At all events, it was not unlikely. Felisa was a true *gitana;* one could more easily hold water in the hand than control her. She was like a flame, blown with the wind, yet which no man could handle. Then, again, she would be gentle as a dove. Ah! if the señor could have seen her! Eyes liquid as an oriental sapphire and limpid as the pool of *los Algibes*. He, Matías, bending over the well, once threw down a stone, and the flashing ripples had made his head swim. Well, it was the same when one looked into the eyes of Felisa.

Of course she had lovers. Every one who gave her a look gave his heart with it ; but she would have none of them. Not one ever touched her heart. He thought then she had none. She was wild and gay as a bird, and sang on every tree. Many a one was snared at the sight of her face at the grating. On the street she would lift her brown lashes for a second, and shoot a glance swift as an arrow, — it was the work of a second, like the flash of the matador's sword. But no lover's hand had ever reached through the grating, or lover's foot had crossed the threshold. She left them all at the door, as she took off her red ribbons at bed-time, and never lost a second's sleep for the sound of guitars under the window.

Antonio was so proud of her! No wonder. If she loved any one, it was he. He was her lover. When he came home from the mountains she hung on his neck. What a necklace they made, those arms! There were those ready to be strangled by them. She had always kind words for him then, and he could refuse her nothing. He brought her little red shoes from Tangiers, and stockings of open lace embroidery from Seville.

"We always left her alone when we were off on our business to Ronda, Gibraltar, or Malaga," said Matías. "In those days Antonio was young. To molest Felisa would be to try the edge of his knife, which he could handle very prettily. I should have been in love with her like the rest, only I was twice her age. She treated me like a brother. Once I was near making a fool of myself, — she sat on the floor mending the fringe of her petticoat, — she looked at me and laughed till I was angry, the little sorceress!

" Well, at the first we were at Cadiz. We went

to bring some silk over the mountains. But our enterprise failed, the coast-guards were on the lookout, so we returned sooner than we expected. Felisa was gay as a lark. I noticed it, for when we were unsuccessful, she was sympathetic, and consoled us with promises of better luck the next time. But this time she asked no questions, nor seemed at all interested in our undertaking ; only she danced about like a madcap, and got four reals from Antonio to buy a silver pin she had seen at the silversmith's, to fasten her mantilla. When we set out again, to try our venture the second time, she stood in the doorway, with the mantilla on her head, her hair shining smooth on her forehead, where it was fastened at each temple with a crimson pink. Antonio asked her where she was going in all her fine clothes, — she had on her best, — but she only laughed and pouted her lips at him, and bade him mind his mule and she would mind the geese. Well, we came back after three weeks. It was evening, and we saw Felisa's light when we turned the corner. It happened I was first, so I entered as usual, without knocking.

" Felisa sat on a bench by the wall, and beside her was a man. He was dressed in the Spanish fashion. But he was not one of us, the *gavacho!* I knew by the cut of his cloak and the little mustache which turned up at the ends. He was one of your countrymen, señor. Before I was in-side the door he was on his feet, and before I had taken a step Felisa had pushed him out of the back door, leading into a sort of court-yard with a low wall, by which one might gain the street in the rear. I was so astonished that I stood still till Antonio behind me pushed me to one side. I knew by his face he had seen everything. But he said nothing. He looked at Felisa, who stood with her back to the door where the Frenchman had gone, — she was confused for a moment, — then he went out to look after the mules in the yard. I knew not which to do, to stay or to follow him, till he had shut the door, — then I stayed. Felisa had recovered herself. She plied me with questions, laughing and singing as if nothing had happened. I replied the best way I could, not daring to catch her eye. She began to get our supper. I was so nervous that I overthrew a pile of oranges on the table. ' How awkward you are!' she said, laughing and showing her pretty teeth, white as almonds. When Antonio returned she ran up to him and kissed him. But he said not a word. When she asked questions I answered them, for the silence was terrible. It must have been the devil that kept up her spirits while we ate supper. She chatted with me who felt like a dead man; told me about the fair, — it was the feast of St. John, — and how the people had hissed Miguel, who had broken his sword on a bull in the *plaza.*

" When supper was over she crossed the room to where Antonio was sitting silent in the corner, and began to fondle and talk to him as she used to when he returned from the mountains. ' Had he brought her anything from Cadiz?' I knew what he had in his sash, but when he took it out I thought it was his knife. It was a fan, and when he gave it to her he looked in her eyes as one looks in the sun, with a dazed expression. But she was gay as a bird. She examined the fan minutely, opening and shutting it rapidly. It fluttered in her hands like the wings of a martlet. When she went up to bed she kissed him, paying no attention to his silence and gravity. I dreaded to have her go and leave me alone with him. For a while I could not open my throat, but I made some remarks at last about our affairs, to which he replied by a shake of the head, a nod, or a monosyllable. He never moved except to roll a cigarette. I was worn with fatigue, and, rolling my cloak into a pillow, I went to sleep on the wooden seat.

" The next morning it was just the same. Felisa came down singing, but I could see there was wickedness in her eyes. The humor of Antonio began to wear upon her. She went after breakfast over to the door leading out into the courtyard, but it was locked. She looked at Antonio, who sat by the other, with a laugh. She wore a pink in her corsage, which she unfastened and

threw to him with a gesture of reconciliation.
But it lay on the floor where it fell. She gazed
at him for a moment in dismay. Perhaps his revolt astonished her who had led him always like
a lamb. I saw the storm coming in her eyes.
'Have your own way!' she exclaimed, contempt-
uously, dropping all her airs and running up to
her room.

"All this would wear out the patience of a
saint. I perspired with anxiety. I rushed into
the street to breathe and see the sun. Old Raquel,
who sold fruits and nuts, was on the corner. She
knew everything that happened in Granada. Felisa had met the Frenchman at the bazaar; she had
seen him follow her down the Carrera del Darro.
But she paid no attention. Every one knew Felisa was no sleeping weasel. This was some weeks
ago, when we were first away. After that she
saw them together often. Pedro Ximenez, who
brought snow from the mountains, swore to her
that he had seen them together beyond the ravine
of Los Molinos. Well, then she began to watch.
The *gavacho* came to the house several times. He
lived at the Leon de Oro; she had seen him at
the café eating ices.

"Well, evening came, and Antonio had not left
the house. I began to be alarmed. So I went
back again; but the lower room was empty. The
pink on the floor made me start. I thought it
was blood. The door to the stairs leading to Fe-

lisa's chamber was open, and I went up with a
fear in my heart that kept it from beating. Antonio was there, — he had just gone up, — no one
else. The bird had flown. My tongue was loosed,
I felt relieved, for Antonio's manner had frightened me. I told him what Raquel had said to me.
It was clear Felisa had gone by the window into
the court-yard, and escaped by the little door into
the street. I was for going here, there, everywhere; but Antonio bade me to follow him. He
has the gift of second sight," said Matías, with
simplicity.

"He went straight to the Leon de Oro. The
man whom we described had been gone several
hours. No one could tell us where, but he had
paid his account and had left orders to send his
trunk to Malaga. That gave me an idea. If
Felisa had gone with him, she would get horses
at the Venta San Rafael, where there was one she
always rode. She could ride with the best of us.
And true enough! Felisa had taken two horses,
and was gone about three hours.

"In the wink of an eye we were in the saddle,
and on the road we have just passed over. But
luck was against us. It was the rainy season, and
the river was swollen. In that gorge which we
passed, the bridge was gone. The water boiled
like a witch's pot; no horse could stand in it.
We were obliged to retrace our steps and make
a long circuit. When we reached the *venta* at

Alhama it was three hours past midnight; I knew by the stars on the top of the Tejada. Our horses were jaded, and we stopped to exchange them for fresh ones and to make inquiries. I struck a flint at the door of the stables, and the first thing I saw was the horse of Felisa. It was for this we had come, but now my heart began to beat again against my vest, — it misgave me for what was to happen. 'Stay where you are,' said Antonio, and he went out with the look in his eye which he had when Felisa threw the pink at him. Two minutes were as long as two hours. I could wait no longer, and went into the house. But I had time to see that only one horse stood in the stable, — Felisa's. There were some others, — sorry nags fit only for the *plaza*, — which had never eaten hay in the stable of San Rafael.

"While I was waiting, this had happened. Felisa, doubtless, was wakened by the noise which Antonio had made at the door. Every one was asleep. God knows what the poor little one thought when she opened her eyes and found herself alone! The villainous rascal had left her; he had gotten up in the night and stolen off like a thief, — and she lying there asleep! Poor Felisa! When I saw her she stood in the middle of the room, her face looking as though she had a knife in her heart. She had on only her red petticoat and her black mantilla wrapped about her bosom and shoulders. Mother of God! the sight wrung my heart, which had not a tear in it for twenty years. I had no anger but for the wretch who was fleeing like a coward over the mountains. This was the thought, too, of Antonio. He stood trembling, with his eyes full of pity. All this takes time to tell, but it was the affair of a minute. While I looked, Felisa went up to him as she used to when we were back from an expedition. She drew from the pocket of her petticoat the fan he had brought her from Cadiz, making believe to put it in his sash, and looking all the while in his eyes. He put out his hands, — when she made a spring backwards out of their reach. It was all over, before one could move a step. I was watching the handle of his knife, which protruded above his sash. I was afraid, in a moment of anger, he would use it. I saw her fingers about it, and then — she was lying on the floor with the blade in her heart. She knew the blow, — a down stroke between the shoulders," said Matías, with an explanatory gesture.

"Pardon, señor, permit me to use your fire." His cigar had gone out while he was telling his story.

"And the — other?" asked Roger, who was profoundly affected.

"Never," replied Matías, between his teeth. "He escaped us."

He was less talkative during that part of the ride which remained. The memories which he

had so vividly revived checked the flow of his
spirits. As for Roger, this story, related in the
dreary defile, haunted him. He went over it again
and again, walking the deck of the steamer and
dozing in the compartment of his carriage during
the long night ride to Paris ; till, once more in the
press of his duties, it faded from his mind and
Antonio was forgotten.

XXI.

BEFORE the fireplace of the Rue du Bac, one autumn evening, were gathered three men who had reached the same stage as the fire which illumined their faces. It no longer blazed fiercely. There were no more any showers of sparks, or hot, leaping flames; but only a red glow, shining without a flicker, and changing slowly into ashes white as the hair of those beside it.

"I received a visit to-day, M. Lande, from your son," said M. Michel.

"The good boy!" said M. Lande, out of his dark corner. "I can never be too grateful to that old gourmand whose gout first led him to Beauvais, and who was the means of making him known to you."

"Ah, you think so! Well, listen. To-day, I repeat, he makes me a visit. If he wished to borrow of me a thousand francs at a good interest, that would not surprise me; or a book which I value, but which he will replace if he tear so much as a single leaf. That happens every day But not a bit of it! He says simply, 'Monsieur, you have a niece, — give her to me!'"

"God be praised!" exclaimed M. Lande. "Ah, my good friend" —

"Your good friend!" interrupted M. Michel, testily; "to what use will you put him, — your good friend? You are a pair, you two."

M. Lande, unprepared for such an explosion, was half persuaded that it was serious.

"And Mademoiselle Rénée, what" — he began to say.

"Mademoiselle Rénée! Parbleu! c'est un fait accompli. It is not a request but a confession that he makes, your good boy."

"To grant absolution is a privilege, — is it not," said M. Lande, appealing to Father Le Blanc.

"When it is not a necessity," interposed M. Michel. "Do you think I did not see the point of the rapier under the robe of the penitent? 'Monsieur, the hand of your niece, if you please,' which, being translated, is, 'Come, old miser, she is mine; surrender!'"

Father Le Blanc laughed aloud.

"And you also laugh, you who are at the bottom of this marriage!"

"I? a marriage?" exclaimed Father Le Blanc. "I do not make them; I bless them."

"That is to say, you make the best of them, as I do. When the rains have fallen on the Upper Nile, one cannot dam the river at Cairo."

"Then you consent," said M. Lande, taking heart.

"Consent! No, I do not consent; I am pillaged!"

M. Lande said nothing, from pure satisfaction. He had waited so long for the realization of dreams that, now one had come true, happiness stifled him, and he drugged it with silence lest it should render him beside himself. To the demon of disappointment and frustration which had so long mocked him without subduing him, he kept repeating softly, "I knew it; I told you so."

"When do they return?" asked Father Le Blanc, breaking the silence. He was thinking neither of Roger nor of Rénée.

"This week. And do you know what I have done, old fool that I am! Come and see."

He lighted a candle and led the way through the library into the vestibule, where he opened a door, and, holding the light above his head, motioned them to enter. The room was a boudoir, recently furnished. One could see the new lustre of pearl-gray satin, and, between the curtains of a door beyond, a bed white as innocence.

"I have made a nest for a bird that will not stay in it," said M. Michel.

"And the convent," said Father Le Blanc; "had you forgotten that?"

"No, I remembered it. But when I close the door, the bird flies out of the window," he replied, leading the way back to the fire, and replacing the candle on the mantel.

"Put it out," suggested Father Le Blanc; "it is more pleasant. You remember," he continued,

when the light was extinguished, " I warned you —
I even prophesied."

" Do you offer that as a consolation ? Well,
at least I am more favored than Job, who had
three friends, while I have but two."

" Come, come ! " said Father Le Blanc, " be
honest with us.   Is there nothing which condones
this robbery ?   Have you no — no recollections
— which " —

He hesitated, shading his eyes with his large
hand.   The semi-obscurity of the room and his
own sincerity had led him upon delicate ground.

" No," replied M. Michel.   " When all the garden was budding, I was in the shade."

" God forgot you, my friend," said M. Lande,
gently.

Father Le Blanc looked at the speaker specu-
latively, from under the shade of his hand.   How
was it that this man who, deceived by the sirens,
had plunged so early into the sea of disappointment, could keep his eyes fixed upon the stars ?

" Yes, I suppose so," replied M. Michel, mus-
ingly.   " For I, too, must have been capable of
folly, and might have had in my drawer a faded
rose, or an old glove, whose perfume could still
intoxicate.   But I have none," he added, naively.

" Listen to this appeal of your own heart.   It
is stronger than the young lover's, for he has no
past, and you have one.   It is stronger than the
voice of wisdom, or the arguments of experience

Why? Because first love is an instinct; every other is a philosophy. It is at once a gift and a sacrifice, — every other is a bargain."

"Good bargains are always good bargains," hazarded M. Michel, thinking of Madame Lande. He did not dare employ too boldly the *argumentum ad hominem.*

"A gift is never a bargain," replied M. Lande, warmly. "What a dull, miserable business, to go to a shop, to exchange values at fixed rates, to be exact to a centime! Love, trust, veneration, are not made for buying and selling. The man who seeks for one worthy of them is the man who is deceived. They are the wealth of his own nature, and he must give them freely, without afterthought. And this gift increases the world's stock; it enriches the poorest heart. It is such offerings, from the depth of our own nature, which, received by us from heaven and given again to the world, increase its capital. Nothing comes of a bargain. Oh, I know of what you are thinking! All this, you say, is very fine in principle, but 'details are melancholy;' in theory we hit the mark fairly, but in experience every stroke glances. And what of that? Will you ask our friend here to discard all those beautiful symbols which he made use of at mass this morning, and which, like lenses, aid our eyes to apprehend the great tragedy of redemption, because our poor eyes still remain blind? You will not be able to stop there," he continued, following up his simile, " you will send the good God himself back to heaven because He makes a poor bargain."

" My friend," said M. Michel, slowly, " you are at once the saddest and the happiest of men."

Continually carried away by his feelings, M. Lande was easily recalled to a sense of his audacity, between which and timidity he swayed like a pendulum.

" The man who is truly happy is the man who has seen the truth and is not dismayed by it," said Father Le Blanc, replying for him.

" I wish," said M. Michel, after a long silence, " I wish your maxim was also a recipe. I know some one to whom I would give it."

" To whom ? " asked Father Le Blanc, stirring the embers.

" To my sister Stéphanie."

"She is not happy ? " said the priest, looking up from the fire, and wondering how much this man really saw who said so little.

" Well," replied M. Michel, " do you think so ? "

" Perhaps it is so."

" I do not know; it is only a thought that I have."

M. Lande, who was not a close observer, listened.

" She will not find happiness in lovers," Father Le Blanc continued, after a pause ; " nor anywhere else till she seeks it where she is now unwilling to look for it."

"I always thought she would make a better nun than Rénée. She has a good deal of the religious element in her nature," said M. Michel.

Father Le Blanc's astonishment grew as he listened. "I never thought of it," he said, candidly. "She has a great deal of religious principle, if you will, but no religious sentiment."

"Well, that is better than to be all religious sentiment without any religious principle, — like M. de Marzac, for example. You see," continued M. Michel, watching the priest's efforts to reconstruct the fire, "there are some to whom God reveals himself in the world, in its beauty or in its love. They cannot look in the sun. But to some He unveils his own person, and speaks face to face."

"Yes, you are right," said Father Le Blanc, abstractedly. "But sentiment is of great value. There is more religion in the Litany than in all the encyclopædia of theology." To tell the truth, he was thinking so intently of Stéphanie that he hardly knew what he was saying.

"Who said anything of theology, my friend?" replied M. Michel.

Father Le Blanc made no answer. He had gathered together the charred pieces of wood and had at last succeeded in coaxing from them a little blaze, which played furtively among the fragments. "She comes back with Rénée, I suppose," he said, sitting up in his chair and watching the flames.

"Yes, next week."

"And does she remain in Paris this winter?"

"She does not say. But why not? There is the marriage of Rénée" —

"True," replied Father Le Blanc, leaning back and closing his eyes, "I had forgotten." His little blue flame had disappeared again.

"Suppose," said M. Lande, after another silence, "that in losing a niece you should gain a sister."

M. Michel looked at him in the fading light, incredulously.

"Oh, I know you," replied M. Lande, with a nod of complete understanding. "You would not move to the Boulevard St. Germain, but Madame Milevski, who is to reside in Paris all the winter, might preside over the Rue du Bac."

"I should not think of it," said M. Michel, quickly, "nor she either. We love each other at a distance."

Father Le Blanc laughed again.

"I am such an old fellow, you know. With Rénée it was different; I began when she was young. Besides, madame has too many servants, They would distract me; and she brings a new one from Spain, a sort of courier — you remember — Antonio — of whom Rénée wrote to us."

"Oh yes, I recollect," said M. Lande. "I see him already, in his sash and leggings."

Here Baptiste and candles put an end to their talk. He brought the coffee, and there was also a little flagon of brandy for Father Le Blanc, with which he flavored his.

M. de Marzac, Baptiste said, had called in the afternoon to inquire when Madame Milevski would return.

To M. Michel this inquiry was only an act of politeness, but in reality it was much more. M. de Marzac had latterly been undergoing a process of which this inquiry was, in a sense, the culmination; a process begun, indeed, long ago, at Kief, where the idea, "how beautiful she is!" had dropped like a ferment into his affective nature, and that had now developed into a fever which prevented judgment from holding the balance between his thoughts and his emotions. Men like M. de Marzac, whose moral principles are not wrought into their nature as moral qualities, but are put on, as garments are, to adorn or to conceal, fall more easily a prey to such fevers. They are like bubbles of air, mere shells of external decoration without resisting power, swaying in the lightest air and collapsing in the storm. A stern moralist would have classified him, without the slightest scruple, among the thoroughly bad. And it is true that he was brave only so long as he had the advantage; that he possessed an unlimited number of fine moral sayings, which fell from his lips under his feet; that he was resolute and persevering only because selfish and vindictive; that his prudence was but caution, his principle but policy, and his wealth and influence the means of self-gratification only. But to stop here would certainly be doing him injustice. Standards may be set too high. It is well to have high ideals for one's self, but in dealing with one's neighbors it is indispensable to forget them. Did not M. de Marzac discharge the ordinary duties and debts of life with regularity and precision? Tradespeople pronounced him just, servants called him generous; and what his wealth did for this class, his ability (ever enlisted on the side of public security, moral order, and religion) did for another. There were hundreds who only knew him by the signature at the end of his articles in the "Univers," who read the man in his utterances. M. de Marzac might have died quietly in his bed in the Avenue Friedland, after receiving the sacraments, leaving no one the wiser. Does not many a man with the heel of Achilles escape a wound in the vulnerable spot, and die unsuspected of weakness?

The truth is, M. de Marzac had heretofore managed to escape strong fire. He was not easily stirred. He took life quietly, with a philosophy that accommodated itself without revolt to every circumstance. His passions were not deeply or readily excited, and, says one, "If you wish to know the man, stir his passions." M. de Sacy, who won from him forty thousand francs at a sitting, had not been able to; he lost with *sang froid* and a perfect equanimity. Neither the Radicals nor the Bonapartists, whom he fought with his pen, had ever betrayed him into an imprudence which required him to draw his sword. Mademoiselle Celimène, of the Theatre Comique, broke with him and went to Berlin with a German banker without having had a scene. How did it happen that Stéphanie Milevski could make him betray himself? He had often asked the same question. His fever had begun with an appetite which rose and fell with the presence and absence of the excitant. In the Kief ball-room it was only a pleasant emotion, barely lingering through the drive back to his lodgings. In the year of his intimacy with her which preceded the visit to Frohsdorf, this appetite had been more constantly excited, and he had grown more definitely conscious of it, till, at the close of the year, it was no longer an appetite, but a desire. Moreover, long continued and long thwarted, it had ceased to produce pleasure ; it was now a discomfort and a pain. On the way back from the ball M. de Marzac had played with it, smiled at it, — now it stood over him with a whip of fire. He would gladly have escaped this tyranny ; but, at the first, vanity precluded retreat from a course in which he had taken so many steps, and he moved in the line of least resistance. The same was still true, but to a greater degree. To retreat now, in the strength of his heightened desire and wounded pride, required unselfishness and virtue. M. de Marzac had a strong will, but how should any one expect him to will an act of unselfishness and heroic virtue when neither unselfishness, heroism, or virtue were within the range of his reflection or experience? Pears, as Antonio said, do not grow on elms, and will is only another name for intelligence. All the thoughts and feelings of his past, even those which, at the time, had seemed most ephemeral, were stored up in his organization, and were now the forces latent in certain springs of action, or the chains which bound others.

During the year alluded to, his close intimacy with Stéphanie, a long concentration of thought and desire upon her, together with an overweening confidence in himself, had led to a habit of mind, — that of looking upon her as a part of his own life, — and the sudden destruction of his hope had destroyed his reason, or, as he said, his temper. After Stéphanie's departure for Spain, he often looked back to those interviews he had had with her as acts of folly. But these lucid intervals were neither long nor frequent. What had at first been a spasm of anger and disappointment gradually became a chronic sullenness and moroseness, less violent but more persistent. Madame Milevski had come to be his right after having so long been his desire. Pride, obstinacy, caprice, — these were sufficient to explain her. He himself had been abused. Were not lovers masters, who only played the part of slaves?

M. de Marzac was especially fond of two things, government and irresponsibility. His life was a more or less unconscious effort to marry them, to enjoy enough of one to save the other. While Stéphanie was in Paris he could, he thought, control events; but in Spain, with Rénée, she escaped him; his hand missed the lever. His plans were too vague, too unsettled. for confidence. He mistrusted everything. Shut off by the interruption to M. Michel's receptions from all sources of information, he had remained ignorant of her illness until after Roger's return, and this episode disconcerted him. Roger's journey and delayed return still further irritated him. There was no one who could tell him what he wanted to know, except, possibly, Madame Valfort, and she had gone to Rome for the winter with her husband. He waited like a mariner who, having lost his compass, and being driven on by the wind, listens anxiously for the sound of breakers, and waits impatiently for the morning.

When he inquired of Baptiste the day of madame's return, he had reached the limit of his endurance, and the few days which still intervened he spent in a restless wandering between the club, the café, the bureau, and the Avenue Friedland. On the evening of her arrival he walked down the Boulevard de Sebastopol, not actually going to the station, yet impelled in that direction, — hoping, perhaps, to see without being seen. Then followed a day of indecision. On the next one he passed by her house in the Boulevard St. Germain, and saw the gate was open and the *persiennes* drawn. She had returned. To his relief he received, the next morning, an invitation from M. Michel, who resumed his reunions. He had yet forty-eight hours to kill, and, on the day in question, he anticipated the evening by dining earlier than usual, and commencing his toilette immediately after dinner. All this caused François, his valet, to wonder. When at last Baptiste had taken his hat, and he stood at the door of M. Michel's salon, he hesitated. When he thought of action everything became confused, and, as he steadied himself, seemed to melt away and elude reflection. He glanced at his attire, made an effort, and entered smiling.

The rooms were full, and there were faces unfamiliar to him. Something unusual seemed to be going on. Rénée was a centre of attraction. In her rear stood M. Lande, looking very happy and much pleased with himself. There were no quiet groups of *causeurs;* an unusual animation prevailed. He did not see Stéphanie, so he pressed forward with others and paid his compliments to mademoiselle.

" It is worth while to have gone to Spain," he said afterwards to M. Michel, " to meet witn such a reception."

" It seems to please everyone — except myself," was the reply.

M. de Marzac did not understand it, but as he passed on he met Father Le Blanc, who told him of Rénée's betrothal. It was not wholly unexpected, yet it set him a-thinking.

" Did not Madame Milevski return with mademoiselle ? "

" Yes, she has entirely recovered. That is, I am told so ; I have not seen her."

" Then she is not present to-night."

" No, M. Michel says she desired to be excused."

" Ah ! " said M. de Marzac. What wonder ! he thought to himself. This was Rénée's "day." It could hardly be an agreeable one for Stéphanie. What ! able to make a journey from Granada to Paris, but unable to ride from the Boulevard St. Germain to the Rue du Bac ! Bah ! he knew better. A little flutter of hope stirred in his heart. He pictured to himself a woman alone, forgotten, and unhappy, and he determined to go at once. He saw Roger, but avoided him. He waited his opportunity when Rénée was less occupied, and approached her to make his adieux with something of his old assurance.

As he did so, he stopped suddenly, his eyes riveted upon an object which she held in her hand. It was a fan, small but of striking beauty, which a young blonde, the niece of M. Scherer, was examining with expressions of admiration.

" I never saw one at all like it," she was saying. "What is this covering? It is not silk, no, nor paper. Ah! here is M. de Marzac," she exclaimed, looking up; "he is a connoisseur in such matters. What is this material?" she asked, holding out the fan to him; "we cannot decide."

His fingers trembled as he took it in his hand. A flood of recollection rushed over him. He was no longer in the Rue du Bac. The hum of his quickened blood sounded in his ears like the rushing of a river which he had once heard smiting the rocks in the defile of the Sierra. He was fleeing again amid gusts of rain, listening above the wind for the voices of pursuers, holding hard to the saddle on a road lost in the blackness of night.

"Well," said Mademoiselle Scherer, impatiently, "you cannot tell us?"

"Yes, mademoiselle," replied M. de Marzac, rallying as he knew how to, and in his politest manner; "it is vellum, but it is not common. Where, may I ask, did you find it, mademoiselle?" looking at Rénée.

"I bought it in Granada."

"What pretty ones they make in Spain," exclaimed Mademoiselle Scherer, taking the fan again.

"Not prettier than in France," replied M. de Marzac; "only, in Spain they know how to use them."

"Have you been there?" asked Rénée.

"No, never," he replied, calmly.

"How do you know, then, that the Spanish ladies use the fan so much better than we do?" asked Mademoiselle Scherer, who was studying the picture painted on the vellum.

"By reading M. Gautier, who says so."

"I do not believe your Monsieur Gautier. At all events, he is very ungallant. But see, Rénée, here is a name on the trunk of this tree, F-e " —

"The artist's," said M. de Marzac, leaning over and examining it in his turn also.

"No, it is a woman's, — Fe-li-sa, — besides, it is written in pencil."

"I knew it!" exclaimed Rénée, with animation. "I told Antonio it was not a new fan. The folds are a little worn with use — do you see?" she said, pointing to the marks on the seams. "Do you think this could be the name of its owner?"

"At all events, it is a very pretty one," said Mademoiselle Scherer. "Felisa! Félicité! She ought to have been happy with such a fan. Let me look again, Rénée," she continued, with a mischievous smile in her eyes; "there ought to be another name there on the tree, after the fashion of lovers. No, nothing. What a pity! It was almost a romance. N'importe! we can write two others, can we not, M. de Marzac? Have you, perchance, a pencil?" and she laughed gayly.

"Anne!" said Rénée, endeavoring to be stern

and beginning to grow red. She had seen Roger approaching.

"What is it that amuses you, Mademoiselle Scherer?" he asked of the young girl, who was dying of laughter.

"Ah, M. Lande, is it you? We have found on this fan of Rénée's, which she thinks has belonged already to some one, the name of its owner. Do you see, there, on the trunk of that tree by the fountain?"

Roger, who had the fan in his hand, and could read the name easily, started involuntarily. Matías' story came back to him.

"Oh, have no fear!" exclaimed Anne, laughing again, "it is a woman's — look, Felisa."

"Where does this fan come from?" asked Roger, gravely.

"Why, it is Rénée's, I have told you. She bought it in Malaga, in Granada, in Spain somewhere. Well, what is the matter!" she exclaimed, looking from Roger, whose face was flushed, to M. de Marzac, whose lips were bloodless.

"Mademoiselle," said Roger to Rénée, who, perceiving his emotion, was as much astonished as her companion, "will you give me this fan? It has a history; some time I will tell it to you. Not now," he said, curtly, to Mademoiselle Scherer, whose amazement was becoming a curiosity, "have a little patience; it is worth it." And he offered his arm to Rénée.

"Mon Dieu! what a mystery!" exclaimed Mademoiselle Scherer, after they had gone.

"A lover's quarrel — already!" said M. de Marzac, with a fine smile of irony.

The young girl shot a swift glance of dissent from her wondering eyes, and turned, perplexed and troubled, at the result of her discovery, to M. Scherer.

Left alone, M. de Marzac sought the door. On hearing of Rénée's betrothal, he had resolved to go to Stéphanie. But this incident had driven her completely from his thoughts. When he went out, he turned down the Rue du Bac to the river, and then up the street along the quay. What did he know? — this man who had stepped unconsciously between Stéphanie and him, and who now held in his hand Felisa's fan. And Antonio! that name, in his thoughts only, it made him shiver. All this was so sudden; like light poured into a chamber he thought locked forever. The quiet and solitude of the quay, the dull noise of the river, oppressed him. He crossed the bridge and took the Rue de la Paix to the Boulevards. It was broad noon there; but the brilliant shops, the thronged sidewalks, the cafés overflowing with lights and the hum of voices, the roar of wheels on the roadway, all this tumult so familiar and so dear to him, could not drown the haunting voices of fear which pursued him. Even conscience, wasted to a superstition, dogged him revengefully. He passed the door of the club. There was the carriage of M. de Sacy, whose livery he recognized, standing at the curbstone in the blaze of gaslight, the coachman on his box with his whip on his knee. But he went on without pausing. Behind the plate glass of the Café Anglais he saw some of his friends, who saluted him and beckoned him to a place at their table. But he sent them back a forced smile, with a nod of recognition, and kept on. Now and then he gave a glance at the windows whose reduplicating mirrors were arranged to catch the eye of the loiterer, and which formed the background to all this tide of life passing before them, — seeing everything, yet recognizing nothing. This wide street through which, like an artery, poured the feverish blood of civilization, how different from that narrow crevice of the Zacatin! Yet it was there he was loitering. An array of fans, suspended from their silken tassels and spread open on velvet cushions, made him shudder, and urged him forward again down the Boulevard. He straightened up, occasionally quickening his gait, with a smile of self-contempt.

Still he went on, by the Maison Dorée, across the street, down the Rue de Choiseul, into the Rue de Richelieu, circuitously, yet ever towards the river, like a man who has an appointment but is in advance of the hour. And this was the fact. M. de Marzac had an appointment. Whether he knew it or not, it drew him on to the place and the hour fixed. Fate, which he had so often pictured as the current of life, enveloped him, sweeping him on he knew not where with the steady set of a tide.

Arrived at the Pont des Arts he lingered a moment, leaning on the railing; then, with a gesture of impatience that seemed to say, " Well, be it so! I yield to you!" he recrossed the river and took his way straight to the Boulevard St. Germain.

The gates were closed, but a light burned in the concierge's window. He rang the bell firmly, his eyes fixed on the polished brass knob till it turned to the pull of the cord. He entered the passage-way, exchanging a look with the concierge through the window, and crossed the court-yard. Jacques himself opened the door. Was Madame Milevski at home?

" No, monsieur, but she is expected every instant. Will monsieur wait?"

Yes, he would wait.

He ascended the stairs to the little room he knew so well. At the door his courage had begun to fail him; now he was more easy. Nothing was changed in this room. He knew every article of furniture. There was the seat in the window overlooking the garden, and a handkerchief, delicate, with its faint perfume, on the cushion. He sat down there and waited. How many things it said to him, that handkerchief, abandoned carelessly, within his reach! The clock ticked on the mantel with its familiar *timbre*. He seemed at home; everything was so cosy and natural, and lost in his thoughts he waited patiently in the window. What should he care for a fan! Spain was leagues away. He was thinking of Stéphanie. She must be his now; they would go — they would go — far away, — and he began to dream.

Suddenly he remembered everything.

It was no longer Stéphanie for whom he was waiting, but Felisa, dark with vengeance and reproach. He started to his feet and looked at the clock. He had been there an hour. He rang the bell, but no one answered. Was it a silly terror which benumbed his feet and chilled his blood in this warm and pleasant room? No one was there to alarm him. No one hid in the curtains hanging motionless before the window. Yes, some one was there. At the hour appointed, the senses become acute. He seized his hat and gloves, and opened the door. The stairway was dimly lighted, and he descended noiselessly. His hand was on the door when he turned, — did not some one call him? — to see the face of Antonio at his shoulder. All his courage leaped into his muscles. At bay, nature came to the rescue. He turned with a mighty spring upon his assailant, — but it was too late. A shock, cold as an icicle and changing in an instant to a stinging heat, paralyzed the muscles of his neck; everything swirled before his eyes, and he sank with a gasp on the stone floor of the vestibule.

XXII.

LYING on his bed in the chamber of the Avenue Friedland, his face white, his eyes closed, M. de Marzac called for pity. To-morrow, as he makes his last earthly journey, those who have never heard his name will take off their hats, not to him, indeed, but to the monarch whom all his courtiers know and to whom they uncover when the cortege passes by. Even M. de Sacy, who really cared but little for his friend, was here at his bedside, with that mingled awe and tenderness which Death inspires. The summons possessed majesty, because it was one he also in his turn should hear.

He met the physician as he ascended the stairway.

" Has he no chance? "

" None."

There was a momentary pause of embarrassment.

" What a frightful catastrophe! " said M. de Sacy, with a gesture of helplessness.

The doctor nodded gravely. He was chary of words. He had made a dozen visits that morning, and had yet as many more before him, besides a room in which people were already beginning to gather, awaiting their turns.

M. de Sacy opened the door of the salon. François, M. de Marzac's valet, was there, standing at the window looking drearily into the street. He had the appearance of one who is waiting for something to happen. He replied by a sign of the head to the question which M. de Sacy asked with his eyes, and the latter pushed gently the door leading into the chamber, and entered on tiptoe. M. de Marzac opened his eyes and exchanged with him a glance of recognition.

"My dear friend," began M. de Sacy, standing at the bedside. He wore his light gloves, and had his hat still in his hand. Brilliant, witty, never at a loss for a word, M. de Sacy could say absolutely nothing. Did his friend enjoy his embarrassment? From out those hollow eyes, darkened already by the shadows of the night to come, he looked at him curiously.

"Water!" he said at last, lifting his hand.

M. de Sacy filled the glass on the table, and handed it to him timidly.

"Let go. I can hold it."

"What a frightful catastrophe!" repeated M. de Sacy; "but you will soon be better — in a few days" —

M. de Marzac on his pillows, the glass at his lips, gave him a peculiar look.

"I am sure of it," continued his friend, remonstratingly. "I did not expect to see you. You are looking "—

"What did he tell you?" interrupted M. de Marzac, glancing at the door.

"The doctor? Absolutely nothing. I only passed him on the stairway."

"And you asked him no questions? You had so little curiosity?"

"You are unreasonable. When one throws away hope, one throws away the last chance. Have courage."

The sick man closed his eyes.

"What can I do for you, my poor friend," said M. de Sacy, with emotion. "The cowardly villain! But he will be found!"

M. de Marzac opened his eyes again.

"Do you think so?"

"How can you doubt it! In Paris, in broad daylight almost! I myself will "—

"On the contrary, you will do nothing."

The two men looked for a moment at each other without speaking.

"You know him?" said M. de Sacy.

"I have just made a deposition, and I know nothing. But you, my best friend," in a tone in which it was impossible not to detect a faint irony, "naturally you would do all in your power to aid justice, to bring the guilty to retribution. Do nothing, I tell you. The retribution is accomplished."

He paused, for the effort of speaking exhausted him.

"The papers will say that justice is defeated, and that the police are imbecile. And they will be right. The one is blind, and the other leads her into the ditch. The blood is paid for — with blood."

M. de Sacy listened in astonishment.

"I repeat, you are my friend; you wish to do something. Do nothing. Do you understand?"

The noise of a door opening in the adjoining room caught his ear, and he stopped to listen. In the low murmur of voices which followed, there was one which was a woman's.

"Do you promise?" he said, still listening.

"Most certainly."

"One thing more, — it is the last. Pardon me, time presses; I wish to save my strength. Go out by that door, — no, the other, — through the dining-room; you know the way. But give me your hand."

M. de Sacy's shook as he gave it.

"Bah!" said the sick man; "have courage, as you say. It is only another comedy finished. Adieu!"

It was a dismissal, not a farewell. But it was a relief to M. de Sacy to go.

The door had scarcely closed behind him, when François appeared at the other.

"Yes, let her come in," said his master, anticipating him, "and — shut the door."

"Wait for me here," said Stéphanie, in the adjoining room to M. Michel, who had accompanied her.

"As you please," replied her brother, who understood nothing of this visit she had asked him to make with her.

She entered the door which François held open for her. M. de Marzac, reclining on his pillows, motionless, pale, his hair clinging to his temples damp with perspiration, still possessed his air of the salon.

"I cannot rise, madame, to receive you. Will you do me the honor to be seated?"

Mechanically Stéphanie took the chair near his bed, and a silence followed in which he watched her attentively.

"You sent for me, M. de Marzac," she said at length. She was a woman, and the spectacle touched her heart.

"Yes, to look at you," he replied, slowly, his eyes still fixed upon her. "I do not thank you for what would not be given except as one happens to be dying. Oh, do not justify yourself," he said, in answer to her movement. "I know what you said to yourself: this man, assassinated in my house, and about to die, I must go to him; it is the least I can do. I do not misunderstand you. I have said already that I only wished to look at you."

His manner checked her utterance. "Why will you speak of these things," she said, imploringly.

" Because they interest me. Did you come to
compose a sermon with me for the ' Univers ' ?
— Do not interrupt me," he said, closing his eyes
with impatience; " can you not see every word
costs an effort ? I have only a few hours. Give
me the liberty of disposing of them as I please ; it
is a luxury. Moreover, I know your catechism by
heart."

" Do you think I came to reproach, to judge
you ?" she asked, sadly.

" Naturally not, for you no longer fear me."

Her pride rose up at his words, but the place
and the hour triumphed. " I have given you unhappiness. I wish to ask your forgiveness. Look
into the past, and search for me."

"You think you have a duty to perform, and
you set about it bravely. But it is needless. I
do not complain of you. When a man risks all
for a woman who cannot help it, who does not
even know it, why blame her ? It is in the system. She is only a tool like the rest."

She did not reply. In the presence of death
one cannot quarrel, and argument becomes entreaty. Perhaps M. de Marzac detected a difference in her demeanor; she was not wont to receive insults so calmly.

"Something has changed you. What is it ?
— Have no fear. Dead men tell no tales — well,
never mind, then," he said, after a pause. " You
were very good to come. Were you not afraid

that to-morrow Paris would be talking about you? People are so thoughtless, — and then the gossips, you know, — they stop at nothing."

"Why will you speak of these things, M. de Marzac?" she said, clasping her hands on her knees, and bending towards him. Her voice trembled. "I came to help you."

"True; I believe you. But the gossips, — will they see in you the Sister of Mercy?"

She turned wearily to the window. The cold persistency of his banter chilled more than it pained her.

"You would make a very pretty one," he continued; "it is not a bad idea. I advise you to think seriously of it."

She came back to the bedside. He had touched a deeper chord than he knew. "Ah! so you have thought of it already?" he said, reading her thought in her eyes. "But it's too late. To-morrow it would be needless."

She felt ashamed of her pity. Could he really see only such motives, or was he still playing with her?

"And your diamonds, — what will you do with them? The Church is fond of diamonds, — or will you give them to Rénée?"

She rose with a sense of helplessness and humiliation.

"Forgive me," he said, quickly; "I am selfish. Are you going?"

"I cannot stay."

"Because what I say pains you? You do not know what a luxury frankness is. But the test is too great. Try it yourself, on the next person whom you meet, — on Mademoiselle Rénée, for example. Well, then, on me. Tell me, frankly, why did you come here?"

"You cannot dream," she said, as if speaking to herself.

"Yes, I can," he replied. "You were, to begin with, a little glad; then you also pitied me a little; and then, since you are to become a nun, you wished to pray, I suppose."

The tears started to her eyes.

"Do you remember," he said, abruptly, "that night at Kief when I first saw you? It seems so long ago, — except as I see you. You have not changed."

"Can you not think of the future, M. de Marzac? It is nearer than the past."

"The future? It is like a white page with nothing written upon it. What interest is there in a blank leaf? But the past — is a book we read over and over. Each has his own volume. Did you ever think what curious things would happen if we could exchange them with each other? What prices they would command in the market? And when you enter the convent, do you expect to rid yourself of the past?"

"No," said Stéphanie, "nor when I die."

“ You wish to frighten me.”

“ I wish to talk seriously with you, to influence you, as I might have done in the past, when I thought only of myself. Life, after all, is so little a thing.”

“ You did not once think so.”

“ I was wrong. I have wasted it.”

“ You have been talking with the priests,” he said, angrily. “ They wish to persuade you, who are an angel, that you are a miserable wretch. I tell you you are a saint. Do you think I do not know ! ”

“ Hush,” she said, gently. “ You do not know what you are saying.”

“ Mon Dieu ! it is enough to raise the dead ! Why have I sent for you, but to kiss the hem of your dress ; to tell you, not that I love you, but worship you ! And this is the very thing which hurts you most ! Ah ! if I had the time,” he said, in a hoarse whisper, exhausted by his long effort, “ I would undeceive you ! I would tell you a story which would put an end to your humility.”

“ It is not you, but God, who is my judge, M. de Marzac,” said Stéphanie.

He lay quietly, breathing heavily, till, his excitement subsided, he scarcely seemed to breathe at all. “ Priests ! ” she heard him mutter. “ As for prayers, I would rather have yours than a thousand priests’.” Then he began to wander, opening his eyes at times without seeming to recognize her. She heard strange names and places, confused sentences of which she understood nothing. She grew alarmed, and rose to call some one; but he heard her movement, and put out his hand. "No, kneel down — pray something — what you will." She burst into tears; and when, after a time, kneeling at his bedside, she tried to pray, his hand stole along the coverlid and took hers. And when the door opened again softly, and the priest entered with the sacraments, she knelt there still, praying.

XXIII.

EXTRACTS.

" I am alone.

" Alone!   Is not this why I find my pen in my hand when, after Baptiste has wished me good-night, I seat myself in this chair?   I have no longer my dear 'Egypt' before me.   The last proof-sheet has passed from my hands.   In good reason I ought to close the ink-pot and rest the pen. — Twenty years!   How well I remember the first word on the first page.   What a task!   But it is done.   It is a long flight *a posse ad esse*, — so long that the wing continues to flutter though the work is done.   Rest?   What! for a pen that has traveled over the lines for twenty years?   There is no more rest for it than for the Wandering Jew.   Then I am alone — except Father Le Blanc.   Good father! he waits for the last office.

" In harvest time, the farmer, tired with his day's work, sits a while by the door.   The milking is done, the cattle fed, the cheeses turned.   Between labor and sleep comes this hour of twilight and evening, when he lights his pipe and thinks, or dreams.   I can see Maître Lande now, in the farm-house at Brienne.   And I am arrived at the same point. My work is finished, and before I sleep God gives me these evening days in which to think and to remember. 'T is a blessed thought to compare death with sleep, — sleep, the rewarder of to-day's toil and the mother of to-morrow's labor. For surely, Maître Lande is thinking of to-morrow; of the field he will plow, the Breton cow he will buy. Would he lay down his pipe and put on his night-cap so complacently, if, in going to sleep, he was to surrender all these? And I, in my twilight, will be complacent also. I will purchase, to-morrow, a new pasture. Who knows into what ink-pot I shall dip my pen? I heard a man yesterday, at Père-la-Chaise, delivering an oration. Death, he said, is an eternal sleep. That was enough. I came away. It is so easy to deal in infinities. How grandly these fellows abdicate the kingdom of self!

.   .   .   .

" A year! How much has happened in this year. I do not complain of it; I only state it. Confession of sorrow eases the heart, as confession of sin lightens the conscience. First, Rénée. She pretends she is still mine, little sophist! Then, M. Lande.

" I took a walk the other day with Stéphanie to St. Cloud, and we talked of these things. There are some pines there which must have wandered from the north. They make a strange contrast among our chestnuts and limes, and they talk a strange language, too. They do not rustle and gesticulate as we Frenchmen do. They have a stately manner up there in the north, and these pines have a speech in keeping with their grave forms. It is said that even when there is no wind they sigh and whisper just the same. We sat down in the sombre shade. It was one of my sombre days. I used to be even-tempered, but now in my old age, with no occupation to absorb my attention and keep my thoughts from my losses, I am sometimes fretful. Are there not some axioms for bald heads, which to curly ones are paradoxes? Is not labor rest, and work the synonym for Eden? 'Do you know what they say, my brother?' said Stéphanie. 'Who?' I asked. 'The pines,' she replied, gazing up into the branches over us. 'No, what do they say?' 'Peace! peace! life is very short,' she answered. From her lips these words had more weight than if read on the page of a philosopher. If I had heard them at first hand, from the pines, perhaps I should not have remarked them. Since that day I hear often the murmur of these trees, rising at intervals and subsiding again into a whisper, and this is veritably what they say. And now she, too, is gone. Ah! but that makes me angry. Rénée, it was natural, — M. Lande, it was time, — but Stéphanie! it is not right. I will never admit it.

"It seems that I have been loving more than I

suspected. Occupation has also its disadvantages. It closes the door of the library, and shuts out laughter with strife, — the sun as well as the cold. Fancy an old man who thought himself in love with Thothmes and Psammetichus, waking up at near seventy, to find that, while absent in Egypt, a little girl had crept into his heart and curled herself up on its hearthstone. Ah, these loves and friendships! I thought them lamps to light my pathway, and lo! they were the stars in the firmament, growing brighter as the night deepened.

"Roger, — he is a good boy, but he is not worthy of her. Doubtless she chose him for that reason. The use to which the good are put seems to be chiefly that of a leaven. A good work, surely, but I am something of an aristocrat. I would have them soar in their own heaven. I defy any one to remember one of those children of light without a pang for their condition. They all wear a ball and chain. Was I not myself Rénée's first? Has she not dragged me up these fifteen years who knew nothing of it till the lifting power of her wings was withdrawn? What stuff did not the child read to me when, after my sickness, I thought my eyes had given out — Eutychius — and Hartmann! Heaven forgive me! Probably she did not understand a word of it, and it had no more power over her than the flames of the king's furnace over the angel. But what a risk! Wisdom comes so late in life — that is my chief complaint. Misfortune, pain, — I will not struggle with such giants of mystery, — but tell me why wisdom comes when the feast is over, the wine drunk, and the guests under the table, — she, the hostess, who prepared the viands, pressed the vines, and knew the good from the evil? For my part, I would not quarrel with that personage who gave to us the knowledge of good and evil, but that he withheld the secret of discerning between them.

"No, I say, he is not worthy of her. He is neither a villain nor a rogue, — but he is blind. All her life must be spent in opening his eyes. Of what use is it to her that he cuts off a leg well and lectures in the École de Médicine? — she is not ambitious! But I am incompetent to argue. I have not loved, and have no premises. Then I am a man who grows by appropriating, by absorbing everything, like a tree, from the air and soil. Woman has a different principle of existence, — she comes like a pure stream from the springs of the mountain to waste itself in the valleys.

"How gay I was the day of the wedding! Should I spoil everything with a gloomy face? Moreover, no one would have believed me if I had shed tears. At the door of the church they stepped into a carriage and whirled away, leaving me standing alone on the sidewalk in my white gloves and waistcoat. Then the smiles were of no use, and disappeared. There was a great crowd.

I heard some one in the throng say, 'Marriage de fille, funérailles de père!' M. Lande walked home with me, — he was not sad, not he! It must be very easy to marry a son, — but a daughter, there is somewhere there a difference. He was gay enough for two on the way home, and I would not confess to him. So we went along merrily together, and drank a toast to the bride at Véfour's, and in the evening we sat down before the fire, we two alone, and played at being merry. Baptiste brought in the coffee. 'I will smoke a pipe, if you please,' said M. Lande, ' now that there are no longer any ladies.' ' By all means,' I said to him, bravely ; ' make yourself at your ease.'

" Then after a while the children came back. They had gone to Beauvais, — it was Rénée's wish, — and after a week there they sent for me. Rénée, especially, implored me to come ; but I was too wise. Is she happy ? Certainly she is happy. The bud is wide open in the sunshine ; God grant it do not drink up its dew ! She runs about, from home to the Rue du Bac, from the Rue du Bac to the Bois, among the shops, to the opera. Does she think ever of her Breton ponies and Beauvais, I wonder ? — Certainly she is happy. Only she thinks all these treasures of happiness lie scattered about the streets for whoever will gather them ; but they are all in her own heart. When nothing but a vintage of 1800 will warm it, when feet are cold away from the fire, and eyes are blind without spectacles, it makes a huge difference. M. Lande would dispute this à l'outrance, were he here. I am safe in grumbling. Moreover, one does not believe all that one says.

"They asked me to pronounce a eulogy over my friend. I refused. I loved him too well. It is strangers who write eulogies. For that reason, also, I do not speak here of him. I find it easier to go at noon, when the sun is warm, and sit among the violets at Père-la-Chaise. It is Rénée who plants these violets. Sometimes we meet there, but I endeavor to avoid it. It gives her pain to see me there. . . .

"There is something in Stéphanie which I do not understand. I am persuaded that Father Le Blanc knows this mystery, — that assassination which no one comprehends, that visit to M. de Marzac. I did not think gentleness could so become her till after she came back from Spain; and after Rénée was married I began to believe God had sent her to me in my old age. But that dream is over also.

.   .   .   .

"Yes, yes, Baptiste, I am coming! Here, at least, is a faithful old dog who extinguishes my candle and says, 'Good-night.' Mon Dieu, what an ingrate I am! No, I am not alone, —

> . . . "'comme un flambeau céleste
> La bonté de Dieu nous reste,
> Elle nous garde et nous suit.
> Bonne nuit! Bonne nuit!'"

The convent church was crowded. In the tragic play of human destiny there are always the spectators. They climbed the steps and poured down the aisles, an eager, curious throng, filling the chairs while yet the sacristan was lighting the lamps in the great gallery along the nave. From that lofty place, where his taper moved like a wandering star, and above which the arches rose into a gloom the lamps could not dissipate, they appeared so many pigmies whose bustle and murmur the vast spaces overhead swallowed up and silenced.

The choir alone was brilliant with light. It shone in the faces of those nearest the railing, and reached up to the white statue of the Holy Mother high above the altar.

Near the great aisle some seats had been reserved. People looked at them and whispered. When an old man with white hair came into the light, leaning on the arm of Rénée, whose face was very pale, every one leaned forward to look at them. Presently came Father Le Blanc with another priest whom Rénée did not know. It was Father Roche, who had just returned from Rome.

Seated between her uncle and Roger, Rénée moved her chair close to her husband's. She had not yet recovered from the surprise of the day before, when Father Le Blanc had told her of what was to be. She had chosen her part out of a pure heart, and misgivings rarely shadowed it.

—except as now and then some thought of the past, or of Sœur Ursule, came to her when alone. But that Stéphanie, who had herself pacified her doubts, should step into the place she had once thought to take, filled her again with trouble. She clung to her husband with a feeling of mingled happiness, reproach, and awe. She had often imagined this scene, and what she thought once herself to do gladly she now waited for another to accomplish with a nervous fear. It seemed cruel to her now. She had grown to love Stéphanie, in spite of that unknown barrier to her heart, which she knew she could not pass. Some tender words and kindly acts of Stéphanie's in the days before her marriage, a kiss on the marriage day which she had never forgotten, — these things came back to her as she sat there waiting, and a mist blurred the lights about the altar.

The silence had now become complete. Those who came late, and endeavored in vain on the outskirts of the throng to reach a better position, could scarce be heard by those who, near the chancel, watched the glass doors of the choir whence the procession would issue. It was a winter night, clear and cold. All the stars looked down on the great city without, whose streets were full of lights and people. It was the hour of the theatres, of music and revelry, when the jester puts on the mask of Pleasure and the fool shakes his bells. But within the church no light or sound penetrated from without. The rose window above the organ was dark; no one would ever dream of the symphony of color imprisoned in its great outlines. From one window only, high in the transept, a pale light from the moon traversed the glass and painted a cold blue lozenge on the black wall above the yellow shimmer of the candles.

Suddenly, without warning, the organ sounded, the cantors burst into song, " O Gloriosa Virginum, sublimis inter sidera," and the procession entered the choir doors. How exultant the voices, as they rose and echoed overhead like the tide of a sea on the shore. " Thou art the gate of the Supernal King; thou the refulgent palace of light." As Rénée saw the long files of the Religious, habited in their black church-cloaks and bearing their tapers, follow the cross-bearer to their places, this triumphant song buoyed up her heart; and often again the hymns of the cantors and the peal of the organ gave her courage, as the martial strains inspire the soldier in the long day of battle. She had seen the figure, between the Mother Superioress and assistant, whom she knew by its secular dress to be Stéphanie; but she had not dared to look in its face, and, as the procession approached the sanctuary steps, she had shut her eyes, struggling with the sob that rose from her heart to her throat. When she heard the words of the bishop, " Pray for her, O Holy Mother of God," she opened them wide again.

Stéphanie was alone in the middle of the choir, the Religious kneeling on either side. She saw the bishop sprinkle the candle, and the novice-elect, led by the Mother Superioress, rise and receive it from his hand at the altar. But when she turned again to resume her place in the centre of the choir, Rénée shut her eyes and held fast to Roger's arm. She could not look yet into the face she loved. All through the sermon she sat motionless. Sometimes the voice of the preacher reached her, but he could not chain her thoughts. They went backwards to the days that were over, and when she lifted her eyes it was not to the preacher's face, but to that figure sitting alone in the great choir, on whose hair the lights shone and on whom the Mother above looked down.

From these dreams she awoke with a start when, in reply to the question of the bishop, " My child, what do you demand ? " she heard a voice which thrilled her : " The mercy of God and the holy habit of religion." Clear and sweet it fell upon her troubled heart as the words of the Master upon the waters of Galilee, " Peace, be still ! " and, when clothed in the habit, Stéphanie reëntered the choir, and the joyful words of the Antiphon rose above the organ, " Who is she that cometh up from the desert, flowing with delights, leaning upon her beloved ? " she could look into her face. How true the words were, " Thou art all fair, my beloved, meek and beautiful. Come, my spouse from Libanus; come, thou shalt be crowned." Would Stéphanie not look at her? She was hungry now for a blessing from those eyes. She saw the cincture girded about her, and the veil placed on her head. She watched her as she received the black church-cloak and took her taper in her hand. She heard again the clear voice rising like the morning star above the mists of earth and fading in the celestial day : —

" The empires of the world, and all the grandeur of this earth, I have despised for love of our Lord Jesus Christ, whom I have seen, whom I have loved, in whom I have believed, and towards whom my heart inclineth."

The choir caught up the words : —

" Whom I have seen, whom I have loved, in whom I have believed, and towards whom my heart inclineth."

Rénée watched her with an eagerness of hope and desire. Would she not look upon her now before she received, prostrate at the steps of the altar, the last benediction, and passed forever beyond earthly eyes? Yes, as she turned to the vast audience, her gaze rested for the first time upon the little group near the chancel rail. Father Le Blanc crossed himself and sighed. Did he think of the part he had played in this human life? Was he thinking of the woman at whose white throat he had so often seen the flash of the czar's diamonds? Whose heart he, better than any other, had known and gauged, and whose eyes said to him now, "It does not hurt, O Pætus!" It would be difficult to tell whether the good father's sigh was one of anguish or exultation. It was only for a moment, — but for that moment all the light of the choir seemed to radiate from that single face. Then the veil fell over it, the Religious rose from their knees, the acolytes took their places, the procession moved again to the song of the cantors and disappeared, file by file, through the choir doors.

Still the audience remained silent, till the curtain fell behind the screen, shutting from view the moving lights, and the last echoes from within, heard faintly as from a world invisible, had ceased. "In thee, O Lord, have I put my trust: let me not be confounded forever."

In the great throng of the porch, Rénée, clinging to her husband's side, whispered, "Did you see her face at the last? It was a prayer."

And Roger, who in the compass of that last look had seen the past, from its first unknown pain to its final peace, answered, "It was more than a prayer; it was a benediction."